The
London Times
acclaims June Thomson

"Here is a crime writer to be encouraged with shouts and cries. . .

"Two qualities chiefly provide the pleasure that Miss Thomson can give. First, she writes very well about the countryside. No blather, no romanticizing, but quiet observation plainly conducted with love, a love that comes off the page.

"Second, she understands people as well as she understands the processes of nature. Observation and compassion play their equal parts here, and especially her portrait of the Inspector . . . eschews any of those marker flags of some eccentricity which most other practitioners rely on. He is a real person, quiet, with passions, with a listened-to-instinct, with shynesses. I am ready to join him in the unhurrying chase whenever he sets off again. But such qualities are not altogether enough for successful crime entertainment. What is needed as well, above all, is a story. And this she provides. That is the recipe for success. Bake more, Miss Thomson."

Death Cap

By
JUNE THOMSON

BANTAM BOOKS · TORONTO · NEW YORK · LONDON

To my mother

This low-priced Bantam Book
has been completely reset in a type face
designed for easy reading, and was printed
from new plates. It contains the complete
text of the original hard-cover edition.
NOT ONE WORD HAS BEEN OMITTED.

DEATH CAP

A Bantam Book / published by arrangement with
Doubleday & Company, Inc.

PRINTING HISTORY
Doubleday edition published May 1977
Bantam edition / March 1980

ISBN 0-553-13314-4

1

It was a Monday morning, routine and undistinguished in every way, except for the weather which was perfect; one of those cloudless sunlit early autumn days that are in some ways better than high summer; with a faint tang in the air that sharpens the senses and raises a feeling of expectation in the blood.

Not that there was much hope of anything exciting happening, Detective Inspector Rudd told himself, as he sat hunch-shouldered at his office desk. The case he had been working on, a burglary, had been satisfactorily concluded—if you could call it that. Two teenage boys, with no talent for crime, had broken into a shop and stolen some transistor radios, leaving their fingerprints everywhere. As they had been in trouble with the police before and were on record, they had soon been rounded up. Rudd had been in court the Friday before to give evidence and to see them sentenced to Borstal training.

I need a challenge, Rudd told himself. I'm getting stale and middle-aged. All the same, he could not help smiling to himself as he thought it, his pleasant countryman's face that put many people in mind of a farmer's, creasing up with amusement at his own self-pitying mood.

Something would turn up. Something always did, even if it was only another amateur thief or a crooked car dealer.

At that moment, there was a discreet knock at the door and the police constable from desk duty downstairs came in with the Inspector's mail, which he placed on the desk and then withdrew.

Rudd picked the envelopes up and sorted swiftly through them. Not much there, he decided. Several replies to correspondence that he had been expecting. A couple of reports he had been promised.

But the last one in the pile was different. Rudd had had enough experience of anonymous letters to recognise this as one as soon as he saw it. It was addressed in crude capital letters to: The Inspector, Murder Investigations, Police Headquarters, Chelmsford, Essex.

The handwriting was obviously disguised. No one could have naturally produced those ill-formed characters that sloped in several directions. He noticed automatically that it was written with a ballpoint pen and that the envelope, of a cheap, thin quality, was postmarked Market Stratton for Saturday the 12th September. He picked it up fastidiously by its very edges and, slitting it open with a penknife, shook out on to his blotter the single sheet of paper it contained.

The message on it was short and was printed in the same awkward capitals: "Mrs. King of Abbots Stacey was poisoned on purpose. It was murder."

Detective Sergeant Boyce entered the office at that moment and Rudd called him over. The Sergeant was a big, burly, deep-voiced man who usually worked with Rudd on investigations and the two men got on well together.

"Come and have a look at this, Tom," Rudd said to him.

Boyce came heavy-footed across the floor, making the glass in the window-frames vibrate gently, and peered over Rudd's shoulder.

"Poison pen," he said briefly.

"I know that," said Rudd a little irritably. "Do you know anything about a Mrs. King dying at Abbots Stacey? Has any report come in?"

Boyce shook his head.

"No," he said, "there's been nothing. But I know the Seregant at Abbots Stacey; name of Holbrook. I was on a course with him a couple of years ago. He's no fool. If there was any funny business, he'd've smelt it out and been on to us straight away. You'll probably find out that this Mrs. King, whoever she was, was ninety-two anyway, died peacefully in bed and some old biddy with nothing better to do than stir up trouble wrote that letter hoping for a bit of excitement."

Rudd pulled at his lower lip doubtfully.

"You're probably right," he said. "But it'll have to be followed up, all the same."

He wondered, as he spoke, why Boyce, like a good many other people, always jumped to the conclusion that anonymous letters were written by elderly and embittered women, usually spinsters.

He slid the envelope and the sheet of paper into two plastic bags, sealed and labelled them and handed them to Boyce.

"Get these sent up to forensic in London, Tom," he said. "And get photostat copies made of them as well. And you might check on the reports that have come in over the past few days, just to make sure we've nothing on Mrs. King's death."

Boyce took the bags and gave a grin.

"You're hopeful, aren't you?" he asked. "I bet I can tell you right now what the bright boys in forensic will say: the paper and envelope are the cheap sort you can buy in any Woolworth's; the only distinguishable fingerprints will be the postman's or the constable's who sorts out the mail and the saliva test will prove the person who licked the stamp belongs to the 'O' blood group, along with a few million other people."

Rudd grinned. He knew Boyce's contempt for the technicians who, according to the Sergeant, were on to a cushy job and never got their feet wet in the real job of police investigation, that of door to door inquiries.

"At least we'll have tried," he said.

Boyce suddenly showed more interest in the bag that contained the letter and carried it over to the window where he held it up to the light.

"There's a smudge of something here in the corner," he announced.

Rudd joined him at the window.

"Where?"

"There," said Boyce, stabbing a forefinger.

There was indeed a small dark patch in the top left-hand corner of the paper as if something liquid had been dropped on it and dried, leaving a faint stain.

"That'll give the boffins something to work on," said Boyce with satisfaction. "I hope it's something to make them scratch their heads over, like . . ."

He paused, unable to think of anything bizarre enough.

"Bat's spit?" suggested Rudd, and Boyce laughed and went out with the plastic bags.

Before telephoning Sergeant Holbrook at Abbots Stacey,

Rudd went over to the far wall where a large-scale map of the county hung. He knew Market Stratton well. It was a small town about eighteen miles away and not much of a place, in Rudd's opinion. Abbots Stacey he knew too, but not so well. He had driven through it many times but had never stopped there. As he found it on the map, he remembered that it was one of those long, straggling villages, spaced out along a road that had a sharp left-hand bend in it by a public house. He always had to slow up when he came to it. Apart from that, he remembered cottages and houses of various periods, a little row of shops, a village hall with a corrugated iron roof and a Victorian school building, like the one he had gone to as a child, with steep gables and a little belfry that had once housed the school bell. He could recall nothing else about the place. It was one of those nondescript villages that is not picturesque enough to be really memorable.

He verified distances on the map, although he already had a shrewd idea how far apart they were. Abbots Stacey was roughly fifteen miles from Chelmsford and six miles from Market Stratton, which would be the nearest town and shopping centre for the village.

Rudd returned to his desk and, having looked up the telephone number, rang Sergeant Holbrook at Abbots Stacey.

When Holbrook answered the phone, Rudd identified himself and went on to say, "I'm making inquiries into the death of a Mrs. King of Abbots Stacey. Can you give me details?"

"Mrs. King, sir?" Holbrook sounded surprised. He had a deep voice, not unlike Boyce's but overlaid with a country accent. "Well, she was found dead on Friday morning. Dr. Foreman, the local doctor, was called in and he's made arrangements for a postmortem and a coroner's inquest."

Holbrook hesitated and then continued more slowly as if choosing his words with care. "I gather it was accidental death. Mind you, I can't say for sure what she died of, but the doctor seemed to think it was something she ate. There seemed no reason to suppose otherwise, so I didn't report to C.I.D."

Rudd felt sorry for the man. He was clearly distressed at the call from headquarters and by the thought that he might have been negligent in some way.

"You were quite right," said Rudd briskly. "But something's turned up here today to suggest there might have been foul play."

He heard Holbrook take a quick, inward breath. Rudd continued, "I don't want to discuss it over the telephone. Where can I arrange to meet you?"

"The police house is just before you get into the village," Holbrook said, "on the Chelmsford road. It's the last in a row of council houses."

Rudd glanced down at his desk, at the other unopened letters and a half-written report.

"I'll be round this afternoon about two o'clock," he said.

Holbrook seemed to have regained his composure.

"Very good, sir, I'll be expecting you," he replied.

There was a tiny pause and then he added with a disarming air, "I'm off duty for a couple of hours this afternoon and I'll be in the back garden, so if you could give a good loud knock at the front door . . ."

Rudd laughed.

"I'll come round to the back and find you," he said and rang off.

He liked the sound of Holbrook. The man had not rushed into hurried explanations and excuses as someone else in his position might have done. Nor had he been over-deferential in his attitude to Rudd. There was nothing the Inspector disliked more than obsequiousness. And if Boyce said the man was no fool, that was praise indeed. Boyce was not the type to hand out compliments unless they had been truly earned.

Rudd spent the rest of the morning conferring with his superior officers and clearing up the paper work that remained on his desk. As he had hoped, he was put in charge of the investigation into Mrs. King's death. He had the necessary experience and there was no other outstanding case that demanded his attention.

After lunch, he drove over to Abbots Stacey. Nine miles out of Chelmsford he passed through the Comptons, the collective name for the group of villages that all bore variations of the same placename; Long Compton, Little Compton, High Compton, Castle Compton and Compton Green. It was a part of the countryside he knew well from childhood; he had lived in a village not far away and it still remained an area that had changed little over the years.

The harvest was in and the shorn fields stretched away

across the flat landscape, broken into irregular shapes by the hedgerows, with here and there a spinney or a cluster of houses and a church. In places the men were still burning off the stubble and the columns of smoke rose almost vertically into the still sunlit air with the flickering line of dark flames below. It had been a good harvest and Rudd was glad.

He passed through the Comptons and turned left at the crossroads on to the Abbots Stacey road and after another six miles came to the outskirts of the village. The council houses were on the right-hand side and Rudd parked the car and walked up the garden path of the police house and round the corner to the back where Sergeant Holbrook was working in the garden, burning the debris of summer.

As soon as he heard footsteps, the Sergeant looked up and, acknowledging Rudd's presence with a nod of his head, walked to the edge of the garden. Rudd strolled down the path to meet him.

"I won't shake hands, sir," said Holbrook, holding his out to show the dirt. "I'm all mucky from the garden."

He was a big man, both tall and broad, and in the open neck of his shirt a thick mat of gingerish hair could be seen, curly and dense.

He continued, "We'll go into the house. I'll get the wife to keep an eye on the bonfire. It's burning up nicely and it seems a shame to put it out."

"It does," agreed Rudd. He watched the heat haze over the fire shimmer upwards, distorting the air and the outline of the apple tree that grew behind it against the fence. "We may not get many more fine days like today," he added.

Holbrook cast a knowing eye at the sky.

"I reckon it'll hold for a while yet," he said.

The two men walked up the path, Holbrook leading the way. Like all countrymen, the weather and the crops were their first interest and topic of conversation.

"It's been a good harvest," remarked Rudd.

"It has that," replied the Sergeant. "The farmers have nothing to grumble about this year, for once."

At the back door, he took off his boots and exchanged them for a pair of slippers that stood ready on the coconut mat just inside the kitchen door.

Mrs. Holbrook, a big, placid woman, was in the living-room, ironing and listening to the wireless. She made as if to turn it off but Rudd said pleasantly, "I don't want to disturb you."

"The Inspector and I've got business to talk about, Betty," Holbrook said. "Keep an eye on the bonfire, will you, and a cup of tea wouldn't come amiss. Unless," and he eyed Rudd speculatively, "you'd prefer a glass of beer."

"Beer would suit me," said Rudd and knew he had said the right thing when the Sergeant smiled.

"It's home-brewed," he said later, after he had gone off to wash his hands and fetch the beer and the two men were seated in his office. He unstoppered the bottle and poured the dark brown liquid into the glasses.

Rudd drank and nodded appreciatively. Holbrook drank more deeply, wiped his mouth and said in way of explanation, "I was fair parchee."

The Inspector put his glass down and hitched his chair nearer to the desk. It was time to get down to business.

"Now about Mrs. King," he began.

Holbrook pulled a solemn face as Rudd continued.

"I received an anonymous letter this morning, suggesting that her death wasn't accidental; in fact, that it was murder."

Holbrook started to speak but Rudd went on, "I'm not for a moment saying that there's been any negligence on your part. Indeed, I've had good reports on your work but, as you must realise, this allegation must be investigated thoroughly. I'll let you see a photostat of the letter, by the way, but at the moment it's at forensic going through the usual tests. The handwriting's obviously disguised but we may be able to pick up a few clues as to the identity of the person who wrote it. Now, Holbrook, what I want from you at this moment is a detailed account of Mrs. King and anybody connected with her who might have been concerned with her death."

Holbrook swallowed heavily and looked unhappy.

"Yes, sir," he replied. "I quite understand. I've got my report here on the finding of the body. A copy was sent to divisional headquarters at Market Stratton but, as I said on the phone, I didn't think it necessary to send one to County C.I.D."

Rudd waved a hand.

"Don't worry yourself on that score."

He was anxious to put the Sergeant at his ease and to get him talking naturally about the case and the people involved.

"And I don't want to read your official account, not at the moment, anyhow," Rudd went on, giving Holbrook a grin. "I get enough reports to wade through, and damned dull reading they are, too. What I want from you at this stage is a chat. So loosen your braces, mate, cop us some more of that beer and let's get down to a good old gossip."

As he said these words, the Inspector slipped deliberately into the local dialect with its flattened vowels and soothing sing-song intonation. The Sergeant recognised it for what it was; partly a joke to put him at his ease, partly an admission by Rudd of the country origins that he shared with Holbrook. The Sergeant laughed and, filling up the glasses, said, "Well, it'd be last Friday morning, the 11th, and I was here at home when——"

"Wait a minute," said Rudd. "Before you start telling me about the dead woman, let's get some idea of the living one for a start."

Holbrook blinked his eyes rapidly. He seemed surprised at this unusual line of approach.

"Mrs. King, you mean?" he asked. "She was a very nice woman. A very nice woman indeed. She kept a shop in the village, the Bandbox it's called; sold children's clothes, women's blouses and jumpers, knitting wool, bits and pieces of haberdashery, that sort of thing. She'd been here in the village getting on for three years——"

"Not local then?" said Rudd.

"Oh, no. She came from London originally, the East End somewhere; Whitechapel, I believe. Her husband was in the wholesale clothing business and when he died a nephew took over the firm and she moved down here and bought herself this shop. She said she'd always fancied a little country business. I got the feeling that she'd lived in the country once and like the life. Perhaps she'd been evacuated during the war as a child. She'd be about the right age, in her early forties. She once spoke to me about Wiltshire.

"Anyway, she settled down here very well. I reckon her husband had left her comfortably off and she had the shop done up and the rooms over it modernised into a nice comfortable flat. Proper little palace it was up there; pale green bathroom suite, fitted carpets, the lot. The business did well, too. Her nephew used to supply her with stuff wholesale; a van came down once a fortnight with fresh stock, so she always had new goods to display and she was able to keep her prices low. The women in the village used to go to her for clothing rather than shop in Market Stratton. I'd guess she was doing very nicely. She was obliging, too, and very pleasant to talk to. Always ready for a laugh or a joke, she was. If it was murder, I can't see how anyone had a motive, I can't honestly."

Holbrook looked and sounded genuinely distressed.

"What did she look like?" Rudd asked. "Are there any photographs of her?"

"Wait a bit," said Holbrook. "Betty might have one."

He left the room and returned shortly with a shiny print which he handed to Rudd.

"That was taken earlier in the summer," he said, "on the church outing. Rene King liked to join in village life; as much as she could, that is, with the business to run. I remember she closed the shop down that Saturday in order to go on the excursion with the others to Clacton. That's her."

He pointed a stubby finger at a woman in the forefront of the picture. Rudd held it towards the light. It was a group photograph and did not show much detail but he got the impression of a dark-haired, plump, smiling woman, more smartly dressed than the others. There was something about the tilt of her head that he found attractive. There was gaiety in it and a kind of amused challenge.

"I like the look of her," he commented.

"You couldn't have asked for a nicer woman," Holbrook said. "You ask round the village. I don't think there's a soul that disliked her."

"Somebody did, though," Rudd pointed out. "According to that letter."

Holbrook lifted his massive shoulders in disbelief.

"That's as may be, Inspector, and you've got your duty to do in following it up. But if you want my opinion, she died accidental, like we thought at the time we found her."

"Let's get on to that now," said Rudd, laying the photograph down on the desk. "Tell me what happened."

"Well, sir, it was like I said, last Friday morning. Dr.

Foreman, he's the local doctor, telephoned me here at home saying that Mrs. King had been found dead and would I go round to her shop to assist him."

"So you didn't find her?" Rudd asked.

"No. Mrs. Youngman did. She lives in the village and used to be Mrs. King's daily help. I gather she went to the shop as usual at a little after nine o'clock, found it still locked up, let herself in with her key and discovered Mrs. King dead.

"She ran straight across the road to the doctor's house which is more or less opposite and the doctor telephoned me."

"I see," said Rudd. "Well, go on."

Holbrook swallowed painfully.

"I've seen a few nasty accident cases in my time, sir, and one death by drowning, but I hope to God I never see anything like that again. Mrs. King was lying on the stairs upside down, if you get my meaning, with her head lower than her body and her legs in a heap a few steps up, all tangled up in her nightie and her dressing-gown. She'd been—well, sick isn't the word for it. It fair turned my stomach up, I can tell you.

"Dr. Foreman was examining the body and he asked me to see if I could find any food left in the kitchen, especially any mushrooms."

"He specified mushrooms, did he?" asked Rudd.

"Yes, he did. Well, somehow I clambered past Mrs. King's body and got up the stairs. There was vomit everywhere up there, too. Poor woman! She must have suffered something terrible to be as sick as that, and that nice little flat of hers, usually as neat as a new pin, all messed up. Well, I poked about in the kitchen and didn't find much. There was some tinned food in the cupboard and a bit of steak and a small leg of lamb in the fridge. Anyway there was a little basket like the kind they put soft fruit in and some mushroom peelings and stalk ends in the waste-bin. I told the doctor and he sent me over to his house to get some plastic bags and some specimen jars. I don't mind telling you, I was glad of the excuse to get out into the fresh air.

"I packed up the stalks and peelings into the bags and then the doctor asked me to find the address of her nephew, seeing he was her next-of-kin.

"She used the back room behind the shop as an office and I had a look through the desk and found his address and telephone number. I'll say this, she was a good business woman. All her papers were in apple-pie order. She even kept a day ledger and a petty cash book.

"By this time, the doctor had finished his examination and he rang through for an ambulance. He told me he wouldn't be signing a death certificate and it would mean a post-mortem and a coroner's inquest. He said he'd arrange that as he knew the coroner personally and he'd leave me to get in touch with the nephew.

"The ambulance arrived and Mrs. King's body was taken away to the mortuary at Market Stratton. I saw the place was properly locked up, after me and the doctor had left. I've got the keys here, by the way, sir," Holbrook added, opening a drawer and producing a small bunch which he placed on the desk in front of Rudd, pointing to each one in turn.

"Those are the keys to the front and back doors; that's the safe key and the little silver one belongs to a leather box in the bedroom. I didn't open it but I reckon it contains personal possessions, jewellery and suchlike."

"Is this the only set of keys?" Rudd asked as he put them in his pocket.

"There's one other key to the door of the shop that Mrs. Youngman, the charlady, had but the doctor said he'd ask her for it himself. It seems she was pretty cut up over finding Mrs. King and the doctor thought it better that I didn't go round to see her until she'd got over the worst of the shock."

"So far as you know it's in his possession?" Rudd asked.

Holbrook nodded.

"And nobody's been in the flat since you and Dr. Foreman examined the body?" the Inspector continued.

Holbrook looked uncomfortable.

"Not to my knowledge, except for the men from the Council. You see, thinking it was just a question of accidental death and bearing in mind the mess everywhere, the doctor got in touch with the Public Health Department and a couple of men came over to take away the bedding and some of the carpets for burning. It couldn't have been left in the state it was in. The weather was still warm and there'd have been complaints."

"Of course," agreed Rudd, but thought to himself that it would complicate the business of fingerprinting the flat. "Were the men supervised at all?"

"Oh yes, sir," Holbrook said a shade eagerly as if on the defensive. "I let them in myself and waited until they'd finished to lock up behind them."

"Which rooms did they go into?" Rudd asked.

"Only the stairs, the landing, Mrs. King's bedroom and the bathroom. They came in and left by the shop door. I gather Dr. Foreman had asked permission of the nephew for it to be done. Being next-of-kin, I suppose he'll come in for her property."

"What do you know about the nephew?"

"I can't tell you much about him, sir. After I'd left Mrs. King's flat on the Friday morning, I came back here and got in touch with him by phone and told him of his aunt's death."

"How did he take it?"

Holbrook wrinkled up his nose in thought.

"Hard to say, sir. When I told him, there was a bit of a pause and then he said, 'How did it happen?' I said the cause of death hadn't been established and there'd have to be an inquest. He seemed surprised but I can't honestly say he was all that upset. I told him Dr. Foreman had done the examination and I gave him the doctor's address. The nephew said he'd be down from London that afternoon. I didn't see him myself but I gather he went round to the doctor's, had a word with him and then went straight back to town. I've seen him in the village on previous occasions; leastways not him but his car parked outside Mrs. King's; about twice all told."

"Did they seem on friendly terms?" Rudd asked.

Holbrook gave the Inspector a look that was at once startled and knowing.

"As far as I know, yes, they were," Holbrook said. He sounded subdued. "But I don't know much about him. In fact, I've never set eyes on him. I've only ever heard Mrs. King mention him the once."

"What did she say?"

"Nothing much," Holbrook replied. "She'd been doing out the shop window and she'd come on to the pavement to have a look at it from the outside. I happened to be passing at the time and I stopped for a bit of a chat and said how nice the display looked. She smiled and said, 'My nephew knows the kind of things I like and that sell well,' or something like that. Mrs. Youngman ought to be able to tell you a bit more about him."

"You didn't see his car, or hear of it being seen, in the village on the Wednesday evening or anytime on the Thursday?"

"No, I didn't see it. I wasn't up the village either of those times. Nor have I heard of anyone saying they've seen it. But if someone did, they'd be sure to remember it. It's a distinctive car, light blue. You couldn't miss it."

He paused and looked down at the desk, nervously handling some papers on it. When he looked up again his eyes were strained.

"I don't think . . ." he began and then stopped.

Rudd knew exactly what he was going to say; that he didn't think it was murder; that nobody, least of all the nephew, her own kin, could have wished her dead. Rudd understood and in a way sympathised with Holbrook. Despite the Sergeant's years of experience in the police force, there was something innocent about him. He still remained at heart a man who trusted in human goodness and the fundamental decency of his fellow men.

It crossed Rudd's mind that Holbrook had lived too long in the cosy and isolated world of a small community. He had grown soft. It might do him good to be in a tougher area where crime took on more violent forms than the occasional case of Saturday night drunkenness or chicken stealing.

"Go on," he said, half hoping that by voicing his thoughts Holbrook himself might become aware that his objections were based on sentiment rather than logic.

"Well," Holbrook said slowly, "I'm not yet convinced it was murder but, if it was, then I can't see the nephew doing it. I know he probably stood to gain by her death and that gives him a motive. But, according to the doctor, it was poisoning, probably something in the mushrooms. In that case, how would he know she was having mushrooms for tea that evening? It strikes me only a local person would know that."

Rudd looked at the Sergeant with renewed respect. Holbrook was, after all, capable of looking at the facts objectively.

"You have a point there," he admitted. "Now about these mushrooms. Let's assume for the moment that it was the mushrooms. Any idea where they might have come from?"

"I've made a few inquiries," said Holbrook. "For a start, I checked that she hadn't bought them at Abstey's, the green-grocer's next door, although I already had a pretty good idea where they'd come from."

"And that was . . . ?" prompted Rudd.

"Stan Spurgeon's farm," replied Holbrook. "I had a word with him yesterday, just casual like, and he admitted he'd taken a little basket of mushrooms round to Mrs. King's place the Wednesday evening before she died; the 9th that'd be. Right upset he was, too, about it. He'd heard she'd died and he didn't take kindly to the idea that the mushrooms he took her might've been the cause."

"Who's this Stan Spurgeon?" asked Rudd.

"He's a local farmer, sir. He lives about two miles out of the village on the Latching road. It's not much of a farm and the Lord above knows how he manages to make a living out of it. He keeps a few chickens, pigs and cows, and farms about a dozen acres mostly on the cash-crop basis, relying on casual labour for harvesting. He sells a bit of produce at the side of the road and supplies Abstey's and one or two other local shops round about with fruit and vegetables. He's in his forties, I'd say; married, but his wife left him a good few years back. He's got one child, a boy called Kenny, who's got a bit missing up here," Holbrook added, tapping his own forehead significantly. "The lad goes to a special school at Market Stratton. Old Mrs. Spurgeon, Stan's mother, keeps house for them, if you can call it that. Whenever I've gone round there, though, it looks as if nothing's been done to the place for years. Anyhow, to get back to the question of the mushrooms; it's common knowledge that Stan Spurgeon used to take a bit of produce round to Rene King's whenever he went there to play cards. He was round there for a hand of whist on Wednesday, as usual, and he admitted straight out he took her some, ones he'd picked himself from the field behind the farmhouse."

"I see. Now tell me more about these Wednesday card parties," said Rudd.

"There's not much to tell, really. I gather Mrs. King enjoyed a game of whist and about twice a month she'd have Stan Spurgeon and the Leacocks round to her place to make up the four. Like I said, she was a jolly sort of woman who liked a bit of company, but with the business to run she didn't get a lot of free time. She supplied a supper for them, ham sandwiches, beer or coffee or what-have-you and they'd meet at eight o'clock and play cards until about half-past ten. It was all very respectable," he added hastily, catching sight of Rudd's expression. "No gambling or anything like that. You wouldn't catch Amy Leacock going round there if it wasn't all above board."

"What do you know about the Leacocks?" Rudd asked.

"They're near neighbours of Mrs. King's; brother and sister, neither of them married. He owns the hardware shop a few doors up from Mrs. King's. It's an old family business, started by his grandfather. Miss Leacock keeps house for her brother. I can't think why Mrs. King ever got friendly with them, except they were neighbours and about her own age and you can't pick and choose your friends in a place this size. They're a quiet couple. She has quite a bit to do with the church but Gilbert Leacock's never been one for mixing socially. I don't think he even goes to the men's club in the village hall for a game of darts or billiards and neither of them would dream of setting foot inside a pub. They're much too respectable. Mrs. King used to pull Gilbert's leg sometimes. 'You're in the wrong business,' she'd tell him. 'You'd've made a smashing under-taker.' But she was like that. She'd have a joke with anybody and no one could take offence; it was all done so friendly. Now, as for Stan Spurgeon, I can understand her taking to him. He's one for a laugh himself. In fact, in some ways, you might say he's a bit of a rogue."

"What do you mean, 'a bit of a rogue'?" Rudd asked.

"Nothing much, sir," Holbrook replied. "I've had no real trouble with him, mind; but on one occasion a lorry driver going to Ponder's farm with a load of seed potatoes found, when he got there, that he'd lost a couple of sacks off the back. He got in touch with me and I made inquiries along the route he'd followed. As he'd passed Spurgeon's place, I dropped in there to ask. Oh yes, said Spurgeon, he'd got the potatoes in his barn; found them lying in the road so he'd shifted them out of the way and if he'd known I was out looking for them, he'd've got in his van and come straight round to tell me. I knew damned well he'd intended hanging on to them if nobody'd asked any questions, but what could I do? I couldn't pinch him for theft although

I did warn him about stealing by finding. He just grinned and said he'd been looking after them until the owner turned up. So I had to leave it, although I was sure he was pulling my leg. But that's Spurgeon in a nutshell, sir. If he does anything wrong, there's no real malice in it."

Holbrook stopped and Rudd cocked his head interrogatively.

"I can't think of anything else to tell you," Holbrook said. "As far as I know, Stan Spurgeon and the Leacocks are the only people who had much dealings with Mrs. King, outside of business, apart from Mrs. Youngman; but she's a simple sort of soul who wouldn't hurt a fly. Besides, I know for a fact she was grateful to get that job with Mrs. King. Youngman's a cowman at Ponder's farm and doesn't earn much and they've got five young kiddies to bring up. And I believe Mrs. King was very good to her, gave her things for the children out of the shop and let her have her knitting wool cost price. As for the rest of the village, well, I can't think of a person who would want to harm her or could have written that letter, come to that; although, mind you, I've not been here above five years and there may be a good bit going on under the surface that I've not twigged on to yet."

"Fair enough," said Rudd. "I've got plenty to be going on with for the moment. Can you give me Dr. Foreman's and Mrs. Youngman's addresses?"

"Dr. Foreman's house is in the main street, almost opposite the Star. You can't miss it. And Mrs. Youngman lives in Rectory Close, that's a little cul-de-sac leading down to the church. Hers is the third cottage along the row."

Rudd swallowed the last of his beer and stood up.

"Thanks," he said. "You've been more than helpful."

"I'll see you to the door," said Holbrook.

On the way out, Rudd said good-bye to Mrs. Holbrook who was laying the table for tea. The two men stepped out into the garden where Holbrook turned to face the Inspector with a troubled look.

"I hope you can find it's an accident," he said. "God knows, her death was bad enough as it was, but I wouldn't like to think anyone caused it deliberately. It'd be like . . ."

He paused and then added in a sudden burst of words, "I'd have to leave here if it was murder. I like the place and the people but they'd be finished for me if . . ."

"I understand," said Rudd.

2

As Holbrook had said, the doctor's house was easy to find. It was an attractive, square Queen Anne building, in the main street, set back a little way from the road behind delicate iron railings. An old magnolia tree, as old possibly as the house itself, quietly dropped its leaves in the garden.

Rudd went up the three steps to the door and rang the bell. Mrs. Foreman answered it and when Rudd stated his business, she said she would fetch her husband and showed the Inspector into a small study at the front of the house.

It was a pleasant, book-lined room, shabby and well-used. Rudd went over to the window and looked across the street. Rene King's shop, the Bandbox was a little way down the road on the other side. The blinds were down over the shop window and the door but the windows above were uncovered and he could see the ruffled edges of net curtains looped back to make a pretty pattern against the glass.

Dr. Foreman came in, apologising for keeping the Inspector waiting. He was a baggy, elderly man, shrewd-faced and tired-eyed and he came straight to the point.

"Have you come about Mrs. King's death?" he asked.

"I have," said Rudd.

"Official?" asked the doctor.

"Just routine inquiries," said Rudd warily.

The doctor smiled suddenly and Rudd smiled back. In that smile they both acknowledged the fact that they had areas of professional secrecy that would be mutually respected.

"Acting on information received, I suppose?" said the doctor. "And I've a fairly good idea what that means. However, I'm surprised. I was perfectly satisfied it was accidental death."

17

"I think you'll find the inquest will be postponed," said Rudd, "pending further investigation."

"I see," said Dr. Foreman. "Well, I won't ask you any more. I'll only say this; that she was a patient of mine and I shouldn't have thought the type to arouse any deep enmity, but we'll leave it there. I suppose you'll want to hear my version?"

"I understand you examined the body?" said Rudd.

"I'll get my notes," said the doctor. "They're in my surgery."

He returned a few minutes later with a folder, a book and an awkwardly balanced tray of tea things.

"You'll join me for tea?" he asked. "Draw up a chair."

The doctor poured out two cups of tea and spread open the folder on the desk. The book intrigued Rudd and while the doctor sorted out his notes, Rudd spelled out its title upside down. It was *British Mushrooms and Toadstools* by B. D. Hillyard. The cover showed a picture of huge flat yellow fungi, like coarse pancakes covered with dark scales, growing on a tree trunk.

"Here we are," Dr. Foreman was saying, picking up a sheet of paper. "Mrs. Youngman came to the house about 9:10 a.m. on Friday, September 11th, that is three days ago. She said she had found Mrs. King and she thought she was dead. As she said Mrs. King had been very sick, I suspected food poisoning at once. Incidentally, Mrs. Youngman was deeply shocked and if you question her, which I suppose under the circumstances you'll be obliged to do, I must ask you to treat her very gently. She's still under medical supervision."

"Of course," said Rudd.

"I went across to the shop," the doctor continued, "and found Mrs. King lying on the stairs. She had been dead, I estimated, about three to four hours."

"That means she died between five and six o'clock in the morning?" Rudd asked.

"Roughly speaking," replied the doctor. "The post-mortem will no doubt establish the time of death more accurately, but I'd say my original estimate was a fairly good one. The bed had been slept in and she was wearing a night-dress and a dressing-gown which was unfastened. She had already vomited in the bedroom, the bathroom and on the landing at the top of the stairs. Taking these facts into account as well as the medical evidence for the time of

death, including the rectal temperature, my guess is that
she went to bed, woke up early in the morning feeling ill
and was on her way downstairs to fetch help when she
finally collapsed. The telephone was in the office at the
back of the shop."

"And the cause of death was poisoning?" Rudd asked.

"No. The immediate cause was, I should say, asphyxiation. Again, the post-mortem will confirm this, but my belief
is she died through inhaling vomit. I think she fainted on
the stairs, was sick while she was unconscious and the
windpipe became choked. She had fallen awkwardly, head
first, and the mouth still contained partly-digested matter
and, as far as I could ascertain, the throat also."

"Have you any theory as to what caused the illness?"
Rudd asked, although he guessed the doctor had his suspicions.

"Fungus poisoning seems the most likely," Dr. Foreman
replied. "I made a point of asking Mrs. Youngman if she
knew what Mrs. King had eaten the day before. She told
me she was going to have mushrooms on toast for tea.
Sergeant Holbrook found mushroom peelings in the waste-
bin, or at least what he thought were mushroom skins. I
searched the medicine chest before he arrived and found
nothing there, or anywhere else, to suggest she had taken an
overdose, accidentally or otherwise, of any harmful drug.
I've been doing a little homework myself since her death.
It's the first case of poisoning, or suspected poisoning, by
fungus that I've ever come across and, according to my
medical books, the most likely culprit is the fungus known
as," the doctor referred to his notes, "Amanita Phalloides,
commonly called the Stinking Amanita or the Death Cap.
Like the time of death, the post-mortem will confirm this,
but personally, I'm in little doubt.

"You see," the doctor continued, "deaths from fungus
poisoning are not all that common but they're not as rare
as you might think, although these days with plenty of
cultivated mushrooms in the shops, not many people, not
even country people, bother to go picking them in the fields.
Now the Death Cap is the one that most resembles the
ordinary edible mushroom and it accounts for over ninety
per cent of deaths through fungus poisoning. It has no
taste and no smell, despite its name Stinking Amanita; at
least, it smells only in its final stage and in its early state
it looks very like a button mushroom. It peels, too, and

that's often the test that a lot of people mistakenly go by. If it peels, they say, it must be all right to eat. Anyway, that's the information I got from this," added the doctor, tapping the book that lay on his desk. "I wanted to read up as much background information as I could."

"And the symptoms?" Rudd asked.

"Unpleasant," the doctor replied, pulling a face. "Violent stomach pains, vomiting, diarrhoea and intense thirst. These symptoms occur from six to twenty-four hours after the fungus has been eaten. According to Mrs. Youngman, Mrs. King was in the habit of having tea at about half-past six, after she had closed up the shop. So if my estimated time of death is anywhere near correct, she began to feel the effects about eleven to twelve hours after eating. Incidentally, my theory that she died through asphyxiation is supported by the symptoms of Death Cap poisoning. Normally, the patient appears to recover from the first onslaught of sickness. Then in two or three days the symptoms return more intensely. The nervous system becomes paralysed and the patient collapses and passes into a coma. Death from actual poisoning can take place anywhere up to five or ten days after the fungus was first eaten."

"As long as that?" Rudd asked, surprised.

"Yes, which makes me think that her death so soon after she had eaten was only an indirect result of poisoning. But, look here, do borrow this book if you'd care to. It gives a lot of information about the fungus and where it's found and some medical information as well. I'd be grateful if you could return it to me before too long, though. It's borrowed from the public library at Market Stratton."

"Thank you," said Rudd. "I'll get it back to you in a day or two."

Dr. Foreman handed him the book and Rudd noticed, as he did so, that it fell open at the page on which Amanita Phalloides was featured, as if that section of the book had been well used. He ran his eye quickly over the photograph that illustrated the page. It showed the fungus in two stages of growth. In the mature stage there would be no mistaking it for a mushroom. The gills were white and closer textured. But in the earlier state, the young fungus did indeed resemble a button mushroom with its white cap protruding from the ground and the gills invisible. The setting in which it was photographed, however, puzzled him.

It was a close-up study but the surrounding tall grasses and foliage suggested a woodland background rather than an open field in which wild mushrooms grew. Rudd glanced briefly at the text. Yes, he was right. "Found in deciduous woods from August to September."

The doctor was saying, "I don't think there's much more I can tell you. I examined the body thoroughly. There seemed, at the time, no reason to suspect foul play, so I arranged for the body to be taken to the mortuary at Market Stratton, ready for a post-mortem examination, and I sent along with it some specimens of the vomit and the mushroom peelings and stalks for detailed analysis. I've been in touch with the coroner and arranged for an inquest to be held. Sergeant Holbrook phoned Mrs. King's nephew in London, a Mr. Roland King, and he called to see me that same afternoon. I explained that he would be called on to give formal identification of his aunt's body. He seemed," the doctor added dryly, "to be torn between concern over his aunt's death and anxiety to get back to his business in London and I was under the impression that his business commitments were the more important. However, that's merely an old man's bitterness at the indifference of the young."

"I suppose, as next-of-kin, he's likely to inherit his aunt's property," Rudd said with seeming casualness.

Dr. Foreman gave him a surprised look, as Holbrook had done, but his professional control was better and he merely replied, with equal casualness, "That may very well be so."

"And you say he seemed distressed by his aunt's death?" Rudd asked.

"Distressed is perhaps too strong a word," the doctor replied. "He was anxious to establish the facts and he did express some warmth of feeling for her. He was worried that she might have suffered a lot of pain and said it was a terrible way to die. He certainly wasn't grief-stricken, nor was he entirely indifferent to her death. But no doubt you'll interview him yourself and form your own opinion."

He glanced at his watch.

"Is there anything else you want to know?"

"There's only the question of Mrs. Youngman's key to the shop," Rudd said. "Sergeant Holbrook said you were going to ask her for it."

"Of course. I have it here," Dr. Foreman replied and, feeling in his pocket, produced a key which he handed over to the Inspector.

"Mrs. Youngman hasn't been back to do any cleaning?" Rudd asked.

"I suppose you're thinking of fingerprints," the doctor said. "No, she hasn't. She was much too upset. But I'm afraid I'm responsible for having the carpets and bedding removed."

"Holbrook told me about that," Rudd said.

The doctor gave him a wry smile.

"I suppose it's complicated your job," he admitted, "but it had to be done. At the time, I didn't suspect anything worse than accidental death. Apart from that, I think you'll thank me. It was bad enough in there on the Friday morning. Even Holbrook was looking pretty green. So God knows what it would have been like today. The Public Health Department will be able to give you the names of the men who came. The ambulance men were from the Market Stratton General Hospital and they merely carried Mrs. King's body out. They didn't go into any of the upstairs rooms or the office."

"I can check on their prints if need be," Rudd said, getting to his feet.

"Perhaps it won't be necessary," the doctor replied as he escorted Rudd to the door.

"Perhaps," he replied guardedly.

The two men shook hands.

"You'll be present at the inquest?" Rudd asked.

"I imagine I shall be called," the doctor said. "They'll probably need formal evidence on the finding of the body. And you?"

"I expect I shall be there," said Rudd, "holding a watching brief, as they say, at that stage of the proceedings."

"I don't want to teach you your job," the doctor went on, pausing at the door, "but I shouldn't take too much notice of 'information received.' People say, and write, things they don't always mean. I get it myself, as a doctor, and I learn to turn a deaf ear and a blind eye on most occasions."

Rudd smiled but said nothing. But he thought to himself as he went down the steps that turning deaf ears and blind eyes was the one thing which a policeman could never afford to do. And in a case like the one he had just begun to investigate, any scrap of information would be more than welcome. He wondered how much the doctor knew of his patients. More than just their physical ailments, Rudd was ready to bet. He was a shrewd old man, after all. He hadn't needed telling that the Inspector had received an anonymous letter. He had been on to that fast enough. Rudd regretted that professional secrecy would prevent him from sitting down with the doctor and gossiping about the people in the village, because he would almost certainly know the neurotics and the emotionally unstable people who might have written that letter. He might even have a good idea of the most likely candidates for a murderer, although at that stage of the investigation, murder had not yet been established. It was simply a word, an idea, that someone had scrawled on to a piece of paper in awkward capital letters. It might be nothing more.

Outside, it was still early and the light had not yet faded. The air had that calm, suspended quality of a still evening without a whisper of wind. A leaf fell slowly, turning over and over, and came to rest in the gutter. The little row of shops opposite were all closed and although the public house on the corner, the Star, was open and the lights had been turned on inside, it seemed empty of customers.

Rudd crossed the road and strolled along the pavement. The Bandbox with its drawn blinds showed him nothing, although he felt that the clean white paint and bright pink facia board with the name of the shop written on it in curly black letters, picked out in gold, told him something of the gaiety of the personality that had been Rene King's. The blind was down over the door only of the Leacock's hardware shop, two doors further down and Rudd did not linger. He merely took in, as he passed, the dirty window-pane, the pyramids of dusty tins of paint, the faded red crêpe paper that lined the window bottom with the dead flies lying on it, shrivelled and dried up in the sun.

He continued walking, absorbing the atmosphere of the place; past the Red Lion, more pretentious than the Star, advertising snacks at the bar and a garden at the rear. He caught a glimpse of it, too; all trellis and metal furniture and hydrangeas in white-painted concrete tubs. The landlord, he guessed, was influenced by the proximity of a new estate of detached, red-brick bungalows on the outskirts of the village. They had nothing to interest him and he dis-

missed their wrought-iron gates and standard rose trees and
turned back towards the older part of the village.

There was, after all, very little to it. A motorist passing
through would hardly register the place unless he stopped
to buy cigarettes at the tobacconist's at the end of the row
of shops, closed now for business and presenting only an
intricate window display of dummy cigarette packets and
bars of chocolate.

He passed the doctor's house again and turned left just
beyond it into Rectory Close, with its row of cottages,
dominated by the church at the far end. Holbrook had
told him that Mrs. Youngman lived in the third cottage.
He hesitated to call on her but it had to be done.

Pausing at the gate, he caught a glimpse of a face at
the upstairs window of the cottage next door. Someone
was watching him with evident interest. Rudd grinned to
himself and, pushing open the gate, walked down the long
front garden to the door of the Youngman house. It was
a combined flower and vegetable garden and Rudd guessed
the cottages did not have much land at the rear. Runner
beans, their leaves already yellow, and winter cabbages
grew among the asters and Michaelmas-daisies. There was
a row of dahlias, too, carefully staked and tied, with an
upturned flowerpot, stuffed with hay, crowning each stake
as an earwig trap. Rudd had not seen that for years.

Youngman opened the door to his knock, in braces and
collarless shirt, chewing lustily but still managing to radiate
suspicion.

"Well?" he asked.

Rudd explained who he was and that he wanted to talk
to Mrs. Youngman. He was expecting trouble, but Youngman was not the sort of man to stand out long against
authority.

"You'd better come in, then," he said and showed Rudd
into a tiny front room that opened straight from the door
and was crowded with furniture and photographs. A row
of geranium plants on the window sill cut out much of
the light. Mrs. Youngman, coming no doubt to see who
had called, appeared at the inner door that led into the
back room and Rudd had a glimpse over her shoulder of
a big table set for tea and several children sitting round
it, their faces all turned in his direction.

"Who is it?" she asked.

She was a round-faced woman with dark hair that was drawn straight back behind her ears and fastened with two hair-slides. It was impossible to imagine her ever being young. She was the sort of woman who seems always to be surrounded by too many children, harassed and over-worked, with bad legs and soap-scoured hands.

"It's Detective Inspector Rudd," said her husband.

Immediately her eyes filled with tears and she fumbled in her apron pocket for her handkerchief.

"You've come about poor Mrs. King," she said.

"I'm afraid so," replied Rudd, moving his shoulders about restlessly. He always hated interviewing tearful witnesses, especially women of Mrs. Youngman's sort: good, simple people, inarticulate through distress. He noticed, at the same time, however, that neither Mrs. Youngman nor her husband seemed surprised at his visit. Perhaps they accepted it as a routine matter for the police to make inquiries in any case of sudden death.

"Go gently with her," Mr. Youngman pleaded. "She's been upset enough over it as it is, what with her finding Mrs. King and all."

"I'll try," said Rudd. "But there are some questions I must ask."

"Sit you down easy, now," her husband told her, "and I'll fetch you through one of your tablets."

Mrs. Youngman sat down and Mr. Youngman went out of the room, leaving behind him an odour of cow and new milk, strong but not unpleasant. Rudd seated himself opposite to her on the other side of the fireplace. The room was so tiny that their knees almost touched.

Mrs. Youngman wept and dabbed her eyes and tried to tell him what she knew, but all that Rudd could make out with any certainty was that she had liked Mrs. King, that she was "a lovely lady" and that Mrs. Youngman would miss her and the job and the money it brought in.

"It wasn't no skivvying job," she said several times, "and Mrs. King treated me like a friend."

Mr. Youngman returned, carrying a cup of tea and a minute white tablet which he gave to his wife on the huge flat palm of his hand. She took it obediently, swallowed it down and immediately became more cheerful, although Rudd suspected that its fast-acting effect was psychological rather than pharmacological.

"I have to have them for my nerves," she explained to Rudd, giving him a faint, apologetic smile.

But what he learned from her now that she was more coherent added little new and merely confirmed what he had already been told. She had found Mrs. King and had gone at once to fetch the doctor. Then being "all shook up" as she called it, she had gone home. The doctor had visited her later that morning, brought her some pills and asked her at what time in the evening Mrs. King usually ate a meal. She had told him it was about half-past six in the evening and Mrs. King would have a cooked tea, usually something on toast, like egg or tomatoes. On the Thursday, she was going to have mushrooms.

Rudd went on to ask her about her job and Mrs. Youngman cheered up even more and became quite chatty. She had evidently enjoyed working for Mrs. King and Rudd got the impression that Mrs. King treated her well. The work consisted largely of housework, of keeping the shop and office clean and tidy and preparing a midday meal for the two of them.

"She always made me eat a dinner with her," Mrs. Youngman said. "She used to say, 'Dolly, you're not going out of here until you've got a warm meal inside you.'"

Mrs. Youngman smiled and then dabbed her eyes again and Rudd realised in her something of the warmth and generosity of Rene King's personality.

"Did you prepare the mushrooms that Mrs. King had for tea on the Thursday evening?" he asked.

"Oh, no!" she said, widening her eyes in horror at the thought. "I saw them in the fridge, though, on the bottom shelf. They were in a little basket. They looked all right, nice and fresh, but, mind you, I didn't take any particular notice of them."

Rudd moved on to the question of where they had come from.

"I believe Mr. Spurgeon sometimes gave Mrs. King a few mushrooms," he said casually, but Mrs. Youngman would not be drawn.

After exchanging a quick look with her husband, she said carefully, "I couldn't say, I'm sure."

Rudd knew that she was not being obstructive or deliberately withholding information. It was a countrywoman's natural reticence about discussing a local person with a stranger. So Rudd left it there and went on to the subject of the Wednesday evening card parties. Mrs. Youngman became more relaxed and talked quite freely on this subject.

"Yes," she said. "Mrs. King enjoyed a hand of cards and, what with the shop and not being able to get out much, she looked forward to them. Mr. and Miss Leacock always came round, being near neighbours, and Mr. Spurgeon made up the four. Mrs. King used to give them supper. I know that because she used to ask me to get the sandwiches ready in the morning, to save her doing it later."

"Did you prepare them for last Wednesday's party?" Rudd asked.

"Yes, the same as usual. Mrs. King asked me to go round to Tingley's, the grocer's, and buy half a pound of sliced ham and I cut the sandwiches before I left and wrapped them in foil and put them in the fridge, so as they'd be nice and fresh for the evening. She telephoned the Star and they sent round one of those big cans of beer. That was in the fridge, too. Mr. Spurgeon preferred a glass of beer to coffee and, from what Mrs. King said, Mr. Leacock would have one with him; not that he usually drank, mind you. Mrs. King used to laugh about it. She said once, 'Poor old thing, the only time he gets a drop of beer is round at my place.' His sister, Miss Leacock, is dead against pubs and drinking but, seeing as it was a social occasion, she couldn't say much, could she?"

Miss Leacock, Rudd thought, sounded a proper old spinster. It crossed his mind that she might have written the poison pen letter. After all, it was the conclusion that Boyce had made: that the letter writer was some old biddy, who liked stirring up trouble.

"What's Miss Leacock like?" he asked casually. But Mrs. Youngman immediately became cautious again.

"Oh, she's very respectable," she said. "A regular church-goer but she doesn't mix much in the village. I feel a bit sorry for her, in a way. She hasn't many friends."

"But she became friendly with Mrs. King?" Rudd continued.

"Well," Mrs. Youngman said carefully, "I wouldn't say exactly friendly. They were on good terms, mind you, but I think Mrs. King found her a bit strait-laced. 'I've never heard that woman laugh,' she said to me once. And, when I came to think about it, I hadn't either. Mrs. King liked people who were jolly."

"And Stan Spurgeon was jolly?" Rudd hinted.

"Oh, yes," Mrs. Youngman replied, unconscious of the innu-endo behind the question. "He's always been one for a laugh."

"I see," said Rudd. He paused for a moment wondering how to introduce Roland King into the conversation.

"I believe Mrs. King's nephew was very good to her," he remarked, crossing his legs casually.

"Oh, he was," Mrs. Youngman replied. As Rudd had hoped, she did not regard the question as at all suspicious as Holbrook and Dr. Foreman had done. "She often said that if it wasn't for him, keeping her supplied with stock regular, the business wouldn't be what it was. He'd send her just a few of each item, see; just one or two blouses, not the half-dozen some wholesalers make you have; and he'd take back anything that didn't sell and credit her for it. Then there were special cheap lines he had in sometimes or samples. That way she kept her prices down. I know for a fact that I couldn't buy children's clothes cheaper anywhere else."

"Did he visit her often?" Rudd asked.

Mrs. Youngman hesitated.

"Well, I wouldn't say often. Mind you, Mrs. King under-stood. 'He's a busy man, Dolly,' she'd say. 'He can't get away as often as he'd like.' He has called on her, though, several times to my knowledge."

"So you've met him?" Rudd asked.

Mrs. Youngman gave her husband a timid, questioning look, but she must have found some reassuring expression on his face for she said, "Yes, he's called in three morn-ings when I've been there, the last time about a fortnight ago. I made coffee for them and took it through to the office behind the shop. He was going over the books with her, something to do with the accounts. He's called other times, too, from what Mrs. King has told me; sometimes in the afternoons and occasionally in the evenings, but not that often. As Mrs. King said, 'It's a long drive down from London after a day's work.'"

"Pleasant young man?" Rudd asked, leaning one elbow on the arm of the chair and assuming the position of an interested listener. But Mrs. Youngman was not easy to draw out. Perhaps she had a natural timidity at expressing an opinion or perhaps Roland King's position as her em-ployer's nephew made her reluctant to speak freely.

"He seemed nice enough," she said hesitantly. "He was

always in a rush to get off, mind. He was very nicely dressed; drove a big blue car."

She offered these last pieces of information eagerly as if hoping the Inspector would be satisfied with mere physical details.

"Did he seem fond of his aunt?" Rudd asked.

"Fond?" Mrs. Youngman repeated the word as if testing its validity. "Well, he always kissed her goodbye and said 'Look after yourself.' I think . . ."

She stopped and looked down into her lap.

"Yes?" Rudd encouraged her gently.

"I felt she was fonder of him than he was of her. She was always a bit sad after he'd gone although she tried not to show it. She's never said a word against him, mind, but I felt she was disappointed he didn't come more often or stay a bit longer. 'Are you stopping for a meal?' she'd ask him and he'd always say, 'Sorry, I can't this time, auntie. Perhaps another day.' And I know she'd bought something special for dinner just in case he'd say yes. It was lovely pork chump chops once. 'All the more for us, Dolly,' she said, but I could tell she was a bit hurt."

"Selfish," Mr. Youngman said.

Until that moment he had kept totally silent throughout the interview, although Rudd had been aware of him, sitting on an upright chair by the door that led into the living-room; a listening presence, his forearms resting on his knees, his head supported in his hands, sometimes turning towards the door as if aware of the children at tea behind it, but most often watching his wife with a tender, anxious and yet encouraging expression on his face.

His sudden remark was, therefore, all the more surprising.

Mrs. Youngman looked flustered.

"I wouldn't say exactly selfish," she began.

"Too busy to bother," Youngman continued. "He's got that big car but he never took her out in it for a drive, not once. Haven't I said that to you, Dolly, that you'd think he'd come down of a Sunday and take her out for a drive?"

"He does live in London," his wife said deprecatingly.

"It's not all that far, not by car. Look at the time before your mother died. You were off every blessed afternoon, ten miles by bus, rain or shine, and a mile walk the other end, but you did it willingly."

Mrs. Youngman looked distressed, but whether at the

memory of her mother or of her husband's obvious displeasure at Roland King's lack of family feeling. Rudd
could not tell. But one thing was clear. The Youngmans
had discussed King's attitude to his aunt and found it wanting, although whether it was sufficiently lacking in feeling
to lead to murder was another matter. Certainly King had
not been devoted to his aunt and his greatest interest in
her seemed to have been on a business rather than a personal level.

Youngman's outburst had obviously upset his wife. She
sat trembling and fumbling with her handkerchief. Rudd
felt it was time to go. He rose, holding out his hand.

"Thank you," he said. "You've been very helpful. I hope
my questions haven't tired you too much."

The remark, meant to be kindly, only added to her
distress. Tears welled up in her eyes and Rudd, excusing
himself, went quickly to the door.

Outside, the light was fading rapidly. A few streaks of
colour in the sky behind the church was all that remained
of the day. A late bird flew homeward and in the dense
shadows of the yew trees that surrounded the churchyard
the bats were already out, swooping in silent flight under
the dark branches.

Rudd walked back to his car. The windows of the Star
were now bright with the lights inside and he could hear
voices and laughter. Heads were visible in the clear panes
above the Victorian patterned glass that filled the lower
halves of the windows. He wondered whether or not to go
in and then decided against it. The mere presence of a
stranger would be enough to cut conversation short and if
he started asking questions, he could imagine the shuffling,
embarrassed replies he would receive. Like Mrs. Youngman,
they would not talk easily about their neighbours except
among themselves.

He glanced up at the windows above the row of shops.
Mrs. King's were, of course, in darkness. So too were
the Leacocks'. They evidently did not use the front upstairs
room in the evening. Possibly they lived in the room behind
the shop, the one Mrs. King had turned into an office. It
was too late, he decided, to call on them and he unlocked
the car and drove out of the village.

He felt disappointed over the day's work. Although he
had gathered a lot of information, he was no further in
establishing whether the case was a criminal one or one of

those tragic accidents for which no one was to blame. Mrs. King sounded a nice woman. She was jolly. She was friendly. She enjoyed company and a game of cards. She was, as Mrs. Youngman had said, a "lovely lady" and she had died under particularly unpleasant circumstances.

He was disappointed, too, that there had not been time to interview the Leacocks or Stan Spurgeon. Apart from the nephew, who might have stood to gain from her death, he was interested in the farmer. If Dr. Foreman was correct and Mrs. King had died as an indirect result of Death Cap poisoning, it appeared a strong possibility that the fungus had been introduced into the basket of mushrooms that Spurgeon had taken to her on the Wednesday evening, although until the pathologist's report came through, the cause of death had not been established. But he would have to interview both men all the same.

Meanwhile, Rudd had his reports to write up and arrangements to make for the dead woman's shop and the flat over it to be thoroughly examined. After that he could go home. He was looking forward to an evening spent sitting in an armchair reading the book on mushrooms and fungus that Dr. Foreman had lent him.

At the office, he settled down at his desk, leaving Boyce to organise the search. Later, the reports finished and the arrangements completed, he drove home, where his widowed sister, who kept house for him, had lit the sitting-room fire for the first time as the evening had grown chilly. His dog, Cairn, welcomed him at the door, ecstatic at his return.

Rudd's sister served his supper and, after he had eaten, he withdrew from the table to his favourite armchair. The fire crackled up, making the room almost too hot. Rudd took off his jacket and, slippered and comfortable, with Cairn asleep at his feet on the floor, he opened the book.

Again he noticed how easily it fell open on the page that featured the Death Cap fungus and a faint stirring of suspicion made him examine it more carefully. Holding it up to the light, he squinted down the spine. As he had suspected, it had been bent back so far as to crack the binding. He sat thinking for a moment. He could not imagine the doctor handling it in so rough a manner. His book-lined study suggested a man for whom a book was an object to be treated with respect.

Rudd turned to the front where the library's dating plate was stuck to the flyleaf and he ran his eye down the dates stamped on it. The last was for the 26th September, the day on which presumably the doctor was to return it. The date before that was the one that interested Rudd. It was for the 8th September. Somebody else, then, had borrowed the book and returned it only days before the doctor had' taken it out.

And yet the stamp immediately before that was for the 21st February, eight months previously, and the one before that for October of the year before. The book was, therefore, not a popular one. Not many people wanted to read about British Fungi. Yet twice within a month, two people had borrowed it: the doctor, whose interest in it was understandable following the death of Mrs. King; and someone else who had taken the book out of the library shortly before Mrs. King's death and, if Rudd's surmise was correct, had turned back the page relating to Amanita Phalloides so roughly as to crack the binding.

Rudd stroked his lower lip thoughtfully. There might be nothing in it at all. It might be one of those coincidences that sometimes turn up and confuse an investigation. All the same, he was taking no chances and, calling to his sister to bring a clean plastic bag, he slipped the book inside it. Forensic should be able to raise some fingerprints on its shiny cover and on the page itself, although Rudd could imagine the confusion of prints that would be found. His certainly and Dr. Foreman's and the librarians'. Other people, too, could have handled the book quite innocently. He could see Boyce, heavy with displeasure, chasing round fingerprinting a dozen or more people and all, perhaps, in the end to no purpose. The book might have been borrowed by someone quite unconnected with the case. There might, in the last analysis, be no case at all. It could be a mere hoax; a malicious hoax certainly, set in motion by someone who liked stirring up trouble; by some old woman with a grievance, as Boyce had suggested; by somebody a bit mad.

Well, that was something he had to put up with. It was all part of his day's work. All the same, deprived of his evening's reading and feeling rather bad-tempered, Rudd had a bath and went early to bed for once.

3

"So what it boils down to is this," Boyce was saying, "if Mrs. King was murdered, the most likely suspects are Stan Spurgeon who supplied the mushrooms, assuming it's a case of fungus poisoning; the Leacocks who were round at her flat the evening they were delivered; Mrs. Youngman who did her cleaning; and the nephew."

They were in Rudd's car, with the Inspector at the wheel, on their way to Abbots Stacey. Rudd had taken the opportunity of discussing the case in more detail with his Sergeant during the drive as the time spent at the office had been largely taken up with organising the details for an inspection of Mrs. King's flat. Another police car that was following behind them contained three constables and a photographer, whom Rudd had arranged to travel together in order that he and Boyce could discuss the case between themselves.

"That's about it, Tom," Rudd replied. "They're the only people who so far have entered the case. We may turn up others as we go along. As far as I'm concerned, it's still wide open."

"Too wide open, if you ask me," Boyce commented. "I like a murder case that I know is a murder case; a straight-forward stabbing or a bashing over the head with a blunt instrument; none of this messing about with possible accidental death. You don't know where you are half the time."

"It's kid glove tactics rather than throwing your official weight about. If it turns out to be accidental death, I don't want anybody suing me for wrongful arrest. Nor do I want any innocent person suspected, and once gossip starts in a village, you know only too well the kind of thing it can lead to."

33

Boyce looked thoughtful.

"True enough," he replied, "but you can't make inquiries without picking on someone to question."

"Then we go carefully and we don't have anyone in at this stage to make an official statement until we're certain of the facts. I intend keeping it on as informal a level as possible until I'm forced to act otherwise. It'll be nice friendly chats with the people so far concerned and an ear kept pressed to the ground for any useful tidbits of gossip or rumour that we can pick up as we go along."

"From what you've said, both Holbrook and the doctor seemed convinced it was an accident," Boyce remarked.

"Holbrook still thinks it is," Rudd said, "and I can't say I blame him. It's his patch, after all, and he knows the people. He can't bring himself to think any of them could be a killer."

"So he counts the nephew out as well?" Boyce asked.

"That's shrewd of you," Rudd said. "And shrewd of him too, and I must admit I'm inclined to agree with his line of thinking. If it is murder, it seems more likely it was someone from the village. But, as I said, it's still wide open and certainly the nephew stood to gain by her death. I'm not counting him out at this stage."

"There's the library book," Boyce pointed out. Rudd had already discussed its possible significance with the Sergeant earlier that morning before sending it off to forensic for fingerprint tests. "If it was borrowed from the public library at Market Stratton, I can't see the nephew going to all that trouble to get hold of it."

"I've already thought of that," Rudd replied, "and it still doesn't rule him out because the book may have no bearing on the case at all. We'll follow it up, of course, but I'm not counting on it leading anywhere, except possibly up a blind alley."

Boyce nodded his head in gloomy agreement.

"Come to that," he said, "I don't know what you're hoping to find in Mrs. King's flat. If you ask me that's going to be another blind alley. All we're likely to find are the prints of the people we know were in the flat anyway and that's not much use as evidence."

Rudd suppressed a sigh. There were times when he found Boyce's attitude depressingly negative, particularly when it coincided with his own less optimistic moments, as it did now. The flat would have to be searched, of course, even if, as Boyce predicted, nothing very useful came of it. It was part of the routine of investigation.

He glanced irritably at Boyce only to find the Sergeant grinning at him.

"Don't mind me," Boyce said. "The wife had me up at half-past six this morning; thought she could smell gas. I was on my hands and knees snuffing round the cooker like a ruddy bloodhound, trying to find a leak. So, sorry if I'm not all sweetness and light."

"That's all right," Rudd said, smiling back. "And did you find one?"

"Find what?"

"A leak."

"No, of course not," Boyce said with affectionate contempt. "She has these phases. If it's not gas leaks, it's the drains smelling or dry-rot under the stairs. That's women for you. My old mum was the same, only with her, it was slates slipping on the roof. The slightest sign of damp on a ceiling and she was off round the landlord's complaining. It gave her something to worry about. Anyhow," he added, "that's neither here nor there. To get back to the case; do you want me to interview Spurgeon or the Leacocks?"

"No," said Rudd. "Leave them to me. I'll see Spurgeon this afternoon, after we've turned the flat over. The Leacocks can come later. I'd rather keep you in the background, Tom, if you don't mind, dealing with routine stuff at the office. I don't want to rouse too much comment by having several of us tramping round the village knocking on doors. Until murder's been proved, if it ever is, I'd rather play a lone hand."

They were entering the village, passing the council houses on their right, then a row of Victorian terraced cottages with little slated porches and cramped front gardens. Across the road a group of bungalows faced them, of the 1930s style. A dog sat on the pavement. An old man with a carrier bag walked slowly along in the direction of the shops.

"Not much of a place, by the look of it," Boyce commented. "Fancy spending your life in a dead-and-alive hole like this."

He looked away from the window, dismissing the village and its inhabitants. Boyce, with his city background and upbringing, would never understand the country and the countryman's attitude to life.

They turned the sharp corner by the Star and drew up outside the Bandbox. Holbrook, previously warned by Rudd of the approximate time of their arrival, was waiting near-by, gazing into the window of Abstey's, the greengrocer's next-door, and trying to appear casual and unobtrusive. He walked towards them as the two cars approached.

"No one much about," Rudd remarked, glancing up and down the sunlit street. Apart from a woman who had just emerged from the post-office and was crossing the road, and a child in a pushchair left outside the butcher's, the place was deserted. Even the school playground was empty but it was possible to hear through the open windows of one of the classrooms the tumpety-tump rhythm of a piano and children's voices gustily singing "The Raggle-Taggle Gypsies O."

"It's early yet," Holbrook replied, looking at his watch. "Not many women get out to the shops before half-past eleven and those with kiddies at the school usually do their shopping even later; then they can pick the children up at half-past twelve and take them home for dinner."

"Well, if a crowd does collect," Rudd said, "which seems unlikely, you know what to do."

"Yes, sir," replied Holbrook.

Boyce had emerged from the car with the case of finger-printing equipment and the photographer and the three constables were unloading the camera and lamps from the other car. On Rudd's instructions all the men were in plain clothes and neither car carried any official police markings.

"I think you know my sergeant," Rudd said and left Boyce and Holbrook shaking hands and chatting while he unlocked the door of the Bandbox and went inside.

The cream-coloured blinds were still drawn down over the window and the glass panel in the door and the sunlight striking against them filled the shop with a soft diffused radiance. It was like being inside a tent. There was a heavy sweet smell in the air that struck him as soon as he opened the door and he sniffed it warily. For a second he associated the smell with death and then he realised it was the scent he had come to connect with mortuaries; the all-pervading odour of disinfectant that had grown stale and had lost its first medicinal sharpness.

He glanced quickly about him, absorbing the details of the shop. To his right was a long, glass-topped counter with display drawers underneath it. The same clear-fronted drawers made up a wall cabinet behind. Everything was neatly folded and encased in plastic bags and printed labels gave their contents: ladies' jumpers, socks, gloves, children's vests, baby pants, scarves. Coloured hanks of wool were piled up on shelves and further along a separate cabinet contained reels of sewing silk, darning wool, needles, zip fasteners and buttons. A cash register and a female torso made out of wire, displaying a pink wool twin-set, stood on the counter top.

On the left-hand side were two racks containing women's blouses and skirts, and children's dresses and romper suits. The far corner had been curtained off and, as he passed it, he twitched aside the curtain to reveal a tiny changing cubicle fitted with a full-length mirror and a stool.

"Nice little shop," Boyce was saying. He and the other men were now crowding in. "Where do you want us to start?"

"Upstairs," Rudd replied. "Take the kitchen first. I want the fridge thoroughly printed inside and out. The mushrooms were in it, on the bottom shelf. Then work your way through the other rooms. Stallington can help you with that."

He turned to the other two constables.

"As they finish with a room, I want you to go through all the cupboards and drawers."

"Are we looking for anything in particular?" one of them asked.

"How should I know?" Rudd snapped. A sense of frustration came over him which he masked under an air of irritability. "Use your initiative."

The police photographer stood by the door, his camera slung over one shoulder, with the patient and resigned expression on his face of a man long accustomed to waiting. He was a taciturn Scot.

"Am I to use my initiative too?" he asked.

Rudd knew him well and understood that the remark contained no criticism. "I want general views of all the rooms," the Inspector told him. "Take them from several angles. And photos of any prints that might seem significant, especially in the kitchen."

He looked at the group of men and moved his shoulders restlessly.

"I'm sorry I can't be more specific. As you know, this is an unofficial inquiry. Murder hasn't yet been established. So it's a bit like looking for a needle in a haystack, without being sure that the needle's there anyway. All we can do is turn the place over and hope that something useful comes up."

With Rudd leading the way, they moved towards the door at the back of the shop. It opened into a narrow vestibule from which the stairs rose. The sweet smell was stronger here, almost suffocatingly cloying in the small enclosed space. Another door opposite led presumably to the back room that Holbrook had said Mrs. King used as an office.

They mounted the stairs, their feet sounding hollow on the uncarpeted treads. At the top was a long landing and several doors. Rudd opened them briefly. Bathroom, bedroom, sitting-room. The kitchen was at the back of the house.

"In here," Rudd instructed and they trooped in, Boyce making straight for the fridge and squatting down in front of it while Stallington unpacked the fingerprinting equipment on the plastic-topped kitchen table. The photographer began to set up his lamps and the two other constables, sensing they were in the way, retreated to the landing where they could be heard talking quietly together.

Rudd stayed watching. The kitchen was bright and modern, decorated in blue and white. Like the shop, everything was tidily arranged. On the floor stood a small pedal refuse bin and Rudd eased his way past McCallum, the photographer, and lifted the lid. Inside it a few scraps of mushroom peelings, dried up and withered, still clung to the lining. These did not interest Rudd; Dr. Foreman had already sent specimens off for analysis. What did interest him was the small basket that still lay undisturbed in the bottom of the bin. It was made of thin waxed cardboard, square in shape, the kind in which soft fruit, such as strawberries, are sold. Calling for tweezers and a plastic bag, Rudd picked it up carefully and handed it over to Stallington with instructions to get it sent off to forensic.

The photographer was manœuvring a lamp into position and as there was nothing else that Rudd could do for the time being, he left them to it and went to explore the flat for himself. He wanted to get the feel of the place and the personality of the dead woman who had occupied it.

Everywhere suggested comfort and feminine prettiness. One end of the sitting-room, with its two long sash windows, draped in nylon curtains, overlooking the street, was furnished as a dining area with modern Swedish furniture in blond wood. At the other end, two armchairs and a sofa in moss green buttoned velvet were drawn up round an electric fire that stood in the grate. There were lamps and ornaments on low tables and on the white-painted book shelves that filled the chimney alcoves. Rudd bent down to read some of the titles. Most of them were fiction, historical novels and detective books; there were a few romances and biographies of the lighter sort.

He only glanced into the bathroom before going into the bedroom across the landing which, like the kitchen, overlooked the back of the house. The same pretty feminine comfort was present here, even though some of the gray carpeting had been taken up and the bed had been stripped down to its box-spring base.

There was a photograph on the dressing-table of a smiling middle-aged man and beside it a leather box with silver fittings. Remembering the small key that Holbrook had given him, Rudd took it from his pocket and turned it in the lock, holding the box by its corners and gently easing back the lid. It was fitted out as a jewellery case, with velvet lined compartments but, apart from a few cheap paste ornaments, the tray was empty. Rudd lifted it out by its centre tab. The bottom half of the box contained letters, presumably written to Mrs. King by her late husband.

Rudd replaced the top tray, closed the box and returned to the kitchen where Boyce and the others were still busy. The refrigerator was now propped open and the Sergeant was dusting the shelves and the inner surface of the door.

"There's a box in the bedroom," the Inspector said, "on the dressing-table. Give that a going over, will you? I've left the key in the lock but I don't think you'll get much from the inside. It's lined with velvet."

Boyce raised his eyebrows and Rudd added a little snappishly, "Jewellery, but not much there except the paste stuff. She may not have owned anything of value but I'd like to know who else handled that box besides her."

"Will do," replied Boyce and returned to his task.

There remained only the ground floor to examine. Rudd descended the stairs and turned to the right into the room that lay behind the shop. It was fitted out partly as a store, partly as an office, with racks built against the walls to hold stock and a desk under the window, with an old-fashioned green-painted safe standing in the corner. Another door led into a further room, intended originally as a kitchen. Rudd stuck his head round the corner, registering briefly a sink, an electric kettle and a tray of tea things on a table. There was no sign of a cooking stove. Mrs. King had presumably used the room only for the preparation of hot drinks to save her the trouble of going upstairs. The back door, he noticed, was bolted and on a chain.

He returned to the office and sat down at the desk. It was the pedestal type with a row of little pigeon-holes across the back, holding stamps, labels, paper-clips and other small items. Two deep drawers and a cupboard filled the lower section. Rudd opened them in turn. In the cupboard was a portable typewriter and that was all. The bottom drawer had been fitted out as a filing cabinet and held thin cardboard folders of invoices and receipts, while the top drawer contained packets of stationery and an address book. There was no sign of any of the account books belonging to the shop.

Rudd closed the drawer and went over to the safe which he unlocked with the key. That, too, was empty apart from a long brown envelope which, on inspection, held nothing more valuable than bank statements.

He stood in front of the safe for a moment, thinking, and then went through to the shop and rang up the "No Sale" key on the till. The cash drawer shot open, nearly hitting him in the stomach. A glance was enough to tell him that it contained no money at all.

Rudd strode to the shop door. Holbrook was standing outside on the pavement, chatting to a woman with a pram. As soon as he heard the door open, he glanced in Rudd's direction and the Inspector jerked his head towards the interior. Holbrook, taking the hint, excused himself discreetly. It was so tactfully done that the woman did not even glance round but simply nodded good-bye to Holbrook and went off up the road with the pram.

Holbrook stepped into the shop and Rudd locked the door behind him.

"Where did you say Mrs. King kept her account books?" the Inspector asked.

"They were in the top drawer of the desk," Holbrook replied. "I saw them there when I was looking for the nephew's address."

"Well, they're not there now," Rudd replied. "The till's empty too; there's no money in the safe, either; and the little leather box you mentioned that looks as if it ought to contain some valuable jewellery has a few bits and pieces of paste in it and that's all."

Holbrook looked worried.

"I wouldn't know about the money, sir. I don't know what day Mrs. King went to the bank. But I do know for a fact that she had one or two nice pieces of jewellery she used to wear. You get to notice things like that, just in case there's ever a robbery. Do you think someone's broken into the place? I swear I checked all the doors and windows before I left that Friday morning."

"There's been no break in," Rudd said impatiently. "My guess is the nephew's been down and taken the stuff. Duplicate keys. It seems the obvious answer. Nothing's been forced, not even the safe or the jewellery box."

"Then he had no right," Holbrook protested indignantly. "He ought to have spoken to me first although, of course, I'd've said no. I couldn't give him or anyone permission to remove anything until after the inquest."

"She must have trusted him," Rudd said, half to himself. "And the nephew didn't waste much time in clearing the place of anything worthwhile."

He turned to the Sergeant.

"Make a few discreet inquiries of the neighbours, will you? Find out if any of them saw his car parked outside recently, either just before or after her death."

Holbrook said nothing, merely nodding assent, and went off looking worried. Rudd clumped back upstairs.

Boyce and Stallington had finished in the kitchen which was now occupied by the two constables who were opening drawers and cupboards and turning over their contents with light, practiced fingers. Rudd withdrew his head from round the door and went into the bedroom where he found the Sergeant and the other constable busy with the box on the dressing-table. Boyce looked up as Rudd entered.

"I want you to print the desk downstairs, the safe and the till in the shop. I've handled all three but I don't think I've left much in the way of dabs," the Inspector told him.

"Something turned up?" Boyce asked.

"I'm not sure yet," Rudd replied. He did not want to discuss his suspicions in front of Stallington who had the eager and hopeful air of a dog on the scent of a rabbit. Far too eager, Rudd did not trust his discretion.

Without saying anything more he clumped off downstairs

again just in time to hear Holbrook tapping at the glass in the shop door. Rudd let him in.

The Sergeant had the same eager air as the constable, but suppressed and controlled.

"I've had a word with the shopkeepers on both sides," he said. "The Tingleys who keep the grocer's didn't notice anything but Mr. Abstey saw the nephew's car—at least, he's pretty sure it was his, a light blue Cortina, anyway— parked outside on the Sunday evening about eight o'clock. He was taking the dog for a walk. He didn't see anybody and the car had gone by the time he got back."

"Which Sunday was this?" Rudd asked.

"Last Sunday," Holbrook replied. "After Mrs. King's death. Nobody noticed the car before that, except for about a fortnight ago and that was in the morning."

"Mrs. Youngman mentioned the nephew paying Mrs. King a visit recently," Rudd commented.

"Looks a bit fishy, him letting himself into the shop like that," Holbrook said. There was a faint questioning tone in his voice as if he was asking the Inspector's opinion. Rudd was not going to be drawn.

"I'll get in touch with him. There may be a quite simple explanation. Do you know if the phone in the office is still working?"

"As far as I know," Holbrook replied. "The doctor used it that morning we found her and I haven't heard that it's been cut off. Do you want me to go back outside?"

The last remark was said wistfully. It was clear the Sergeant would prefer to stay inside where it seemed the action was now taking place rather than resume his lonely patrol duties in the street with only the local shopkeepers and a few passers-by for company. But he was disappointed.

"I'll call you if I need you," the Inspector said firmly and Holbrook walked heavily through the shop and let himself out.

Rudd sat down at Mrs. King's desk and lifted the telephone receiver. It was still working and, having found the number of the nephew's business in London on the top of an invoice, he dialled it.

A girl's voice answered, pert and at the same time bored. Rudd asked to speak to Mr. Roland King.

"I'll see if he's in his office," the girl replied indifferently. There was a clicking sound on the line, the girl said

"You're through" and immediately a man's voice announced, "Roland King speaking."

Rudd had always prided himself on his ability to sum up a person's character by voice alone and to adapt his own approach accordingly. King spoke briskly, with total conviction in his own identity and yet in a neutral tone, not committing himself to any reaction until he knew the name and business of the caller. There was the faint nasal ring in his voice of a person who has lived all his life in the East End of London and has picked up, probably unknowingly, a very slight Cockney intonation.

Rudd's voice was equally neutral as he explained who he was.

"I see," said King after a tiny pause. "How can I help you?"

"We're making routine inquiries into the death of Mrs. King of Abbots Stacey," Rudd continued. At times like this he found the slightly pompous official language a very useful cover. "She was your aunt, I understand."

"Yes, she was," King replied carefully, as if he felt safe committing himself in giving this piece of information.

"We have had occasion to examine Mrs. King's premises at Abbots Stacey," Rudd went on, "and we believe someone may have entered them recently and removed certain items."

"What items?" King asked sharply. As Rudd had hoped, this direct approach had drawn King's attention away from the question why the police had been examining his aunt's shop.

"The account books are missing," Rudd replied, "and as far as we know certain items of jewellery also. Naturally," he added, his voice taking on a disarmingly frank and confiding tone, "we thought we ought to contact you about this, as you're a near relative of Mrs. King."

It had its desired effect. When he answered Roland King sounded embarrassed and anxious to explain.

"It's very good of you to get in touch with me, Inspector. As a matter of fact, there's no need for you to worry. I was a bit concerned about certain things of value being left lying about the place as it was empty and I let myself in a few days ago and took them."

"Oh, I see," said Rudd, assuming the cheerful air of a man pleased to have a mystery solved. "We couldn't understand as there was no sign of anyone having broken in. I suppose you had a spare key, sir?"

"Yes. My aunt gave me one in case of an emergency."
King now sounded wary.

"And duplicate keys for the safe and the jewellery box,
too, I suppose?" Rudd continued.

There was a silence and then King said, "Well, no. My
aunt kept a spare set of keys hidden in the house in case
the original ones were ever lost or stolen. I used those.
My aunt never kept it a secret from me where she hid
them."

He was beginning to sound annoyed, like a man who feels
he has been put in the wrong and resents it.

"Look here, there was nothing underhand about it. As
one of my aunt's executors as well as her next-of-kin, I
felt I was perfectly within my rights to remove those things.
The jewellery and the money from the safe and the till are
at the bank, the manager of which is the other executor,
and the books are with my accountant. I really don't see
why the police should be interested."

Rudd hastened to soothe him down.

"It's just a matter of routine inquiries, sir," he said blandly.
"All the same, I'd be grateful if you'd let me know if you
intend entering the premises again. And perhaps you'd be
kind enough to let me have the account books. Again, it's
a purely formal matter."

"Oh, very well," King grudgingly replied. "I suppose it
must be necessary, although I had no idea there was all
this fuss in a case of accidental death. Will it be all right
if I let you have them in two or three days' time?"

"That will do very nicely, sir," Rudd said and rang off
before King could inquire any further into the matter of the
police investigation. He felt he had handled him rather
cleverly. The man was clearly no fool and could have asked
a lot of awkward questions. With a jaunty step, Rudd went
to the bottom of the stairs and shouted for Boyce.

The Sergeant's head appeared over the banister railings.

"I want you down here, Tom," Rudd said. "On your own."

Boyce came clattering down and the Inspector took him
into the office, closing the door after him.

"As soon as you're through here," he told him, "you're
to get up to London and check on the nephew. I'll give
you the address. Find out what he was doing on the Wednesday and the Thursday before Mrs. King died. But make
it discreet, for God's sake."

Boyce looked interested.

"Found something that points to him?" he asked.

Rudd humped his shoulders. His elated mood had gone, leaving him feeling depressed and uncertain.

"I don't know. I've just been on the phone to him. He admits quite frankly removing jewellery and the account books, as well as money. He says he didn't like the idea of them being left here with the property empty.

"That sounds reasonable," Boyce said.

"I know it does," Rudd snapped. "It's quite reasonable, too, that Mrs. King should have given him a spare key to the shop door and that he knew where she kept the keys to the safe and the jewellery box. It's damned sharp of him, too, as well as reasonable. But how do we know what he took? She may have kept a lot of cash on the premises that she didn't bank. It's been known to happen. Fiddling the Income Tax, it's called. And as he's got the account books, there's no way of checking on it at the moment. So we'll check on him first, even if it results in nothing more than crossing him off a list of possible suspects."

"All right," Boyce replied without much enthusiasm. "What do you think he did? Nipped down here from London after the card party and popped a few fungi in with the mushrooms?"

He sounded slightly derisive and Rudd reacted irritably.

"No, I don't. But he could have brought her a present of mushrooms, suitably doctored. And anyway, we'd be wrong to assume at this stage that she died as a result of fungus poisoning, although the local doctor seemed convinced of it. Until the path. report comes through, we can't be certain. For all we know, he might have brought her a cream bun with a dose of arsenic in it. The symptoms, vomiting and diarrhea, aren't exclusive to any one poison; and don't forget, she died of asphyxiation, at least that's Dr. Foreman's theory, although even that's open to question."

He caught sight of the expression on Boyce's face and made a conciliatory gesture with his hand.

"I'm sorry if I sound annoyed, Tom. To be quite frank, this case is beginning to get on my nerves. There's so little to go on. All I know is a woman is dead, possibly murdered, and her nephew stood to gain from her death which gives him a motive and as far as I can see, it's the only motive we've yet come across."

"Right you are," Boyce replied. "That's good enough

reason for checking on him. We should be finished here in a couple of hours. I'll push off up to London as soon as we're through."

"Meanwhile, I'll check on the local angle, assuming for the moment, that Dr. Foreman was right and it was fungus poisoning," Rudd said. "I'll have to interview the farmer, Spurgeon, and the Leacocks who were at the card party, and just hope to God something positive turns up."

He leaned his hands on the top of the desk and gave Boyce a quizzical grin.

"I sometimes wish I was in some restful business," he said, "like dry-cleaning, working regular hours and every weekend off."

"Get away with you," Boyce replied with amusement. "You know very well it's meat and drink to you."

"Perhaps," Rudd replied. "And you?"

"My old woman wants me to give it up," Boyce replied obliquely, "and start a boarding-house in Margate."

He looked at Rudd, his eyes crinkled up with laughter.

"There'd be no getting away from her then, would there? Besides," he added, "I hate the sea; always have done. There's too bloody much of it, in my opinion."

"You'll do, Tom," said Rudd happily, his good humour restored. "Come on, let's get this job sewn up."

Boyce strode to the foot of the stairs and shouted for Stallington. Rudd wandered back into the shop. It was still full of diffused sunlight but he could no longer smell the scent of the stale disinfectant that had reminded him of death. Like a good many other things, he had got used to it.

4

Spurgeon's farm was two miles out of Abbots Stacey, on the Latching road. The house itself was set back a little way from the grass verge, behind a high tangled hedge. It was a small, depressing looking building with a slate roof that looked too large for it. A farm gate, set open, and a deeply-rutted drive led round to the back of the house and to a yard surrounded by farm buildings. Everything looked neglected and in need of repair.

At the road's edge beside the gate, Rudd noticed an old kitchen table with a board nailed to the gate-post beside it, announcing in crude, hand-painted letters: "For Sale. Home-grown Produce. Flowers. Fruit. Vegetables. Eggs." Some bedraggled asters stood in an enamel pail on the ground and on the table were two wooden trays containing apples and pears, and a basket of eggs. There was no sign of any mushrooms.

Rudd drove the car along the farm drive a little way and having parked it against the hedge so as not to obstruct the opening, walked round to the back of the house. There was no one about and after knocking loudly several times at the back door and getting no answer, Rudd crossed the yard to examine the farm buildings. There was a dilapidated barn, a range of dirty styes containing a few pigs; half a dozen young heifers in a pen and a large hen-run in which about fifty chickens were pecking disconsolately at the earth, from which every blade and shoot had long ago been eaten, leaving only clumps of nettles and dock plants. A mud-caked tractor stood in front of the barn but there was no sign of any human life.

A gate led from the yard into a meadow and Rudd guessed this was the mushroom field that Holbrook had mentioned. It was a large field, sloping gently down towards

the farm, and although no horses were in it except one old
white one that was quietly cropping the grass on the far
side, it was evident from the horse droppings that it had
been used fairly recently as a paddock. The mushrooms, too,
were evident. As Rudd climbed over the gate and walked
up the field, he could see their white caps growing in little
constellations among the grass. Rudd strolled about. Although he was no expert, it seemed to him that what he
could see were indeed mushrooms, although the book by
B. D. Hillyard had made it clear that the Death Cap
fungus closely resembled the edible mushroom in its early
stages of growth. Rudd, therefore, looked for the more
mature and more easily recognisable fungus, with its greenish
gills, but as far as he could make out, all the clumps he
examined were of the edible mushroom. The field, however, was too large for him to examine it all.

The far end of the field was bounded by a wood and
the large oak trees that grew on its edge had extended
their branches in places over the meadow. Remembering
that Hillyard's book had stated that the Death Cap could
be found in pastures adjoining woodland, Rudd examined
the grass there with greater care. But, although he walked
up and down several times and stopped to look closely
at every mushroom clump in the vicinity of the trees, he
could see no sign of Amanita Phalloides.

Rudd sighed and straightened his back. The fact that he
had found nothing proved little, except that he might not
have looked carefully enough. The only answer would be
to get a group of men, at least twenty, to make an inch
by inch search of the field. If they found nothing, it would
at least prove something; that however the fungus might have
been introduced into the basket of mushrooms, it had not
been because anyone had picked one accidentally, mistaking
it for an edible mushroom.

The wood presented a different problem. If the fungus
grew there, then someone had either gone out of his way to
pick it deliberately or was ignorant of the fact that mushrooms do not grow in woods. In the first case it would
be murder. In the second, it still remained accidental death.

Rudd was looking over the tangle of barbed wire, broken
fencing and low bushes that formed the boundary between
the wood and the field, wondering whether to try pushing
his way through, when an angry shout behind him made him
turn and he saw a man coming towards him, waving his

arms. It was obviously Spurgeon, come to see why Rudd was on his land, and the Inspector walked forward to meet him.

"What you doing?" Spurgeon was shouting. "This is private land! Clear off!"

Rudd continued to walk towards him without replying. He had no intention of shouting back that he was a police inspector come to inquire into the death of Mrs. King. But he put on a pleasant expression to mollify the angry farmer.

As the two men drew nearer, Rudd could see that Spurgeon was a tall, well-built man in his forties, with coarse brown hair and moustache. Under his tanned skin there was an angry red flush and his bright blue eyes had a furious look in them. But, despite the old working clothes he was wearing and his general unkempt appearance, Rudd could see that the man, if smartly dressed and in a good humour, would be attractive. There was a strength and masculinity about him and a free and easy swagger in the way he carried himself.

A few yards from him, Rudd stopped and stood his ground, letting Spurgeon approach him. He was amused to see that the farmer had shot his bolt and was now so out of breath with fast walking and shouting, that he was speechless. However, he kept his face straight and said politely, "Mr. Spurgeon? I'm Detective Inspector Rudd from Chelmsford C.I.D. I was hoping I'd see you. I'd like a word with you."

"What?" said the man. He seemed completely deflated on learning Rudd's identity. Having worked himself up into a fine rage, which he could no longer vent, he was at a loss what to say.

"Perhaps we could go into the house for a chat?" Rudd suggested. "It's a bit nippy out here for talking."

Indeed a chill little wind had begun to blow. Even the horse felt it and shifted round to be back to it, its tail and mane whipped sideways. Some fallen leaves came bowling down the slope of the field from the wood.

"All right," said Spurgeon unwillingly.

The two men walked in silence down the field towards the farm. Rudd ventured a remark about the weather that was answered with a grunt. The farmer appeared to be deep in thought. Rudd glanced sideways at him and noticed a dark crease between the man's eyebrows. His face had assumed a sullen expression.

As they entered the yard, Rudd saw a battered van drawn up behind the house.

"That your car parked in the entrance?" Spurgeon asked.

"Yes," said Rudd pleasantly. "I hope it wasn't in your way when you drove in."

"Leastways, I didn't hit it," Spurgeon replied with a touch of irony.

"You were out when I first called," Rudd went on.

Spurgeon gave him an oblique look.

"If it's anything to do with you, I'd taken my mother into the village to do a bit of shopping," he said. "There ain't no law against that, is there?"

"Not as far as I know," Rudd replied peaceably.

In a strange way, he was getting to like Spurgeon. There was a directness and an air of independence about the man that the Inspector could not help taking to. Rudd liked, too, his dry and laconic humour.

As they drew nearer to the house, the back door opened and an old woman came out on to the doorstep to watch their approach. Spurgeon shouted at her, "It's all right, Ma! He's not come about Kenny."

To Rudd he added, "There was a bit of bother at the school once over my boy."

Rudd remembered Holbrook telling him that Spurgeon's son was mentally retarded.

"I'll have his hide if there's any more trouble," old Mrs. Spurgeon commented, as she drew aside to let them pass. Rudd wished her "Good afternoon" but got no response, apart from a look full of suspicion. She was a bent, unwashed old woman, with straggly white hair and a hard face. Rudd took in her appearance with a glance as he passed her. She was wearing an old brown woollen dress and a flowered overall, the front of which was so dirty that its pattern was almost obliterated. A pair of downtrodden felt bedroom slippers were on her feet.

The kitchen beyond was ill-lit and, as far as Rudd could see, in the few seconds it took to pass through it to the living-room, as dirty and untidy as might be expected from Mrs. Spurgeon's appearance. A saucepan was boiling on a paraffin stove and gave off an unpleasant odour that Rudd recognised from his childhood as the smell of peelings being cooked up for chicken mash. A cat sat on the draining-board among the dirty dishes.

The living-room was bigger and better lit but was no

cleaner or tidier. Old-fashioned, scarred furniture took up most of the space and there were clothes and old news-papers lying on every chair. An oil can stood on the side-board, a pair of muddy boots on the hearth and there was a strong smell of cat in the room.

"Sit down, if you can find somewhere to sit," Spurgeon said. It was by no means an apology for the state of the room. Rudd took a pile of ragged comics off a chair and sat down, facing Spurgeon who had seated himself by the fireplace and was rolling a cigarette. As he sat down, Rudd noticed the bills tucked in behind the clock on the mantel-piece, several of which, judging by the red print, were final demands. Money, it would seem, was short, unless Spurgeon was careless about paying bills as they fell due. Rudd suspected it was a bit of both. Certainly, neither the house nor the farm gave the impression of affluence.

Now that they were seated opposite each other, Rudd was able to look directly into the man's face. There was no guilt in Spurgeon's expression. The blue eyes were direct and frank and yet Rudd was not sure. The very fact that the man had not yet asked him why he was there could in itself be suspicious. Most people, even those with nothing on their conscience, would be curious to know why a police inspector should be calling on them. Spurgeon had so far showed no curiosity.

"I expect you're wondering why I'm here," Rudd said, coming straight to the point.

The farmer licked along the gummed strip on the ciga-rette paper, rolled it between his fingers to seal it, put it to his lips and struck a match on the tiled hearth.

"It had crossed my mind," he said laconically.

"I'm inquiring into the death of Mrs. King," Rudd con-tinued, watching him closely. A shred of tobacco from the home-made cigarette fell on to Spurgeon's jacket and he bent down to brush it away. When he looked up again, the frank look in his eyes had gone. A dazed expression had come over them, as if the irises had gone dense, clouding out any sign of reaction.

"She's dead," he said.

"I know that," Rudd said sharply. "That's why I'm here."

He was surprised at Spurgeon's reaction. The man had turned into a caricature of the stupid, country oaf. Even his bearing had altered. His shoulders sagged, his head came forward like an animal peering at something it did not understand, the big, capable hands were clumsy and fumbling. As a defence, Rudd could see its advantages. It is difficult to question a big, lumbering fool of a man. Yet Spurgeon was no fool. He might not be educated or possess a particularly subtle or intellectual mind, but he was not unintelligent and had, Rudd was sure, a certain native quickness of thought. The inspector was inclined to call his bluff by saying something like, "Come off it. Don't try the dumb act on me."

But before he could speak, Spurgeon sat up and faced him. The dazed look cleared from his eyes and they were frank again, but troubled.

"I know what they're saying up in the village," he said slowly. "That she was poisoned by something she ate and it was the mushrooms I gave her as killed her. But that ain't true. The ones I took her that evening were all right, I'd swear to it."

Rudd was puzzled. He was sure Spurgeon had intended to be stubborn, to deny all knowledge, to plead ignorance. He was sure, too, that the man had decided against this approach and was now pretending to be frank and open. He remembered what Holbrook had told him about the seed potatoes. Spurgeon had been prepared then to be dishonest and to lie. But was he lying on this occasion? He seemed to be genuinely distressed that he should be considered the cause of Mrs. King's death. There was even a touch of anger in his voice that a man in his position might naturally feel against his slanderers.

"I liked Rene King," Spurgeon was saying. "I'd not do anything to cause her harm. And them mushrooms were all right, I tell you. We had some ourselves the same evening as I took hers round. And they were the same lot so I can't see how they could've killed her."

Again, there was sincerity in his voice and manner. When he spoke of Mrs. King, his eyelids trembled a little as if it caused him real emotion.

Rudd decided to reserve judgment and continue with the questioning. When he got to know Spurgeon better, he might be able to form a clearer idea of the man's character.

"The mushrooms were picked from the field behind the farm?" he asked.

"That's right," Spurgeon replied, "The field you was in when I found you."

Rudd looked at him sharply, wondering if the man were being sarcastic, but again he met the frank blue eyes.

"Who picked them?" he asked.

"I did," said Spurgeon. "I went in the morning, straight after I'd done the milking. They're best picked early."

"Did your mother help you?"

"No, not her. She don't like stooping more'n she has to."

"Or your son?"

"In the holidays he might, or at weekends. But he's getting ready for school on a weekday."

"So it was only you that picked them that morning?"

"I thought I'd already said so," replied Spurgeon. There was a fleeting glimpse of an ironic expression in his face.

"And what happened to them after you'd picked them?" Rudd asked.

"Same as always happens," Spurgeon replied. "I took the basket back to the house and set it out on the table by the roadside."

"To sell you mean?"

"Well, they weren't for giving away free," Spurgeon said with a small grin.

"Did you sell any?"

"Not that day. We don't do a lot of trade. Not many cars pass. We sell mostly at weekends, although it's mainly eggs and soft fruit there's any call for."

"And then?"

"Well, they were stood out there all day and come the evening, I sent Kenny out to bring the basket indoors. My old mum cooked some for our tea with a bit of bacon and the rest I put into one of them little baskets we have for strawberries and I took it round to Mrs. King's."

The dazed look came back into his eyes momentarily but was gone so quickly that Rudd wondered if he were not being over sensitive and imagining it.

"That was the Wednesday evening?" he asked.

"That's right. I was going round there for a game of cards and, knowing she was partial to a few mushrooms, I thought I'd take her some. I'd promised her I would the last time I was round there."

This was new information and Rudd pounced on it.

"So you said you'd take her some? She was expecting you to?"

"Yes. I'd been supplying Abstey's, the greengrocer's, with a few baskets the previous fortnight. She pulled my leg about it and said, 'When is it my turn?' So I said I'd bring her some next time I saw her."

It was a small point but it might be important. If Spurgeon had promised to bring her mushrooms on that occasion, the Leacocks and Mrs. Youngman might well have known of the promise. So, too, might others.

"She knew I'd got them growing in my field," Spurgeon was saying, "and I'd taken her things other times."

"What things?" Rudd asked.

"A few eggs; raspberries and strawberries when they were in season."

"Why?" Rudd asked.

"Why?" echoed Spurgeon. "I don't get you."

"Why take her anything?" Rudd persisted. "Or did she pay you?"

The man flushed. "She offered to, but I wouldn't take no money. I liked her, I told you. Besides, the stuff was there. It didn't cost me nothing."

Rudd accepted this. He could see that Spurgeon might offer gifts of produce to somebody he liked and yet the Inspector had the feeling that there was an element of courtship about the presents. Had Spurgeon gone calling on Mrs. King with eggs and mushrooms as another man might take flowers and chocolates?

He decided to leave this for the moment and finish the question of the mushrooms first.

"What happened after you gave her the mushrooms?" he asked.

"She thanked me," Spurgeon replied, "then she put them in the kitchen."

"Where exactly?"

"In the fridge, I think," Spurgeon said. The ironic look returned. "I'd've taken more notice if I'd known it was going to be important."

"And then you played cards?"

"Yes. Amy and Gilbert Leacock were already there. We played whist until about half-past ten with a stop halfway through for sandwiches, coffee and beer. Rene always laid on a supper."

"Did any of you leave the room during the evening?" Rudd asked.

"Rene did, to get the tray of supper things. I helped her

to carry in the beer can and glasses. Gilbert Leacock went
out to the lav. At least, I suppose that's where he went.
I heard the chain pulled."

"And Miss Leacock?"

Spurgeon grinned. "She might have gone to the lav. when
she went out to get more milk for the coffee. But I didn't
hear the chain go that time."

"But she left the room?"

"For a few minutes, like I said, to fill up the milk jug."

Rudd leaned back. That line of questioning seemed to be
pretty well exhausted, but it had established the fact that
both the Leacocks had left the room during the evening
and that either of them could have had the opportunity
to add some of the Death Cap fungus to the mushrooms.
Or Mrs. Youngman the next day. Or any casual passer-by
when the mushrooms were displayed on the table at the
side of the road, although Rudd was inclined to discount
that theory. According to Stan Spurgeon's evidence, he, his
mother and son had eaten mushrooms taken from that
basket and had suffered no ill effects. It seemed more likely
that the fungus had been introduced into the small basket
that Spurgeon had taken to Mrs. King.

Rudd now wanted to clear up the question of Spurgeon's
relationship with Mrs. King.

He offered Spurgeon a cigarette which he accepted, lit
one himself and asked casually, "How long had you known
Mrs. King?"

"Getting on for two years," the farmer replied.

"She'd been living in the village for nearly three years,
I understand?" Rudd said.

"That's right. I didn't meet her straight off."

"And how did you meet her?"

The farmer laughed a little shame-facedly.

"Well, to tell you the truth, I'd been by the shop a few
times, taking stuff to Abstey's and I'd noticed her. She was
a good-looking woman . . ."

"And you were attracted?"

"I'll not deny it. Then one day it was my mother's
birthday and I thought I'd get her something, so I went
into Mrs. King's and got chatting. After that, I used to call
in at the shop about once a week. I asked her to have a
drink with me at the Star but she said she didn't care for
pubs. Then, later on, she said she'd asked Amy and Gilbert
Leacock round for a hand of cards and did I play whist?

I said I did and after that we used to meet about once a fortnight for cards."

"What was your relationship with Mrs. King?" Rudd asked.

Again, the opaque look came into Spurgeon's eyes and his face took on a sullen expression.

"I don't understand," he said.

"I think you do," Rudd replied smoothly. "But I'll put it another way if you like. Had you considered marrying her, for instance?"

There was a pause and then Spurgeon replied, "I'm already married."

"I understand your wife left you."

"It hasn't taken you long to pick up the gossip," Spurgeon said with a jeer.

"It's part of my job," Rudd replied.

"Then no doubt you've heard that she left me and the boy eight years ago, that I don't know where she is, and I don't much care, and she hasn't, as far as I know, put in for a divorce."

"You could divorce her," Rudd pointed out. "Under the new law, either party can get divorced after two years' separation if they agree."

"I don't know nothing about divorce," Spurgeon replied, "except it costs money. Anyway, I reckoned I was all right as I was."

So, thought Rudd, marriage with Mrs. King had crossed his mind. As if the farmer had himself realised this, he added quickly, "Not that I thought of marrying her, or anybody else come to that. I liked her, but that was all."

"You found her attractive?" Rudd persisted.

"That don't mean I fancied her as a wife," Spurgeon said. "You can think an apple on a tree's a good 'un without wanting to pick it."

He gave Rudd a grin, disarmingly man-to-man, and Rudd grinned back and rose to go.

"Thank you, Mr. Spurgeon," he said.

"Is that all?" the farmer asked with an air of relief.

"For the moment," Rudd replied. "Although I would like a word with your mother before I go."

"Why?" Spurgeon asked, suddenly belligerent. The blue glare had come back into his eyes.

"I just want to ask her a few questions," Rudd said, surprised at Spurgeon's reaction.

"Now, see here," the farmer said fiercely, "she's an old woman and I won't have her bothered."

"I shan't bother her," Rudd assured him, and wondered how that dirty and unlovable old woman managed to provoke such a strong protective instinct in her son.

They found old Mrs. Spurgeon in the garden at the far side of the house, among a tangle of asters and chrysanthemums and cabbages, picking mint. She was wearing a man's old raincoat on top of her overall and a pair of wellington boots. As they approached, she straightened up. So much for her not liking to stoop, Rudd thought.

"What do you want?" she asked ungraciously. The question seemed directed as much at her son as at Rudd.

"He wants a word with you," Spurgeon replied, jerking his head in Rudd's direction.

"What about?" she asked.

"I'm making inquiries into the death of Mrs. King," Rudd began.

"You're from the police," she said accusingly. Her eyes were very bright and sharp. Rudd noticed that in one hand she was holding a cigarette burnt down almost to its end. Her upper lip and the front of her white hair that straggled over her forehead were stained yellow with smoke. She dropped the cigarette butt on the ground and stamped on it, with a gesture of finality which suggested she'd like to do the same to the Inspector.

"I'm from Chelmsford C.I.D.," Rudd explained, "and I'm making a few routine inquiries. I understand from your son that he took some mushrooms to Mrs. King the other Wednesday evening."

"What he gets up to is his own look-out," Mrs. Spurgeon replied. Spurgeon grinned in an embarrassed way and looked at his feet. But Rudd thought he could detect in the old woman's voice a suppressed venom directed towards her son.

"He picked the mushrooms on the Wednesday morning, he tells me," Rudd went on.

"If he's told you that, then you won't want me telling you again, will you?" she asked. Spurgeon grinned more broadly. He was evidently enjoying the encounter.

"Did you help him to pick them?" Rudd asked.

"No, I did not," Mrs. Spurgeon said sharply. "I was getting that Kenny off to school and that's more than one person's work."

Spurgeon's grin vanished.

"I've already said she didn't pick any," he said gruffly.

"But you ate some of them yourselves that evening?" Rudd continued.

"We did. Not that it's any of your concern," she said.

"I'm afraid it is," Rudd replied. "Someone has died. That makes it very much my concern."

"Well, you're wasting your time sniffing round here," was the old woman's reply.

Rudd controlled his anger, thanked her and walked away. Spurgeon, a little abashed by his mother's retort, hurried after him.

"She don't mean no harm," he said. "She's a bit sharp-tongued, but that's all."

"That's all right," Rudd replied, accepting the apology.

At the end of the garden, he glanced back. Old Mrs. Spurgeon was standing looking after them, with the bunch of mint clasped in her hand. There was something archetypal in her stance, her white wispy hair blowing in the wind, that stirred his imagination. She represented another generation, another way of life, a different set of values and attitudes that were out of keeping with modern ideas.

He wondered, too, about Kenny. Mrs. Spurgeon's antipathy towards the boy might be nothing more than an elderly woman's understandable impatience with a mentally retarded child. She was not, Rudd imagined, a naturally affectionate person. If she had ever seriously beaten the boy, it might form a motive for the child to seek revenge. He could have picked some of the fungus, knowing it to be poisonous, and put it in the basket, intending to punish his grandmother. The fact that all the family were to eat mushrooms from the basket for tea that evening might not have entered his head. He was, after all, mentally subnormal. But this theory still did not get round the fact that none of the Spurgeons had suffered from fungus poisoning.

Rudd sighed. There seemed no explanation other than that the fungus had been put in with the mushrooms after the Spurgeons had eaten tea and, in that case, no other victim was intended but Mrs. King. And, at the moment, Rudd knew of no motive Kenny could have for wanting to kill her.

As for old Mrs. Spurgeon, Rudd hesitated. She might have felt jealousy towards Mrs. King as a possible daughter-in-law, even though Spurgeon had stated he had no intention of marrying again. It would need looking into, anyway.

His thoughts turned to the anonymous letter writer. Old Mrs. Spurgeon seemed a likely candidate for that role. She was malicious enough, Rudd reckoned. On the other hand, this would put her out of the running as Mrs. King's killer. She would hardly murder Mrs. King and then draw attention to the fact, especially as the death had been at first accepted as accidental. And it had yet to be proved that it was murder.

Rudd and Spurgeon had reached the yard. Both men had been silent for several minutes; Rudd busy with his thoughts; the farmer, judging by his dark expression, brooding over the recent encounter with his mother.

Rudd turned towards him. "I'd like your permission to bring some men and make a thorough search of your field and the wood behind it," he said.

"Please yourself," the farmer replied, shrugging.

He seemed subdued. His blue eyes had a withdrawn, almost distressed look in them.

"I'll let you know exactly when it will be," Rudd continued.

"All right," Spurgeon said.

"And one thing more," Rudd added, suddenly thinking of it, "is there any short cut to your farm from the village, a quicker way than coming round by the road?"

"What?" Spurgeon asked. His thoughts seemed far away.

Rudd repeated the question.

"There's a footpath," the farmer said. "It starts at the back of the church and leads across the fields. It passes just behind the wood and finishes up at the next village, Copse End."

"Does it?" said Rudd thoughtfully. The footpath would have to be examined. From what Spurgeon had said, it sounded as if the wood and the field might be easily accessible from the village.

Rudd thanked the farmer and said good-bye. For a moment the man's eyes rested on him and the expression in them was eloquent of so much unexpected sadness that Rudd, as he turned away and walked to his car, felt uncomfortable.

At the bottom of the farm drive, before turning into the road, Rudd glanced quickly back. Spurgeon had gone. The yard was deserted except for the muddy tractor and the cat that was washing itself in a patch of sunlight.

5

The public library in Market Stratton was a late Victorian building of red brick with dogtooth ornamentation round the windows and two narrow beds of dusty and depressed looking laurel on either side of the main entrance.

Rudd pushed open the swing door and entered a square, dark foyer with notice-boards round the walls announcing local events. The Market Stratton Amateur Operatic Society was putting on a production of *Iolanthe* and the Reverend Harold Digby was to give a lecture at the Assembly Rooms on "The Christian Church in the Far East," illustrated with coloured slides.

Three sets of double doors led respectively to the Children's Library, the Reference Library and the Adult Lending Library which Rudd entered.

The room was high-ceilinged and echoed strangely. Tall shelves of books divided it into gloomy little bays but the girl at the counter was cheerful enough and smiled pleasantly at him as he approached. Rudd produced his official card discreetly and asked to speak to the head librarian. The girl was regretful. The head librarian was having her coffee break and the assistant head was away ill, but could she help? Rudd said he supposed she might and asked if she could check on any members of the library who lived at Abbots Stacey.

"Can you give me their names?" the girl asked. "You see, all our membership cards are filed alphabetically and unless we know the surname, it's going to mean going through the files looking for addresses."

Rudd asked for a sheet of paper and wrote down the Leacocks, Stan Spurgeon, Mrs. Spurgeon and Mrs. Youngman and, for good measure, added Mrs. King and Dr. Foreman as well. He did not want to run the risk of arousing any suspicion by naming only those directly connected with the case.

The girl took the piece of paper away and presently returned. She had, she said, put a tick beside those names that were on the library's files. Rudd ran his eye down the list. The only ones ticked were those of Dr. Foreman and Mrs. King. The others were, therefore, not members.

The head librarian appeared at this moment, a schoolmistressy woman with grey hair and a severe manner, who was not pleased to see her young assistant chatting so affably with a middle-aged man. Rudd again produced his official card and explained his business and the woman agreed, somewhat ungraciously, to have the files examined and to let him have a complete list of everyone with an Abbots Stacey address.

"Although," she added, "it will take a great deal of our very valuable time."

Rudd thanked her and asked next about the book, *British Mushrooms and Toadstools* but, as he had suspected, neither of the librarians could remember it being taken out. It had been too much to hope for.

Rudd made his departure and walked back towards the town centre. There was little in the place of interest, in his opinion. Any pretensions to quaintness had long ago been destroyed by unimaginative and piecemeal development. The narrow high street was just a bottle-neck for traffic, inconvenient and noisy, and the shops that lined it, with their ugly modern façades replacing the original old brick and stone, seemed to offer nothing much except tired vegetables, cheap clothes and tinned food at bargain prices. It was only a very observant passer-by who, glancing up, would notice above the shoddy frontages the uneven roofs of weathered tiles, patched and cushioned with lichen and moss, and the occasional cock-eyed dormer window.

The only attractive feature of the town was the large cobbled square where the market was held, with the white-painted, beautifully proportioned George Hotel facing it. But even that had been spoilt; some nineteenth century local dignitary had caused a statue to be erected to his memory in the very centre of the square and there, in granite trousers and frockcoat, he dominated the scene from his plinth, flourishing in one hand a stone rolled-up paper, looking for all the world, Rudd thought, as if he were hailing a taxi.

There was nothing else that he wanted to do that morning in Market Stratton. Although he could have gone to the
mortuary to view Mrs. King's body, he decided against it.
Nothing would be gained from it and, although he had
seen death in many forms, he still found the official viewing
of a corpse one of the more unpleasant features of his job.

He did, however, call in at the police station and speak
to the Inspector there, asking him to get in touch with the
pathologist to arrange for Mrs. King to be photographed
and her fingerprints taken. It was something he could have
organised through his own staff but he thought it would be
better to let the local police deal with it. After all, he was
in a way poaching on their territory and it would be only
good sense to put them in the picture in case he needed
their co-operation later on. The two men discussed the case
briefly but, as Rudd had guessed, the local Inspector could
tell him nothing. It was Sergeant Holbrook and the people
of the village who would know anything of real use.

From Market Stratton, Rudd drove back to Abbots
Stacey. He intended to interview the Leacocks that afternoon but when he arrived in the village, he found all the
shops were closed for the dinner-hour and, as he did not
want to interrupt the Leacocks at their meal, he went to
the Red Lion for a snack, as the Star did not serve food.

The Red Lion was the kind of pub Rudd hated. It was
both pretentious and uncomfortable, with imitation beams
and banquette seating covered in slippery red plastic. The
middle-aged barmaid tried to be coyly flirtatious and Rudd,
pocketing his change, escaped to the so-called "garden"
where he sat alone among the concrete tubs of hydrangeas
and the wire wastepaper-baskets. The sun was still shining
brightly but a stiff little breeze blew the empty potato crisp
packets across the paving-stones.

Just after two o'clock he walked back along the main
street. The Leacocks' shop was now open and he went in.

The interior was long and narrow and dark. On each
side, brown-painted shelves reached up to the ceiling,
crowded with saucepans, tins of paint, rolls of wallpaper,
bottles of turpentine and all kinds of other hardware. There
was a strange complex smell in the shop, compounded of
paint, paraffin and wood rot. At the far end of the shop,
Gilbert Leacock was standing behind the counter, with his
knuckles resting on its surface, leaning slightly forward as
if expecting a customer.

"Can I help you, sir?" he asked, the moment the shop bell had stopped tinkling.

Rudd stepped forward. His immediate reaction was one of dislike. There was something about Leacock's tall, drooping figure in the brown overall, about the way he held his head slightly to one side, that Rudd found unpleasantly obsequious. However, he kept his voice and expression polite and non-committal.

"Mr. Leacock?" he asked.

Gilbert Leacock seemed surprised to hear himself addressed by name and replied, "Yes?" on a note of uncertain interrogation.

The Inspector introduced himself and produced his official card which Leacock took and read carefully, turning it so as to catch the light.

"I see," he said, pursing his lips slightly. "What can I do to help you?"

Rudd said, "I'm making routine inquiries into the death of Mrs. King and I'd like to ask a few questions of you and your sister."

"I see," Gilbert Leacock said again. It was a singularly inexpressive phrase. He stopped there and Rudd cocked his head inquiringly.

"You'd better come through to the back," Leacock added, opening the door behind the counter.

Rudd followed him. The room beyond was small and dark, despite the brightness of the day outside, and depressingly full of heavy, old-fashioned furniture. There was a huge sideboard with a mirrored overmantel, a big square table and mahogany upright chairs with brown leather seats. There was a profusion, too, of ugly knick-knacks, brass ornaments and painted vases, and a large, slow-ticking clock, supported on ebony columns, presided on the mantelpiece.

A door led through into a kitchen and, almost as soon as Rudd and Leacock came into the room, Amy Leacock appeared in the doorway, her face full of suspicion. Before she had time to speak, however, Gilbert Leacock said, "This is Detective Inspector Rudd, Amy. He's come to make inquiries into Mrs. King's death."

The tone in his voice was expressive of a great many things. Evidently the man had had time to recover his poise since Rudd had first introduced himself. It suggested politeness towards Rudd, respect for his position, regret at the nature of his inquiries and, Rudd thought, a note of warning as well.

Amy Leacock darted a look at the Inspector. "I've been told her death was an accident," she said sharply.

"Now I wonder who told you that?" Rudd asked.

She hesitated and decided to back down. "It's common knowledge in the village," she replied.

"Perhaps you'd like to make us a cup of tea?" Gilbert Leacock suggested. On the face of it, it seemed a reasonable enough suggestion and yet Rudd had the feeling it was made to get her out of the room.

"Sit down," Gilbert Leacock continued and dragging the table forward a little way from the wall, he made room for the three of them to sit down round it. Rudd squashed himself in on the far side. Amy Leacock could be heard rattling about in the kitchen.

"It's a sad affair," Gilbert Leacock said, folding himself into an equally small space. His hands came up to place themselves on the table-top in much the same way as they had been resting on the counter. They were long hands with curiously padded fingertips that gave them a splayed-out look. Rudd remembered Holbrook telling him that Mrs. King had called him "the undertaker." It was a good comparison. There was something about those long padded fingers, the pale eyes, the soft voice and the way he had of holding his head slightly to one side that gave Rudd that impression too.

Gilbert Leacock sighed and said again, "Yes, indeed, a very sad business."

Rudd decided to be brisk. Whether the man was being genuine or not, the Inspector had no patience for his sentiment. "I believe you knew her quite well?" he asked.

"As a neighbour, yes."

"I understand you and your sister went round to Mrs. King's fairly regularly to play cards?"

Again there was that slight pursing of the lips and the hesitation before replying as if Leacock were carefully weighing his words. "Yes, indeed, we did go to Mrs. King's fairly regularly."

"At her invitation?"

"Oh yes."

"And it was usually a Wednesday evening?"

"Always."

"Did she ever come here for the evening?" Rudd asked.

He was finding the interview heavy going. Although Gilbert Leacock answered all the questions with apparent frankness and without the hesitation he had first shown, he confined himself entirely to the question asked and offered little additional information.

"Well, no," Gilbert Leacock was saying, "she didn't come round here ever. She seemed to prefer having people to her place."

Amy Leacock returned at this moment and shoved a tray of tea-things down on the table. Looking at her badtempered expression, Rudd thought Mrs. King had been right. Amy Leacock seemed to find making tea for the Inspector and her brother an imposition. Her face, as she handed him his teacup, was positively hostile.

"There you are," she said ungraciously. "There's sugar in the bowl."

Rudd stirred his tea and thought about the pair of them. They were physically so dissimilar that it was difficult to imagine a blood-relationship. He was tall and thin, with stooping shoulders and a slightly concave chest. His head was long and with fine gingerish-fair hair, going grey, that lay close to his scalp. All his features had a down-drawn mournful cast to them, a saddened hang-dog look that contrasted with an alert and watchful expression in his eyes. He did not, however, reveal his eyes very often. They were usually kept hidden under lowered lids and he had a habit, before looking up, of fluttering his pale eyelashes in a little nervous spasm. Rudd was aware of a listening air about him; the kind of silent intensity that some deaf people have.

Amy Leacock, short and stout, was quite the opposite. Her fat little face had a crushed-up look, like a badtempered Pekingese. But she had her brother's pale eyes and gingerish, greying hair, although hers was permed into a lot of little waves and curls. Like her brother, she gave the impression of weighing her words, but she lacked his soft delivery.

Seeing them sitting together at the table, Rudd was reminded of some married couples he had known. There was about them that air of uneasy truce that some middle-aged husbands and wives develop between them for the sake of peace, in which one partner, in this case Gilbert Leacock, withdraws to a position of almost silent acquiescence which the other learns to respect up to a point. Amy Leacock evidently found her domestic life irksome. Rudd had known women like her before; always complaining, always blaming their husbands for their dull and unrewarding lives. Yet there was a kind of unspoken boundary across which they would not step, for fear of losing all.

Rudd had never seen this kind of relationship between brother and sister before and it made him think of his own sister who had kept house for him ever since her husband's death. Unlike Miss Leacock, she was the silent, uncomplaining type and yet her life was very much the same as Amy's: housekeeper to a bachelor brother; a kind of pseudo-wife.

Rudd stirred restlessly in his chair and cleared his throat. "I would like to ask both of you about the last card party at Mrs. King's," he said, "which was held, I believe, on the Wednesday evening, 9th September?"

"That's right," Gilbert Leacock said and stopped there.

"Would you tell me about it?" Rudd asked impatiently.

Brother and sister exchanged glances as if asking each other silently who should speak. Despite their differences, Rudd guessed there was a strong understanding between them. They knew each other very well after all the years they had spent together; better than a lot of married couples.

Amy spoke, "There's not much to tell. We went round there at the usual time, eight o'clock, played a few hands of whist and left about half-past ten."

It was said in a colourless, grudging tone of voice. Rudd was longing to get her talking freely about Mrs. King, but doubted if she would be drawn. Apart from her natural caution, she seemed to have a personal antipathy towards the Inspector, for what reason he did not know, but possibly just for being there, inconveniencing her, sitting at her table, drinking her tea, asking questions. She did not intend giving anything away if she could help it. It was not in her nature to be generous and forthcoming. Rudd decided, however, to try: "I understand Mr. Spurgeon took a basket of mushrooms to Mrs. King that evening," he said.

"Yes, he did," Amy Leacock replied.

"Did you see them?" Rudd asked.

"No, I didn't," she snapped. "But I heard her thanking him for them."

"Where were they when she thanked him?" Rudd went on.

"They were on the landing. We were in the sitting-room, waiting as usual for Stan Spurgeon. I heard him come up

the stairs and then she said, 'Oh mushrooms! How lovely!'
Or something of that sort. That's all I know."

"So you didn't see what she did with them?" Rudd asked.

"No, I didn't."

"I see," said Rudd. He paused for a moment and drank
some tea. He was finding her as difficult to interview as
her brother but he was getting attuned to Amy Leacock's
style of answering. The replies might be abrupt and merely
factual but a great deal more was implied beneath the
surface. Stan Spurgeon's late arrival was evidently a cause
of annoyance. Even the simple phrase "I heard him come
up the stairs" suggested more than at first seemed. The
slight stress on the word "heard" implied Amy's disapproval
of the farmer's noisy approach. As for her repetition of
Rene King's words, Amy Leacock managed to suggest in
her tone of voice criticism of both Mrs. King's reply and
the gift itself. Amy Leacock evidently thought Mrs. King
was too warm in her thanks and the present was in bad
taste, anyway.

Rudd decided to turn this to his own advantage. He
shifted his chair a little nearer to her and said, copying her
tone of voice with its innuendo, "I'm told he quite often
took her little presents."

"More fool him!" she replied. "He's supposed to be hard
up but he could afford to give stuff away."

"That's his business, not ours, Amy," Gilbert Leacock
said gravely.

Blast him! thought Rudd. Trust him to go shoving his
oar in just when I'd got her going.

But the damage had been done. Amy Leacock gave her
brother a look and promptly shut her mouth.

Rudd returned to a more prosaic line of questioning.

"I understand Mrs. King put the basket of mushrooms
in the fridge in the kitchen. Did either of you notice them
there?" he asked.

Amy Leacock did not speak and after a silence Gilbert
Leacock said, "I didn't see them, Inspector. I didn't go into
the kitchen all evening, although I did go out once to the
. . ." he paused and then went on delicately, ". . . to the
bathroom."

"I see," said Rudd. That corroborated Stan Spurgeon's
evidence. He turned to Amy Leacock. "Did you see them?"
he asked.

"No, I didn't," she replied snappily.

"You did go out to the kitchen," Gilbert Leacock put in. "You offered to refill the milk jug."

"I didn't offer. She asked me to," Amy Leacock replied. It was one of those bickering retorts that Rudd had heard couples indulge in before, the recriminatory "No. I didn't," "Yes, you did," verbal match that tries to establish some quite trivial point. Rudd decided to nip it in the bud but before he could do so, Gilbert Leacock retracted his statement.

"That's right," he admitted. "I remember now. Mrs. King was pouring out coffee and asked you if you'd mind getting more milk."

"I told you," his sister said with a smug, triumphant look. Gilbert Leacock looked down with that quick flutter of eye-lashes and smiled a curious, tucked-in little smile.

Anyway, Rudd thought, one point's been established. Amy Leacock did go into the kitchen but it had not been previous-ly planned by her. Under the circumstances, he could not see how she could be suspected of slipping some of the fungus in with the mushrooms, unless she had gone pre-pared on the off-chance of Mrs. King asking her to per-form some small job, like filling the milk jug, that would take her into the kitchen. Or unless she had been ready to make some excuse herself for leaving the room, like Gil-bert's trip to the bathroom. In that case, she could not be entirely ruled out. Nor could Gilbert Leacock.

"And I didn't see the basket," Amy Leacock was saying. "I filled the jug up from the bottle of milk in the fridge door compartment and took it straight back to the sitting-room."

"You seem very interested in the mushrooms," Gilbert Leacock hinted. "Was it them that caused her death?"

"I'm afraid I can't say," Rudd replied. "The cause of death has not been finally established."

He was being deliberately officious but he had no in-tention of giving anything away to the Leacocks. Nor did he like being pumped for information by the people he was supposed to be questioning. To soften the retort, he got out his cigarette packet and offered it first to Miss Leacock, who said disapprovingly that she did not smoke. Gilbert Leacock took one and Rudd lit them both. Amy Leacock got up from the table to fetch an ash-tray from the mantelpiece which she placed ostentatiously between the two men. It was a hideous object in bright yellow china with a grinning pixie in red and green perched on the rim. Printed underneath were the words "Good Luck from Devon."

Rudd drew on his cigarette and tried to relax. He felt he was handling the interview badly and yet he could see no other way of approaching the Leacocks. Their caution and their respectability acted as a barrier against the gossipy approach and their intelligence made them difficult to trap into making an unwary answer. Rudd surprised himself by that word "intelligence." And yet they were very far from stupid, he realised. Of the two, he thought Amy Leacock was his best bet. She was more emotional than her brother. Less inclined to caution.

He drank his tea and looked about the room, searching for an approach that might wheedle or flatter her into a friendlier attitude. The overcrowded room, he noticed, was scrupulously clean. The ugly brasses shone, the heavy furniture had a polished gloss to it. She was evidently a house-proud woman. Rudd tapped a tiny fragment of ash carefully into the ash-tray and said with a smile, "It's a very pleasant room, Miss Leacock. Everything's beautifully kept."

Her little crumpled face showed the first flicker of response. "I like to keep it looking nice," she replied. "Not that it's easy."

"It can't be," Rudd sympathised. "These older premises are often difficult to run; steep stairs, uneven floorboards . . ."

"Damp," she added, "and the plaster dropping off as soon as you look at it.".

Rudd made condoling noises.

"It'd take a small fortune to modernise the place," she went on. "The kitchen needs doing up for a start. There's the sink and one of those old-fashioned dressers that ought to come out and . . ."

"And it all costs money," Gilbert Leacock said with a mournful air.

It was evidently an old bone of contention between them. Rudd saw her face flush up angrily.

"It's all very well for you," she began, but the tinkling of the shop bell interrupted her and Gilbert Leacock got up and left the room, first nipping out his cigarette and slipping the half-smoked end into his overall pocket.

Rudd was glad to see him go. It gave him an opportunity of speaking to Miss Leacock alone and of introducing the subject of Mrs. King.

"I noticed how nice Mrs. King's flat was," Rudd went on. "She evidently had a lot done to it before she moved in."

Amy Leacock sniffed. "She could well afford to. There was no shortage of money," she replied.

"I believe her husband left her comfortably off," Rudd said, assuming his ready-for-a-nice-chat attitude, with one elbow on the table.

"So I've heard," she said. "He was in business; in the East End."

The slight emphasis on the words "East End" implied her distaste for that area of London.

"She was a very pleasant woman, I've been told," Rudd went on.

"Yes, she was very friendly," Amy Leacock said grudgingly.

"You enjoyed going there for cards?" Rudd asked.

"It made a change," she admitted.

"What did you think of her as a person?" Rudd said.

But Amy Leacock was not going to be drawn.

"I don't believe in discussing the dead," she replied with a snap.

You sanctimonious old bitch! Rudd thought.

"Did you ever meet her nephew?" he asked, trying a new line of questioning.

"I've seen him," she replied. "But I've never been introduced," implying that she did not want to meet him socially, anyway.

"Well-dressed young man, isn't he?" Rudd hinted wickedly, taking up Mrs. Youngman's comment. He had Amy Leacock's measure now and he knew exactly what she would reply.

"A bit flashy for my taste," she answered.

"And selfish, too, so I've heard," he continued, leading her on. "He didn't visit his aunt as often as he might have done."

"I don't know about that," Miss Leacock replied with a sniff. "She never discussed him with me."

That in itself was interesting. Rene King had talked about her nephew to Mrs. Youngman. The remark suggested that she had not been on such intimate terms with Amy Leacock.

Rudd circled nearer.

"I believe she was well liked in the village," he remarked.

Miss Leacock folded her lips.

"Most people spoke well of her."

"Most people? Have you ever heard anyone say anything against her?" Rudd asked.

But the question was put a little too eagerly and Amy Leacock's face closed up. She merely shook her head, making her fat cheeks tremble.

All the same, Rudd decided to continue with the questioning. Now that Gilbert Leacock was out of the room, it seemed a good opportunity to reintroduce the subject of Mrs. King's relationship with the farmer.

"Mr. Spurgeon seemed on good terms with her," he remarked.

"He's never had much sense where women are concerned," she replied, and Rudd thought he recognised in the bitterness of her voice all the pent-up resentment that an unattractive spinster would feel towards someone of the opposite sex.

"Yes, I'd heard his wife left him," he said obliquely, hoping to encourage her.

She gave him a strange look, hard and at the same time questioning, as if she was trying to gauge how much he knew. He could see that he had lost her.

"All that happened a good while ago," was all she would reply.

Gilbert Leacock returned at this moment and stood just inside the door that led into the shop.

"Is there anything else you want to know, Inspector?" he asked. Rudd noticed that he held the door open as if as a sign that he should leave.

He looked at their faces and then down at his empty teacup and crushed out his cigarette.

"No," he said, getting up from the table. "Not for the moment anyway."

He turned to Miss Leacock.

"Thank you for the tea," he said pleasantly.

"You're welcome, I'm sure," she replied in that grudging manner of hers.

Gilbert Leacock escorted him to the shop door.

"I may want to ask both of you some more questions

another time," Rudd said, intending the remark as a reminder of his official role.

Gilbert Leacock smiled, his long mournful face lighting up for a moment.

"Of course, Inspector. Anytime. We want to do all we can to help," he replied.

Rudd nodded to him and walked away. It was only then that he realised that neither of them had expressed any regret at Mrs. King's death. Or perhaps, in their respectable way, they considered it would have been in bad taste to do so.

Rudd dug his hands into his pockets. He had the feeling that there were undercurrents below the surface that he only partially understood and yet were significant. The gloomy shop, the ugly, over-clean room, Leacock's padded fingers and ducking sideways smile, the sister's obvious bitterness and resentment added up to an atmosphere that he found disturbing. It might be nothing more than mutual antipathy between them that had given rise to his own disquieting thoughts, but he could not shake off the conviction that he had been an unwitting participant in some subtle game that was being played out between the pair of them, the point of which he had not grasped.

It again crossed his mind that Amy Leacock might be the writer of the anonymous letter. Despite her veneer of respectability there was a hard core to her nature and she could very well be the type who liked stirring up trouble. But that line of thinking would exclude her from suspicion of murder.

He was passing the post-office and, on an impulse, he went inside and edged his way forward towards the counter. The elderly man behind it seemed deaf for he leaned interrogatively towards the Inspector as he approached.

"I'd like a packet of cheap envelopes," Rudd said loudly.

"Envelopes?" the shopkeeper repeated.

"Yes, envelopes," said Rudd, suppressing a sigh. He had hoped for the opportunity to chat with the postmaster, of gradually turning the conversation to a gossip about Mrs. King, the Leacocks and Stan Spurgeon. He could see now that it would be pointless.

The old man shuffled off and came back with a packet of envelopes. Rudd paid for them and left.

But it had not been an entirely wasted visit. Examining the envelopes later in the car, Rudd was convinced that they were of the same sort in which the anonymous letter had been sent. It was a tiny detail but it established one fact. The letter writer could have bought them locally and in a case such as this one, in which nothing seemed certain and everything conjecture, he was quite satisfied to find something, however small and insignificant, that was tangible.

6

Rudd was still puzzled by Stan Spurgeon's relationship with Mrs. King. Although the man had denied any romantic interest in her and was not free to re-marry anyway, yet Rudd could not get it out of his head that there had been something more than just friendship between them. Spurgeon was attractive to women; the Inspector had been aware of this himself. Rene King was a widow who, as far as he could judge from the photograph and Holbrook's remarks, had been a good-looking and vivacious woman who would enjoy men's company; although, as Holbrook had pointed out, she had a comfortable flat and enough money and Rudd could not see her wanting to exchange them for Spurgeon's decrepit house and run-down farm. Nor could he see any woman, unless she was very deeply in love, wanting to undertake Stan Spurgeon's mother or his son. All the same, the gifts of fruit and vegetables and the very fact that Spurgeon had gone out of his way to get acquainted with her troubled him. It was a point that would need clarifying.

Mrs. Youngman was the obvious person to ask. She had known Mrs. King well and had been in her company daily. What would be more natural than the two women discussing Stan Spurgeon between themselves?

Remembering Mrs. Youngman's distress on his previous visit, he hesitated to trouble her again with further inquiries and yet it would have to be done.

He called on her the following morning. The face was again visible at the next door window and Rudd gave a cheery wave with his hand this time as he walked down the path. He had hoped, out of mere curiosity, to get a closer glimpse of the face but as he got nearer to the cottages, the angle became too oblique and it was lost to sight behind the curtain.

Mrs. Youngman greeted him at the door in a slight tremor of apprehension but she seemed calmer and he was shown this time into the back living-room as Mrs. Youngman was baking and she wanted to keep an eye on the oven.

Rudd sat down at the table and watched her bustle about making tea in the small scullery beyond. The living-room was larger and sunnier than the tiny front parlour in which he had questioned her before and it was pleasantly cluttered. A warm sweet smell of cake cooking filled the room.

Mrs. Youngman brought in the tea and Rudd was pleased to see that she swallowed one of her tablets with the first sip she took. He crossed his legs comfortably, planted an elbow on the table and tried to give the impression of a family friend who had called in for a chat. He began quite deliberately in a casual way, discussing the weather, the garden and the children.

A second cup of tea was poured and Mrs. Youngman, relaxed and at ease, was now talking quite freely. Rudd cast about his mind how to introduce the subject of Mrs. King into the conversation without disturbing the flow.

In the end, it occurred quite naturally. Mrs. Youngman went to fetch the cake from the oven, tapped the bottom of the tin to make sure it was cooked right through and turned it out on to a wire tray to cool. Rudd admired it and Mrs. Youngman said, "Now I don't work mornings, I get more time to do a bit of baking, although I still miss the money."

"I expect you do," Rudd said sympathetically. He could see about the room signs of a struggle to make ends meet and Mrs. Youngman's cardigan was neatly darned at the elbows.

"I miss her, too," Mrs. Youngman added. Her eyes welled up with tears again much to Rudd's dismay. "I shall never get over her death, but there," she added, wiping them away, "as Len says, there's no point to brooding and making yourself ill. Life has to go on."

"I expect all her friends will miss her," Rudd said. "Stan Spurgeon in particular."

Mrs. Youngman hesitated, not quite sure whether to commit herself to saying anything or not. Rudd took a sip of

tea and raised hs eyebrows interrogatively at her over the
rim. It was an old trick but it worked. Invited to speak,
she was trapped into making a reply.

"I wouldn't say they were all that close," she said.

"Really?" said Rudd. "I must have got the wrong impression, then. I thought they were—well—not exactly sweet-
hearts . . ."

"Oh, no," replied Mrs. Youngman. "I don't think there
was anything like that between them. She often spoke of
her dead husband and said there'd never be another man
like him. Mind you, I think she liked teasing Mr. Spurgeon.
But she did that with all the men. There was nothing in
it. I know we've laughed several times over Mr. Leacock.
She said to him once, over a game of cards, 'Unlucky at
cards, lucky in love,' and as he'd just lost, he went as red
as a beetroot, she said, and got all flustered. He's never
been one for the women. I think he's a bit afraid of them.
But, it was never anything more with her than just pulling
the men's legs. I don't know what Mr. Spurgeon's said to
make you think otherwise, but I'm sure she never thought
of him, or anybody else come to that, at all seriously."

"I must have got it wrong," Rudd said soothingly. "It just
seemed natural that someone like Mrs. King should think of
remarrying sometime. After all, she was still comparatively
young and a good-looking woman, too."

"I think she'd had offers," Mrs. Youngman said. "Not
from anyone round here but from someone she knew while
she was still in London. But, as she said to me, 'I'm happy
as I am.' And she was, too. I think she enjoyed men's
company and that was all."

"I see," said Rudd, getting to his feet. "Well, thank you,
Mrs. Youngman. I'm glad to get that point cleared up."

Secretly, though, he was not so sure. In spite of what
Mrs. Youngman had told him, he still felt that a small
question mark of ambiguity remained over Stan Spurgeon's
relationship with Mrs. King.

Outside, he turned down the lane towards the church.
He intended, while he was in the village, to have a look
at the footpath that Stan Spurgeon told him led from
behind the church and across the fields past the wood at
the back of his farm. He entered the churchyard, skirted
the back of the church and was making for the footpath,
when he saw Miss Leacock on her knees, tending a grave.

He gave her a smile of greeting and Miss Leacock nodded

curtly to him in reply. He noticed how well organised she was. She had brough; a little rubber mat to kneel on, a bucket of soapy water and a nail brush and she was busy scrubbing the headstone clean of dirt and lichen. Tufts of long grass that had been rooted out from among the white marble chippings that covered the grave lay in a little pile. It looked an uncomfortable last resting-place, Rudd thought, with its solid kerbs and stony covering.

A white stone vase, placed in the centre of the chippings, contained a bunch of plastic flowers of no recognisable variety.

The lettering cut into the stone declared that it was sacred to the memory of Arthur George Leacock and also his wife, Mary Susan Leacock. Rudd noticed from the dates that Arthur Leacock, Miss Leacock's father, had been dead for fifteen years; his wife for only six.

"Busy, I see," remarked Rudd.

"It's the least I can do," she said shortly. "We have a duty to the dead."

"Indeed," said Rudd, thinking that from the way she was attacking the stone with the nail brush it was a duty that she did not find at all pleasant.

"You keep the grave looking very nice," Rudd said out of politeness.

"It's a pity a few more don't make the effort," she replied with a sniff, looking pointedly at the other graves in the vicinity with their leaning, lichen-covered headstones and grass-grown mounds. All the same, Rudd could not help feeling that they suited the church and its surroundings better than the sterile neatness of the Leacocks' monument.

He was prepared to stay there longer, chatting to her, but he was soon put off any such intention.

"Well, I must get on," she snapped, "there's still plenty to do."

"And so must I," replied Rudd, knowing it had been intended as a snub. "I thought I'd have a stroll along the footpath as it's such a lovely day. Have you any idea where the path leads to?"

He knew very well, but he wanted to find out if she did, too.

"Across the fields," she replied.

"And where exactly does it come out?"

"It's years since I walked across it," she said, implying

that her time was too precious to be spent going for walks, "but it comes out at Copse End."

"I expect it still does," Rudd replied and walked off before he could see her reaction.

The good weather was holding, but signs of fading summer were everywhere. The cows' parsley plants had dropped their clusters of creamy blossoms, revealing the delicate skeletons of the flower heads. The underlying structure of the trees and hedges was becoming visible through the scantier leaves and the blackberries were beginning to change from hard sour green to red, although they were not yet ripe enough to pick.

Rudd strolled on, enjoying the sunlight and the countryside. There was an autumn smell to the air that he liked; a scent of early decay; a faint mustiness of leaves and dying plants that was pleasantly melancholy.

After a walk of twenty minutes, the timing of which Rudd checked by his watch, he reached the wood. The path skirted the further side of it and he had to leave it and walk down the edge of the wood in order to see the mushroom field behind the farm and the clustered roof-tops of the outbuildings and the house. A trickle of smoke rose from a chimney into the still air but there was no other sign of life.

Rudd turned and walked back. He had verified one fact. Somebody could easily have walked from the village, reached the field or the wood and returned in less than an hour. Everyone in the village would almost certainly know of the existence of the path. Probably every person living there had used it as a child, if not as a grown-up, to walk to the next village or to go bird's-nesting, or blackberrying or primrosing. Or even to steal mushrooms from Stan Spurgeon's field.

Rudd walked on, deep in thought, and climbed the stile into the churchyard. Miss Leacock had gone, with her bucket and her rubber kneeling mat. The headstone was still damp and had a scoured look about it, all trace of dirt and lichen removed. The inscribed letters were as sharp and as clear as if they had been newly cut.

The grave next to it attracted his attention. It was older and not so well kept but, as on the Leacocks' grave, a vase of plastic flowers had been placed inside the low iron railing that surrounded it and he bent down to read the names on the stone. They were Leacocks, too; Henry Arthur and Maud Alice and, judging by the dates, they were Amy Leacock's grandparents.

Rudd again experienced that sense of the past that he had felt when, glancing back, he had seen old Mrs. Spurgeon standing in the garden, holding the bunch of mint. These people, the Spurgeons, the Leacocks, were part of the place. Their names, and the other names which, he saw as he glanced about him at the graves, were repeated again and again: the Thorogoods, the Turnbulls, the Sadlers and the Champions, made a roll-call of the generations. Their family roots went deep. They had probably intermarried over the years and, if genealogical tables could be studied, it would no doubt be proved that they shared common ancestors who linked them into an intricate web of blood relationships, remote now and forgotten, but which emerged from time to time in a distinctive physical feature or a quirk of personality that some mutual great great grandmother had handed on to subsequent generations.

Rudd was an interloper in this village. So, too, he realised, was Sergeant Holbrook. Rene King had been a stranger also. Pleasant and friendly and well liked as she might have been, her roots had not been here. After all, what was three years when the Leacocks or their forebears had been here for three hundred?

The old patterns were dissolving, of course. The country communities were breaking up. Young people especially moved on, seeking new jobs and new homes in towns and cities. Yet a nucleus still remained.

Rudd humped his shoulders uneasily. He felt a stirring of something which he could not put into words: the past was linked to the present and the generations joined hands across the years. He could not help feeling that this was in some way significant, although how it could help to solve the immediate problem of Rene King's death he was not sure. All the same, he made a mental note to get Holbrook to introduce him to someone in the village, some elderly person, who had known the neighbourhood and its inhabitants from the past and who might, if he or she did nothing else, rid him of this irritating tick in his intuitive thought that he could not rationalise and yet could not wholly dismiss.

Rudd turned and walked back through the churchyard and into the lane. The face was still visible at the cottage window. Rudd waved and the gesture was returned: a hand fluttered against the glass and then was gone. Rudd wondered who it might be. A sick child, perhaps, whiling away the tedious hours in bed by watching everything that went on in the lane outside. There would not be much to see: the postman or the milkman making their deliveries; a handful of people on a Sunday making their way to church for matins or evensong; Amy Leacock among them, but Rene King no longer a member of the congregation. No doubt Dr. Foreman would visit the patient and the thought of the doctor put Rudd in mind of the library book which he had not yet returned.

He turned right at the end of the lane and mounted the steps of the doctor's house. Mrs. Foreman, a pleasant, grey-haired woman, answered the door and said her husband was busy with his morning surgery. Rudd scribbled a note, briefly explaining the situation and then walked back to where his car was parked.

The afternoon would have to be spent in the office and the Inspector regretted this. The day was too good to waste indoors and yet reports had to be written and he knew he must arrange a properly organised search of the mushroom field and the wood beyond it. Until he had done that, he could not establish the basic fact in the case: whether or not the Death Cap fungus grew in the field and could therefore have been picked in all innocence by Stan Spurgeon or his mother, or, come to that, by his son. Or, if it did not, where it could be found, for until Boyce returned with positive news of King's movements, Rudd could do nothing more but concentrate on the local angle to the case.

When he got back to the station he found that Boyce had returned, looking dispirited. Rudd could tell from his face that his inquiries had led nowhere.

"A complete waste of time," he said, dropping heavily into a chair. "I saw King's wife and went through the usual spiel for this sort of inquiry: street accident, lorry ran over an old lady, looking for witnesses, checking on cars seen in the vicinity, one with a registration number like theirs seen by a passer-by, my duty to investigate, etc., etc. She was quite positive. King wasn't at home that night."

Rudd stirred in his seat and Boyce gave him a quick grin.

"That's what I thought at the time. But wait for the rest of it. He was in Bradford, seeing one or two knitwear manufacturers on business. So I had some discreet inquiries made up there. He checked in at the Court Hotel using his own name and this was confirmed by the night porter who says King uses the place regularly. He certainly wasn't at Abbots Stacey slipping fungus into a basket of mushrooms on Wednesday, and he's covered for the Thursday as well. He lunched at the hotel with some business men and didn't check out until six o'clock."

"Well, he had to be checked," Rudd said, "even if he didn't seem all that likely. At least we've proved that line of inquiry's a dead end if nothing else. What's the wife like?" he added. It was pure curiosity.

"King's wife?" asked Boyce. "Blonde, bored, indifferent. A good figure but a mean mouth. Not much warmth there, I'd say. They've got a flat in one of the new tower blocks down by the river. Not my style at all. All show. No real home comfort. There were lots of women's magazines about and a cocktail cabinet. I suppose that's how she spends her time; that and shopping and going to the hairdresser's. It was one of the reasons I took so long over the inquiry. I called a couple of times and she was out. When I did find her in, she looked as if she'd just come back from having her hair done."

"Do you think she'll say anything to King about your visit?" Rudd asked. "Not that it matters."

Boyce shrugged.

"She might do, but she didn't seem all that interested. By the way," he added, "it seemed pretty pointless coming back here last night to report, so I went to see my old mum at Romford and spent the night there as it's near to London and I was late finishing."

"How is she?" asked Rudd. He had never met Boyce's mother but had often heard the Sergeant speak of her with gruff, half-disguised affection.

"The same as ever," Boyce replied. "She made me an apple dumpling. Funny to be back there; on my own, I mean, without the wife and kids. I slept in my old room. It's not changed much: same bed, same wardrobe and chest-of-drawers and I listened to the trains as I used to do as a kid. It took me back a few years, I can tell you."

Rudd gave him a look of quick understanding. We all have our sense of the past, he thought. It's part of us. Something that can never be taken away.

The people he had become involved with in the case, the Leacocks and the Spurgeons, he had known for only a short time but he had worked with Boyce in close collaboration over several years. Yet, when you came down to it, Boyce himself was an enigma to him. The glimpses he caught of the real man were few enough. Of those others, the suspects, he knew even less. Their motives, their thoughts, their true personalities were almost totally unknown to him.

"Well," Boyce was saying, "what's on the cards for this afternoon?"

"Plenty," Rudd replied, arousing himself from his reverie. "I'm having a thorough search made of Spurgeon's field and the wood behind the farm. I've sent Johnson and Cates over to get precise measurements. They should be back soon. I want a list drawn up of at least twenty men. Transport's got to be arranged and that's only a beginning."

Boyce heaved himself out of his chair.

"I'd better give the wife a ring," he said, "and tell her I'll be home late tonight."

"And I'll phone my sister," Rudd said.

He felt a pang of conscience. Until Boyce had spoken, it had not occurred to him to telephone her, so totally absorbed had he been in his work.

He dialed his home number but there was no reply. Perhaps she was out shopping or taking the dog for a walk. Absurdly, as he replaced the receiver, he felt disappointed that he had not been able to speak to her and fulfil his good intentions.

Later, as the pressure of work in the office increased, with Johnson and Cates returning, people coming and going, Boyce asking his advice, he forgot and it was not until nine o'clock that evening, when all the others had gone home and he paused at the door to turn out the lights, that he remembered that he had not tried to telephone her again, after all.

7

The reports were already coming in. The forensic tests on the letter had been completed and largely confirmed what Boyce had predicted: the paper and envelope were of a cheap, popular brand on sale nearly everywhere; there were no recognisable fingerprints on the letter itself, only smudges which indicated, Rudd thought, that the writer had either worn gloves or had deliberately wiped the paper over to remove any prints. Yet even this piece of negative information told him something. The writer was shrewd and intelligent enough to obliterate any evidence of his or her identity. Prints of both fingers and thumbs belonging, the report stated, to at least two different people, had been found on the envelope but these did not interest Rudd. They were probably, as Boyce had pointed out, the prints of the postman and the constable who sorted out the mail. The Inspector did not think that the writer of the letter would be stupid enough to leave fingerprints on the envelope and yet take such care to leave none on the letter itself.

Two positive facts, however, did emerge. Although the saliva test on the gummed envelope flap proved that the person had indeed belonged to the "O" blood group, as Boyce had gloomily predicted, the person who had licked it had been a smoker. Nicotine tests had been positive. Rudd turned this over in his mind. Stan Spurgeon smoked; so did his mother. Gilbert Leacock did too, but his sister had refused the cigarette that Rudd had offered her. This would, therefore, rule her out as the writer of the anonymous letter and yet Rudd dismissed her reluctantly from that list of suspects. She had seemed such a perfect front runner in the poison-pen stakes, the classic example of the embittered spinster. So much for pigeon-holing people, Rudd thought. The trouble with that line of thinking was that sooner or later you came up against the truth that people can't be classified in that ready-made way.

The second piece of information appeared at first to be more interesting. The small stain in the top left-hand corner of the letter was not, as Boyce had hoped, something exotic and difficult to trace, but paraffin. Leacock sold paraffin in his hardware shop; this leaped at once to Rudd's mind. But then he remembered the Spurgeons had a paraffin stove in their kitchen. Both the Spurgeons, mother and son, probably handled the stove or filled the paraffin can. Come to that, if he made inquiries, he would no doubt find that half the inhabitants of the village kept paraffin on their premises. The evidence of the stain did not lead very far, after all, although it might form a useful link in a chain of other evidence.

No report had come in yet about the library book and Rudd rang through to the lab, hoping that the tests were far enough advanced for him to be given a verbal statement at least. After a short pause, while the assistant went off to make inquiries, his question was answered.

On the cover of the book, which was shiny and retained marks well, twelve different sets of prints had been isolated. The paper of the inside page had not such a good surface but, nevertheless, ten different sets could be distinguished and there might be more as some of the prints were overlying others and this made individual recognition impossible. A written report was being prepared and photographs would be available shortly. The tests on the basket that had contained the mushrooms were not yet far enough advanced for any statement to be made but information on it would be forwarded as soon as possible.

Rudd thanked the assistant and rang off. As far as the library book was concerned, it was as he had suspected and yet he was disappointed all the same. If the worst came to the worst, a positive identification of individual fingerprints might be possible although he groaned inwardly at the amount of work it would entail. It might mean fingerprinting every member of the library and every inhabitant of Abbots Stacey. Of course it could be done. It had been done before in murder investigations. But Rudd hoped it would not be necessary in this case. Apart from anything else murder had not yet been established.

As for the basket, he had been aware himself that not

enough time had yet elapsed for any tests on it to be completed and even when they were the Inspector did not hold out any great hope of anything useful emerging from them. Prints alone would not prove anything positive. Like the book, the basket might have been handled by someone quite innocent. Miss Leacock, for example, might have touched it that Wednesday evening without being aware of it and so might Mrs. Youngman. Under the circumstances, he could not see it providing damning evidence against any of the Spurgeons either. Only if Leacock's prints were found on it could it really be regarded as material evidence in a murder trial for he appeared to be the only one out of that group of people who had no excuse for opening the fridge door at any time between the basket being placed on the shelf inside it and Mrs. King taking the mushrooms out to cook them on the Thursday evening.

The pathologist's report came by the afternoon post and was waiting on Rudd's desk when he returned from lunch. It confirmed what Dr. Foreman had already told him, although the facts of Mrs. King's death were now officially established. She had indeed died through asphyxiation caused by inhaling vomit and the vomiting had been brought on by the ingestion of the fungus Amanita Phalloides. One new fact, however, did emerge. Mrs. King had eaten only a little of the fungus and yet it would have been sufficient to cause death through poisoning even if she had not died through asphyxiation. As the report stated: "A small amount of this fungus is fatal." This was interesting. It meant that only one or two of the fungi, presumably in the button stage when they most resembled the mushroom, needed to be introduced: a small enough quantity to be concealed in the hand or in a pocket.

The time of death had also been established. The pathologist's report stated that she had died between four and five a.m., which was very close to the time Dr. Foreman had given Rudd. Evidently Dr. Foreman knew his medical facts.

There was one more line of inquiry that needed official verification and that was the names of the adults from the village of Abbots Stacey who were members of the Market Stratton public library. As no report had yet come in, Rudd telephoned the library and asked to speak to the head librarian. Here, however, he drew a blank.

Did he not realise, she said snappishly, that a full investigation of the membership cards would take a great deal of time? She hoped he appreciated that there was only herself and two assistants and the ordinary work of the library had to go on. They were, after all, a public service and not a branch of the police force.

Rudd made soothing noises down the telephone which somewhat mollified her and she finally agreed to let him have the list within the next few days. Rudd thanked her and rang off. There was nothing more he could do in that line except wait.

Rudd next went to see his Superintendent, taking with him copies of the forensic and pathologist's reports. Davies was a neat, spare, upright man, of few words and with an air of quiet authority, who believed in letting his detectives get on with the job, while watching carefully but unobtrusively from the sidelines. The two men always got on well together and had built up a good relationship based on mutual trust and respect. "Sit down," Davies said as Rudd entered and the Inspector drew up a chair to the desk.

"Cigarette?" Davies added, pushing a plain, leather-covered box towards him. As Rudd lifted the lid, he noticed the tidy arrangement of the cigarettes inside it, in one compartment plain, in the other filter-tipped. It was typical of the man and very different to the battered packet that Rudd carried about in his own pocket, usually with a telephone number or a name jotted down on the back of it.

"How are the inquiries going?" Davies asked.

"Not very far, sir," Rudd admitted. "There's very little real evidence to go on."

Davies got up and, crossing the room, produced a folder from the filing cabinet and returned with it to the desk. It contained, neatly clipped together, the copies of the reports that Rudd had already written up on the case and had sent to the superintendent's office.

Davies looked the reports over, softly stroking his well-shaven chin as he did so.

"Murder still not established yet?"

"No," said Rudd, "but I'm hoping to get a bit further on with that tomorrow."

He explained the arrangements he was making to have the field and the wood behind Spurgeon's farm searched.

"That sounds reasonable," Davies replied. "Do you need any help with it?"

"I don't think so," Rudd said. "Boyce is back now. He's been making some inquiries about Mrs. King's nephew which, incidentally, rule him out as a possible suspect. You probably read in my report that I was having him checked on."

"That reminds me," Davies put in, "King's solicitor phoned me this morning, very anxious to know when he could have access to Mrs. King's property. It seems that, under the terms of her will, the nephew is empowered to have it and its contents valued and then sold, the money to be paid into the aunt's bank account until such time as the will is proved; unusual but perfectly legal, so his solicitor informed me. He said something about avoiding unnecessary delay."

"And King wants to get started on it," Rudd replied. "He would. He's a sharp operator. You'll see from my report that one of the reasons he came under suspicion was because he'd walked in and taken everything of value out of the place within a couple of days of her death."

"But he's cleared now of any suspicion?" Davies asked.

"Yes. Boyce found he'd got a cast-iron alibi. He had to be checked on of course but he's a Londoner and this case smacks to me of local knowledge, especially now that fungus poisoning has been established."

"And you've checked Mrs. King's flat?"

"As far as we can. It's been fingerprinted and turned over. McCallum has taken photographs. I can't see what else we can usefully find in it."

"So you'd have no objections if King goes ahead with the sale?"

Rudd shrugged his shoulders. "We can't stop him, can we?"

"Not unless we make it an official murder inquiry," Davies replied, "which we can't do. We haven't the evidence."

"And we may never get it," Rudd pointed out.

"Exactly. And I don't want to put us into an awkward legal position. King's solicitor sounded polite but very probing."

"I should imagine King must have got on to him after I'd phoned him from his aunt's shop," Rudd replied. "It's the sort of thing he would do. I've never yet met a sharp business man who hasn't had an equally sharp legal adviser behind him. Anyway, with King out of the case, it looks as if it involves only local people."

"One of these," asked Davies tapping the reports. "Spurgeon, his mother, the Leacocks or Mrs. Youngman?"

"They're the only ones who seem to have had the opportunity," Rudd replied. "It's motive that's the main stumbling block. They all seem to have been on friendly terms with the dead woman. It was the point that Holbrook, the local Sergeant emphasised when I interviewed him. Mrs. King was not the sort of woman to make enemies. In fact, until I received that anonymous letter, it was accepted by Holbrook and the doctor that her death was accidental and neither of them are fools. Holbrook is still convinced it was."

"He may very well be right," Davies pointed out.

"He may," Rudd agreed. "That's why I've had none of them in yet to make an official statement. There'll be time enough for that after I've had the field thoroughly searched and I'm a bit more sure in my own mind just where the fungus is to be found."

"Has nothing useful turned up on the anonymous letter writer?" Davies asked.

"Only what's in this report," Rudd replied, handing over the copy.

The Superintendent ran his eye quickly over it.

"No fingerprints," he commented. "So it's not going to be easy finding out who wrote it."

"It isn't," Rudd agreed. "The village has a total population of 1,800. If you halve that figure to allow for the adult population, it still leaves 900 who could have written it. But there's one thing that bothers me about it. I've seen anonymous letters before and the accusations in them are either of a moral nature, not specified, just mud-slinging of a general sort; or specific charges are made, but usually both the person as well as the charge are definitely named; it was so and so who stole such and such, that sort of thing. Now, in this letter, the charge is definite: murder. But no one is accused by name. Boyce is inclined to think it's pure malice but I'm not so sure. I have an uneasy feeling that the writer of that letter knows something and for some reason won't name the person involved but hopes that, by putting us on to the scent, we'll find out for ourselves."

Davies pulled a wry face.

"I don't like this type of case," he said. "It could drag on for weeks and lead nowhere in the end."

"I agree," replied Rudd with feeling.

The Superintendent gave him a quick, sympathetic look.

"Well, you know you can rely on me for any help you may need," he said. "By the way, I've checked with the coroner's officer. The inquest will be held on Monday at Market Stratton. I've explained our position and there'll be an adjournment. Only formal evidence will be called at this stage, who or what I can't say, but Ridgely will be in charge and he knows what he's doing."

Rudd thanked him and left the office.

The rest of the afternoon was taken up with organising the final details of the search and by six o'clock it was completed. Rudd glanced at his watch to confirm the time, stretched his arms and yawned. Boyce, who was shuffling papers about, trying to look busy, also looked hopefully at the time.

"Finished?" asked Rudd.

"Just about," Boyce replied.

"Let's shut up shop then," said Rudd. "It'll be a busy day tomorrow."

They walked down the stairs together.

Boyce said, "My wife's going to faint, me coming home at this time."

"I expect my sister'll be surprised too," Rudd replied.

Rudd stood with his hands in his pockets watching the twenty police constables slowly working their way up Spurgeon's mushroom field towards the wood at the far end. He was feeling particularly pleased with himself. The arrangements had gone like clockwork. The field was divided by means of lengths of twine into strips about two yards wide and each man was responsible for one of those strips. He had been instructed to search his area carefully and to stick a white marker into the ground wherever he found a mushroom whose identity he was unsure about. Rudd had already briefed them on the appearance and identification of field mushrooms and the fungus Amanita Phalloides before the search began and each man had been given a photocopy of the illustration from the book *British Mushrooms and Toadstools*.

Boyce, Holbrook and another sergeant, armed with a large-scale plan of the field and wood, drawn to scale with the strips marked in, were to walk behind numbering and placing the position of any mushrooms from a doubtful

clump on their plan. The mushrooms in question were then
to be placed in plastic bags, numbered to correspond with
those on the plan and sent later to a mycologist at London
University for positive identification. Rudd had already been
in telephone communication with this expert, a Professor
Harvey, who had agreed to hurry through the tests and
send Rudd a report the next day.

The search was laborious but necessary. Rudd could see no
other way of establishing the first step in this inquiry to
find out whether Mrs. King had met her death accidentally
or not.

Rudd watched the men's progress. They had begun together at the bottom of the field but gradually the line
had broken up as some of them moved further forward.
Boyce, Holbrook and the other sergeant waited in a small
group by the gate that led into Spurgeon's yard, hunch-
shouldered, bored and cold. There was not much they could
do until one of the constables should raise his arm, the
signal for the discovery of a possible fungus. Then they
could move forward with their plan of the field. Rudd could
see it tucked under Boyce's arm, a white oblong. Because
of the wind, it was difficult to spread out. It would have
been better if it had been mounted on a board and Rudd
wished he had thought of it. But, he consoled himself, he
could not have foreseen the change in the weather. The
summer had died overnight and, although the sun still shone,
there was a distinct chill of autumn in the wind. It roared
like the sea in the taller trees in the wood, sending leaves
showering down and disturbing the rooks that flew round
and round, cawing bad-temperedly. Already their ragged
nests were exposed among the denuded branches. Overhead,
great towering grey and white clouds tore past, like sailing
ships driven before a gale.

Rudd smiled. He liked gusty weather. It exhilarated him.
And he was pleased, also, that everything was going as he
had planned. He had even remembered the horse that usually
occupied the field and he had arranged with Spurgeon to
have it pastured in the adjoining meadow. It was looking
over the hedge now, like Rudd watching the activities of
the policemen, with a sardonic expression on its long face.
He strolled over to say hello to it.

He stood stroking its nose for a few minutes, feeling it
blow warm breath into his hand, and then he walked up
the field beside the hedge, intending to scramble through

the bushes at the far end into the wood to check that the markers there had been properly placed, when a piece of paper, caught in the hedge bottom and fluttering in the wind like a small flag, caught his attention and he bent down to pick it out. It was a piece torn from the local newspaper of a fortnight before. It might mean nothing at all but nonetheless he folded it carefully and put it into his wallet and, stooping again, searched among the brambles for anything else that might have been abandoned in the hedge. There was nothing on his side but he could see through the gaps in the twigs another piece of paper on the far side and what appeared to be the remains of a fire. A little further along, a gate connected the two fields and Rudd climbed over it and walked the short distance back.

He had been right. Someone had lit a fire close to the hedge, under its lee. Rudd squatted down beside it and examined the little pile of ash and circle of half-burned sticks. The ash had been blown about by the wind but looked fairly fresh. The second piece of paper that had caught his eye was fluttering nearby, spiked on a twig. It seemed to be from the same newspaper and had evidently been used to light the fire as its edges were charred. Rudd folded it up and placed it in his wallet with the first piece and, searching his pockets, found a piece of string which he tied to the twig where the second piece of paper had been found. He then walked back to the fire and stood looking down at it. Something about the arrangement of the sticks caught his interest and he moved over to the far side of the circle and squatted down on the grass. At that moment a shout from one of the policemen in the adjoining field made him look up and he saw that from where he was now sitting he had a perfect view through a natural opening in the hedge of the mushroom field, the wood beyond and the straggling line of policemen working their way towards it.

Rudd sat back on his heels and pondered. Someone who had lit this fire with pages from a recent copy of the local newspaper could have sat where he was now sitting and could have seen anyone gathering mushrooms in the field beyond or entering the wood. Who lit fires in a field? A child, perhaps. But more likely gypsies or a tramp. Rudd did not think it had been gypsies. They preferred the road's edge were they could easily park their caravans. Besides, gypsies usually left more evidence of their stay in the way of

discarded rubbish. Whoever had lit that fire had not remained there long enough to leave anything much behind
except ashes, burnt sticks and a couple of pieces of newspaper.

Thoughtfully Rudd picked up one of the sticks and sniffed
at it. It still smelt faintly of burnt wood. He was still
sniffing at it when he became aware that someone was
standing behind him and he turned quickly, putting the
stick down, to find he was confronted by a small boy who
was watching him with a wide unblinking stare.

At first sight, the boy seemed just like any other country-
bred child. He was sturdy and strongly-built, roughly dressed
in old jeans and a dirty windcheater and he had that coarse
fair hair that grows straight down over the forehead and
never lies flat over the crown of the head. Then Rudd
noticed the slackness of the boy's mouth and the vacancy
in his light blue eyes and he realised it was Kenny, Stan
Spurgeon's defective son.

"Hello," said Rudd, smiling.

The boy did not answer but went on staring at him with
a fixed gaze.

"Not at school today?" Rudd continued.

The boy did blink at this question, veiling his eyes for a
second with straight stubby fair eyelashes. Rudd was reminded of Spurgeon's lashes fluttering down when he had
spoken of Mrs. King. It was a movement that was at the
same time embarrassed and furtive.

"Someone lit a fire here," said Rudd, leaning forward to
poke at the ashes with the half-burnt stick. "Was it you?"

The boy considered the question, then wiped his nose, that
had begun to run in the cold wind, on his jacket sleeve
and shook his head.

"Gypsies?" pursued Rudd.

The boy again shook his head.

"A tramp, then?" suggested Rudd.

Kenny Spurgeon considered the question, removing that
light blue stare from Rudd's face and looking away across
the field. Then he nodded.

"Do you know his name?" Rudd asked. He dug in his
pocket and produced a fivepenny piece which he held up.
"You can have this if you can remember his name."

Kenny transferred his gaze to the coin and held out his
hand.

"No," said Rudd firmly. "You must tell me his name first."

"Ol' Bi'," said the boy.

"Old Bill?" hazarded Rudd.

Kenny smiled and nodded, delighted to be understood; and Rudd handed over the money. The child's fingers closed over it at once and he turned and ran away down the field, startling the horse which, bored with watching the policemen, had resumed its cropping of the grass.

Rudd climbed back over the gate and sought out Holbrook.

"Old Bill?" said Holbrook. "Yes, I know of him. He's around these parts on and off during the summer months. I've heard old Mrs. Spurgeon slips him a bit of grub from time to time."

"Funny, that," remarked Rudd. "I know some country people won't turn a gypsy away for fear of the Evil Eye but I thought they hadn't much time for tramps."

"Well, Ma Spurgeon's a law to herself," Holbrook said. "Besides, she comes from the same sort of stock. They say her grandfather was a diddecoy and used to go totting for old iron and what-have-you round the district and he spent the last few years of his life living in a little makeshift hut down by the river. Old Bill's been round here for a good few years, so I've been told. When Mr. Spurgeon was alive, Stan's father that is, Old Bill used to come regular every summer to do casual work on the farm, so she's known him from way back."

Rudd asked, "Any idea where he might be now?"

Holbrook shook his head.

"I've not seen him around for nearly a week. I expect he's moved on. But I tell you what, he shacks up in the wood. We could go and have a look round and see if he's there."

"Right," said Rudd. He called Boyce over and told him where he was going. Boyce nodded without replying. He was cold and miserable and he hated the country.

"The tea van'll be here soon," Rudd said, to cheer him up. He had arranged for a mobile canteen to be sent over from headquarters as the search seemed likely to take several hours. "As soon as they've finished in the field, you can call a break before they start on the wood."

"Talk about looking for a blinking needle in a haystack,"

muttered Boyce turning away, only a little cheered by the thought of hot tea. As Rudd and Holbrook walked off, the Inspector thought he heard Boyce add, "Bleeding mushrooms!"

The wood was narrow and composed largely of tangled undergrowth with a few large trees standing up among the lower-growing bushes and scrub. Red and white markers of the kind used as warning signs round road repairs protruded here and there among the brambles and dying bracken like exotic plants. They were placed there to indicate the search lanes.

Holbrook seemed to know the wood well. He crashed through the scrub, holding back branches in a solicitous way for Rudd to duck under and in a few moments they emerged on to a narrow grassy path that traversed the wood. It was not wide enough for both of them to walk side by side and Holbrook went first. Rudd, following behind, kept his eyes open for fungi and saw several varieties; one a great sponge-like growth on a tree-trunk; another, a circle of delicate little dome-capped toadstools growing on slender stalks. But he saw nothing that resembled the Death Cap.

After walking for several minutes, Holbrook turned off between two trees into a space where the undergrowth had been cleared and pointed a finger.

"That's where he shacks up," he said. Rudd stared. At first he could not make out anything that resembled a habitation, however crude. All he could see was a large bush over which wild honeysuckle and old man's beard had draped themselves to form a great hump of leaves and twigs. But, as they approached it, Rudd saw that the bush had been strengthened with pieces of broken hurdle and an entrance hole had been cut in one side. He ducked his head through the hole. The centre of the bush had been hollowed out and dried bracken and straw thrown down in one corner to make a rough bed. A torn piece of tarpaulin was tied to the twigs and small branches over it to keep off the rain. Dirty paper and a few rags lay about on the ground and the place smelt strongly of damp and mould. Rudd quickly withdrew his head.

"Does he really sleep in there?" he asked.

"When he's in the area. Spurgeon won't have him on the farm because of the danger of fire. You know what these old tramps are like, always brewing themselves up tea. But he can't stop old Mrs. Spurgeon from giving him a bit of grub. I've heard she leaves it wrapped up in newspaper by the yard gate. He moves on somewhere else from time to time but I like to keep an eye on him when he's around the district. Apart from the risk of fire, I wouldn't put it past him to nick anything he found lying about. But like I said, I've not seen him now for several days and in the winter, I don't ever see him. I expect he finds somewhere a bit warmer to sleep."

They walked back. At the edge of the wood Rudd said, "I'd like a full description of him that I can circulate round the area and if you see him yourself, I want to be informed straight away."

"Of course," said Holbrook. "I could give you a description right now if you like."

"I'd rather you gave it some thought," Rudd replied. "Ring me at the office this afternoon."

"Very good," said Holbrook. He hesitated and then added with a sideways look at Rudd, "I think the old man's harmless enough. He might knock off a few eggs or washing from a line but he's never been in any real trouble."

"Good," said Rudd and left it at that. He had no intention at this stage of telling anyone why he wanted to question the tramp. After all, there was so little to base anything on; only the ashes of a fire, some scraps of newspaper and a convenient hole in a hedge. It might lead nowhere at all.

When the Inspector and Holbrook clambered back into the field they found it empty. Evidently the search had been completed and the men had gone back to the road where the mobile canteen was now drawn up in Spurgeon's gateway. The policemen were clustered about it, drinking tea out of paper cups. Spurgeon was standing in the yard watching them with a grin on his face.

"Proper schoolboys' outing, ain't it?" he said to Rudd as the Inspector approached. "I hope they've got something to show for all their trouble. Look at that one!" he added derisively, pointing to a young constable who was wiping his boots fastidiously on a clump of grass. "Picked up a bit of horse muck, by the look of it. Leave it on, lad," he shouted at him. "It'll help to keep the wet out."

Rudd smiled. Spurgeon did not appear at all put out by the search. On the contrary, he seemed hugely amused by the situation.

"By the way," the Inspector said with seeming casualness. "Seen anything of Old Bill recently?"

Spurgeon turned his candid blue gaze on him.

"The tramp? No, not for several days," he said. "Why?"

"No reason," replied Rudd. "I noticed someone had lit a fire alongside the hedge and Old Bill's name was mentioned."

"The old fool!" Spurgeon said angrily. "I've told him enough times about lighting fires. He'll have the whole bloody place in flames one of these days."

"Why don't you turn him off your land, then?" Rudd asked.

The farmer looked uncomfortable.

"Well," he said, shifting his feet about, "he's no real trouble and I get him to do a few odd jobs about the place sometimes."

"Like picking mushrooms?" suggested Rudd.

The blue eyes became angry.

"I thought I told you it was me as picked them," he said.

"All right," said Rudd equably. "I was only asking."

He strolled off down the lane to find Boyce.

Boyce was better tempered after his hot tea.

"We'll soon have this lot finished," he said to Rudd. "The wood's not all that big, thank the Lord, and I reckon another hour'll see it done."

"Found anything?" Rudd asked.

With a grin Boyce held up a plastic bag at the bottom of which a small button mushroom lay.

"That's the lot," he said. "Not much to show so far and in my opinion it's not an Amnita Phalldois, or whatever its name is. It's an honest-to-God mushroom and if someone would bet me a quid I'd have it for tea to prove it."

"Better not risk it," replied Rudd. "If you were wrong, I don't think, from what I've heard, that you'd find it a peaceful way to die. Besides, the fungus expert in London wants to test anything suspicious that we find. Anyhow we'd better get them on their feet," he added. "I want that wood searched. And see they clear up all their litter. I don't want Spurgeon making complaints."

Boyce walked off, issued a few orders in his deep voice and the men collected up the paper cups and walked back up the field in twos and threes towards the wood.

Boyce was right in his estimation. It took about an hour

to search the wood and they were rewarded after a quarter of an hour by a shout from one of the constables. Rudd, accompanied by Boyce and Holbrook, made their way in the direction of the shout to find a constable, out of breath and with pieces of twig caught up in his clothes and hair, pointing excitedly at the grassy space at the foot of a tree.

Rudd squatted down to look closely. There seemed no doubt about it. They had found Amanita Phalloides. There were quite a few of the fungi growing there, about twelve in all. Some were just protruding from the ground among the grass stems and fallen leaves and were surprisingly similar to half-buried eggs while the half-grown specimens were indeed like button mushrooms with the thick, white, rounded cap and the short, stocky stalk hiding the underside of the gills. There was no mistaking, however, the fully grown fungus for an edible mushroom. The cap was flat and greenish-white in colour and the white, densely packed gills were clearly visible. One had fallen on its side and Rudd, taking a penknife from his pocket, carefully cut a slice and, spearing it on the point of the blade, sniffed at it cautiously. It had an unpleasantly foetid smell.

"That's it!" he announced. He stood up and rubbed the penknife clean on a handful of grass before returning it to his pocket.

Everything was quickly organised. Boyce and the other sergeant measured out the exact position of the fungi, which were growing about twenty feet from the boundary of the wood and close to the far end of it while Holbrook and two constables made a detailed search of the surrounding area. They found nothing, not even a thread of material caught on a thorn, although Holbrook was of the opinion that someone had been there recently. He pointed out to Rudd several freshly-bruised twigs on a nearby bush and signs that the grass had been disturbed. But that was all. The ground was too deep in dead leaves to hold any foot-prints.

Rudd saw to it that several of the fungi, in various stages of development, were placed in plastic bags for the mycologist in London to examine but he was certain in his own mind what his findings would be. It was the Death Cap right enough.

The rest of the search was something of an anti-climax. No other fungi were found and, although Rudd told the men to look out also for any evidence of anyone having been in the wood recently, the result was negative. At the far side of the wood, Rudd called the search off and the policemen made their way back to the road where a bus was waiting to take them back to headquarters.

Rudd, Boyce and Holbrook walked back to the farm. There was no sign of Spurgeon in the yard but, as they passed the house, Rudd was sure he saw old Mrs. Spurgeon's face peering at them through the kitchen window. She ducked out of sight as soon as she saw them.

At the car, Rudd reminded Holbrook that he wanted a description of Old Bill telephoned through to the office that afternoon.

"Old Bill?" Boyce asked inquisitively as they drove away.

Rudd remembered that Boyce had not been told about the tramp and he described briefly his finding of the camp-fire site and the talk with Kenny Spurgeon.

Boyce looked doubtful.

"Not much to go on," he commented.

But Rudd refused to be disheartened. Since the Death Cap had been found in the woods, he had become convinced that Mrs. King's death was not accidental. Someone had deliberately looked for the fungus. Someone had, as deliberately, introduced it into the basket of mushrooms. Of this he was now certain. And he had the feeling that Old Bill, if he could be found, might prove a useful, if not invaluable, witness.

"We'll see," he said non-committally. It was, after all, rather nebulous when you came down to it; nothing much more than a feeling and yet Rudd could not shake off his conviction.

Holbrook telephoned that afternoon with a detailed description of the tramp. "Aged about seventy. Tall but stoop-shouldered. Long grey straggly hair and beard. Usually dressed in an old army overcoat and carrying a khaki haversack over one shoulder."

Rudd had the description circulated to all police stations and mobile units throughout the country. Meanwhile, he had his report to write up on the morning's search of the field and the plastic bags of specimens to despatch to London for expert analysis. He made a note, too, to call again at Spurgeon's farm and talk to Kenny Spurgeon, not that he held out much hope of getting anything useful from the boy. He seemed barely articulate and, even if he knew something that might be useful to the investigation, he could not be called as a witness. No court of law would ever accept the testimony of a defective ten-year-old child.

He wanted, too, to talk to Mrs. Spurgeon again, this time out of her son's hearing. Old country women often know a great deal about the use of herbs and home-made remedies. Mrs. Spurgeon might very well know the properties of various wild plants and fungi and where they could be found.

He wished, though, that he had more tangible evidence to go on, even if now he was certain of one thing, that the anonymous letter writer had been right and that Mrs. King had not met her death by accident.

It was like lifting up a stone. There it lay all clean and innocent looking but, as soon as you turned it over, all kinds of things scuttled away from the sudden light. Rudd had the feeling that a good many more stones would have to be turned over before he could call the case complete.

8

The inquest on Mrs. King was held the following Monday morning in the town hall in Market Stratton. There was no jury and Dr. Wakefield Ridgely, an elderly man, sat alone behind a heavy oak table. He was both a medical practitioner and an experienced coroner, and Rudd, who had attended inquests held by him before, knew and admired his technique. Ridgely had a mild, courteous manner but he had been known to ask very pertinent questions in a deceptively conversational tone of voice.

Rudd slipped in at the back and sat down unobtrusively in the last row. There was only a handful of people present. Among them Rudd recognised Dr. Foreman and Stan Spurgeon. A young man who was seated in the front he took to be Roland King, Mrs. King's nephew. Rudd glanced across at Spurgeon, wondering why he was there at all. It seemed unlikely that, at this stage of the proceedings, he would be called upon to give evidence. Spurgeon was sitting at the far side of the room so that Rudd could see him in three-quarter profile. He presented a slightly unfamiliar appearance in a conventional dark blue suit and collared shirt with a tie, for the Inspector had only ever seen him dressed in rough working clothes. He sat in an attitude of uneasy tenseness, his arms folded tightly across his chest. From time to time he shifted about on the seat as if he found it uncomfortable and the inactivity irksome.

Although he craned his neck, Rudd could see little of Roland King except the back of his head with a fashionable longer than usual haircut.

Dr. Ridgely coughed politely and the slight hum and stir in the courtroom ceased and the inquest began.

Roland King was called first to give evidence on the

identification of his aunt's body. He answered the coroner's
questions in a deliberately subdued tone, quite different from
the positive and self-assured manner that Rudd had noticed
when he spoke to him on the telephone and the Inspector felt
he had been right in his estimation that King was a shrewd
operator.

He said that his aunt had been very frank with him about
her business affairs and he had no reason to believe she had
any financial worries. Yes, he would say that she was a
cheerful person and she seemed to have recovered from her
husband's death four years previously and to have settled
down in her new life quite happily.

Ridgely expressed his regret at her death and for a moment
King was at a loss. With an uncertain gesture, one hand went
"You may sit down, Mr. King," Ridgely said kindly.
"There are no more questions I wish to ask you."
up to touch his black tie.

King resumed his place at the front seat, without ap-
parently realising that Ridgely had neatly established the
fact that suicide was unlikely. Rudd crossed his legs in an
attitude of comfortable satisfaction. Although it was nothing
to do with him, he felt pleased that the coroner had put something over on King without him being aware of it.

Dr. Foreman was called next and gave evidence on his
examination of the body. Most of what he said Rudd already
knew but he did learn one new fact. Mrs. King had suffered
from a slight heart condition which was not serious but
which might have accounted for her collapse on the stairs. It
was on his recommendation that she had employed domestic
help and she had been told not to over-exert herself.

The next witness was the pathologist who had performed
the post-mortem. He looked so young, with a schoolboy's
lick of hair falling over his forehead and a bouncy, cheerful,
adolescent air about him, that he might have been taken for
a first-year medical student. He gave his evidence quickly
and enthusiastically while Dr. Ridgely scribbled down notes.
It covered all the main points that had been contained in his
report to Rudd, and the Inspector, while still listening, divided
his attention between it and the effect it was having on some
of those present in the court.

Roland King was sitting very upright but, from time to
time, as the more unpleasant medical facts were described,
he passed a hand as if nervously over the back of his hair.

Stan Spurgeon had unfolded his arms and was leaning forward, his elbows on his knees and his head between his hands, like a man awkwardly praying.

"The fungus Amanita Phalloides," the pathologist was saying, with all the enthusiasm of an expert who has done his homework, "contains six principal poisons: phalloidine, a hexapeptide which causes degeneration of the liver, kidney and cardiac muscle and . . ."

Dr. Ridgely looked up mildly over his spectacles.

"I'm sure," he said, "that you have gone to a great deal of trouble to acquaint yourself of this information and the court is grateful. I know I am. But, as it has been established that Mrs. King died of asphyxiation, the poisonous nature of the fungus is not of primary importance."

The young pathologist went back to his seat looking disappointed, like a schoolboy deprived of a treat.

There was a subdued stirring in the court. Roland King, who had been listening intently, relaxed a little. Stan Spurgeon resumed his tense attitude, his arms folded across his chest again and his head ducked slightly forward. From where he was sitting, Rudd could see the muscles in his neck straining like cords and a glistening patch of sweat on his forehead and upper lip among the coarse brown hairs of his moustache.

Dr. Ridgely looked up from his notes and the rustling died down.

"There seems no doubt," he said, "that Mrs. King died of asphyxiation caused by inhaling vomit and the vomiting was the result of her eating the fungus Amanita Phalloides. At this stage, I do not propose calling any more evidence nor shall I pronounce a verdict. This inquest is, therefore, adjourned to a later date to allow further inquiries to be made."

There was a further stirring in the court as he closed his notebook and Rudd took the opportunity to slip quietly out of the door. Once clear of the court, he walked briskly to the carpark. But he did not immediately drive away. He saw Dr. Foreman emerge from the building in company with the young pathologist. They stood talking on the steps for a few moments. The young man seemed to be inviting his older colleague to join him for a drink. Dr. Foreman shook his head and the two men parted, Foreman walking to his own car and driving away without noticing Rudd. Spurgeon came out shortly afterwards, with King following almost directly behind him. In fact, the farmer half-turned to hold the door open for the other man and then, as he realised who he was, Spuregeon gave an awkward little flinching movement with his shoulders and hurried down the steps two at a time. King seemed unaware of the farmer's embarrassment at the encounter. After all, there was no reason for him to know Spurgeon's identity and he had probably not even noticed his presence at the inquest. He stood at the top of the steps, adjusting the lapels of his jacket, and then took his time walking to his car.

Rudd watched Spurgeon approach. The farmer's battered van was parked a few bays down from where Rudd's car stood and the Inspector had a good opportunity to study the man as he walked towards it. The too wide legs of his trousers, out of fashion long ago, flapped over the top of his shoes. The dark crease was visible between his eyebrows. It still puzzled Rudd why Spurgeon had been present at the inquest. Ridgely had clearly not intended calling on him to give evidence; it was much too soon in the investigation. And yet Spurgeon had, for some reason of his own, felt it necessary to change his clothes, leave his farm and place himself in a situation which he had found distressing and in which he had been plainly ill-at-ease. The encounter between the two men at the top of the steps that Rudd had witnessed was, he felt, significant also. But had it been guilt that had made Spurgeon flinch away from any contact with the dead woman's nephew? It might, after all, be nothing more than a natural reticence on Spurgeon's part to avoid a member of her family at the time of bereavement, simply because he did not know what to say to the man.

Rudd sat quietly behind the wheel. Spurgeon had not noticed him. The engine of the old van spluttered several times and then died. A door slammed and the farmer came into the line of Rudd's vision, a starting handle in his hand. Several times he tried cranking the engine and then, with a gesture of impatient finality, flung open the bonnet and ducked his head under it. The engine coughed and then vibrated. Spurgeon emereged from under the bonnet, made as if to wipe his hands on the seat of his trousers and then realised he had his best suit on. Rudd grinned. He had himself been in the same situation many times and he understood the weary resignation with which Spurgeon closed down the bonnet and, holdīng his oily hands awkwardly in front of him, got back into the van and drove off.

Rudd gave him several minutes' start and then too drove out of the carpark and took the Chelmsford road out of Market Stratton.

At headquarters, he was going upstairs to his office, when Boyce met him.

"You've got a visitor," he told Rudd with a grin. "Name of Old Bill."

"Good," Rudd said. "That was quick. Where was he picked up?"

"Out at Stavely. A mobile unit brought him in. You should have heard the driver swear! He didn't half carry on. He's out in the yard now, dusting the car out with DDT powder."

"Well, you can tell him not to bother," Rudd said. "I may need to take the old man over to Abbots Stacey and I'll use the same car. Where is he now?"

"In your office, stinking the place out. I've nipped out for a breath of fresh air. There's a constable with him but you'd better get in there quick before he passes out."

Rudd went on up the stairs, thinking that Boyce was exaggerating. But as he entered his office, he was struck himself by the smell. It was a fierce, throat-clutching odour that reminded Rudd of the lions' house at the zoo. A police constable, with clenched nostrils, was standing behind the desk, as close as he could get to the window, which was open at the top a few inches. As Rudd joined him there and struggled to get the lower half opened, the constable whispered to him, "I've tried that, sir, but the papers on your desk keep blowing about."

Rudd gave up and turned to face Old Bill who was seated in a chair on the other side of the desk. He was as Holbrook had described him: about seventy, although his exact age would be difficult to guess. Grey wisps from his hair and beard had grown together to form a matted halo round his face and under his chin. He was dressed in an army greatcoat which, in the absence of buttons, had been tied round the waist with a bit of stout string. In the gap between its unfastened edges, layer upon layer of other clothes could be seen: at least two jackets, a waistcoat, a cardigan and a pullover, like a section through a cut cabbage. He was nursing a khaki haversack on his lap.

Yet, for all his dirt and degradation, the old man was

not without a certain pride. He returned Rudd's gaze with a straight, angry stare and it was he who spoke first.

"What you want bringing me here for? I ain't done nothing wrong."

"We hope you may be able to help us with some inquiries," Rudd replied soothingly.

"Didn't even have a chance to have me grub," the old man grumbled. "A couple of coppers come up and bundled me off afore I could get me fire lit."

"Haven't you eaten?" Rudd asked.

"That's what I just said, didn't I?" the tramp replied with asperity. "I was gathering up a few sticks in the 'edge bottom when this police car come up and I was took."

Rudd turned to the constable. "Go down to the canteen and get a cup of tea and some sandwiches," he said.

"Any particular sort?" the constable asked.

Rudd looked inquiringly at the tramp who said, "Cheese'll do me. I can't chew on meat no more."

"Cheese," said Rudd, passing on the message as the constable seemed incapable of looking at Old Bill directly and kept his eyes fixed on the Inspector.

"Very good, sir," he said. He was clearly relieved at being able to leave the room.

"And two spoons of sugar," the old tramp called after his retreating figure. The thought of shouting orders at a policeman seemed to amuse him because he began to laugh, wheezing and choking and showing blackened stumps of teeth.

Rudd sat down at his desk and waited for the paroxysm to pass. Presently the old man wiped his sleeve across his face and sobered down.

"May I have your full name?" Rudd asked.

Old Bill immediately became hostile, all trace of laughter gone.

"What you want my name for?" he asked.

"So that I'll know what to call you," Rudd replied.

"Old Bill'll do me."

"Haven't you got a surname?" asked Rudd.

The old man watched him carefully from under shaggy eyebrows.

"I might 'ave," he said. "And then again I might not."

"Then you won't mind if I call you Old Bill?" Rudd asked.

"You can call me Old Nick if you want to," he said, heaving again with laughter. "I've been called a good few names in me time."

Rudd watched him curiously. He was not anxious to begin questioning the old man until he had eaten. A full belly, Rudd hoped, would place him under some obligation to the authority that had provided it, although he doubted if he would answer any questions he did not want to. There was a strong air of independence about the tramp, coupled with a humorous perverseness. But if he couldn't be bullied into answering he might very well be tricked.

The constable returned with a tray containing a cup of tea and a pile of cheese sandwiches on a plate. He put the tray down on the desk and Rudd indicated to Old Bill that he could start. The old tramp pulled up his chair and fell on the food, cramming it into his mouth and Rudd, withdrawing to the window, looked out across the yard to the rooftops and the back windows of the houses opposite. A solitary tree behind the brick wall fluttered a few rags of leaves. The high winds of the past few days had almost stripped it bare. Below, in the yard, where the police cars and vans were parked, came the sound of men's voices and an engine starting up.

A small cough behind him reminded him of the constable's presence. Rudd had forgotten to dismiss him. The Inspector turned and waved him away and the constable thankfully withdrew. Old Bill watched over the rim of his cup. The sandwiches had been eaten. All that remained on the plate were a few crusts chewed down to their very rind. The tramp replaced his cup and wiped a hand over his mouth but a few crumbs remained caught up in his beard.

Rudd sat down again at his desk.

"Now," he said briskly, determined to get down to business at last, "I believe that the other week you were over at Abbots Stacey?"

Old Bill looked at him guardedly.

" 'Appen I was," he said at last.

"And you were sleeping in the wood behind Stan Spurgeon's farm?"

"I might 'a done. There ain't no law."

"No, indeed there isn't," said Rudd. "What I want to know is this: when you lit your fire or when you were in the wood, did you——?"

"What fire?" Old Bill interrupted him.

Rudd sighed. He could see this part of the interview was

not going to be easy. The old man was clearly not going to answer any question straightforwardly and Rudd thought he caught a glimmer of amusement in the tramp's rheumy eyes, as if he was enjoying thwarting the Inspector's inquiries.

"I found the remains of a fire," Rudd explained patiently, "behind the hedge in the meadow next to the field where the mushrooms grow."

Old Bill considered this, gazing down at the floor, and then looked up into Rudd's face. Again there was that flicker of amusement.

"What meader?" he asked.

Rudd pushed back his chair and stood up. He had had enough.

"I'll show you which one," he said and, striding to the door, shouted for Boyce.

Boyce came in, took in the situation at a glance and grinned. The look on the Inspector's face was enough to tell him that the old tramp had got the better of him.

"Cussed old devil," Rudd muttered and then announced out loud that he and the Sergeant were going to take him over to Abbots Stacey and show him exactly which meadow was meant. Old Bill showed no hostility. He picked up his haversack and slung it over one shoulder and they escorted him down to the yard where the police driver, chatting with a colleague, saw them coming and, lifting up his eyes heavenwards in a long-suffering expression, hurried over to open the car door. Old Bill was packed into the back seat and Boyce went through a polite pantomime of holding the other rear door for the Inspector.

"No, in you get," Rudd said. It quite restored his good humour to see the expression on the Sergeant's face and, as he got into the front seat beside the driver, Rudd could not resist turning round and asking Boyce, "Comfortable?"

Boyce, huddled away in his corner as far as possible out of contact with his fellow passenger merely grunted in reply and Rudd turned back to say cheerfully to the driver, "Abbots Stacey, the Latching road. I'll tell you where to stop."

They drove with all the windows down, the draught whipping up Old Bill's beard and hair so that he looked like some wild Old Testament prophet. Presently he leaned forward and tapped the driver on the shoulder.

"Look, boy," he said, "put that winder up, will you? I'm perishin' with cold here in the back."

The driver gave Rudd a sideways look and, as he nodded assent, slid the window closed. Rudd heard the old man wheezing gently with laughter. He seemed perfectly well aware why the windows were open and he did not in the least mind.

The rest of the drive was completed in silence, except for Rudd giving instructions as they neared the village. The car turned left on to the Latching road and drew up in the gateway of Spurgeon's farm. Old Bill was helped out and stood, blinking and looking about him in the bright afternoon sunlight.

"You remember this place?" Rudd asked him.

" 'Course I do," he replied contemptuously.

Hearing the car, Spurgeon came out of the barn and stood watching them for a moment before strolling across the yard towards them. He had changed out of the dark blue suit he had worn at the inquest that morning and was dressed in his usual working clothes. As far as Rudd could see, the farmer did not seem at all put out by Old Bill's presence. He nodded to him in an offhand way before turning to speak to the Inspector.

"What do you want this time?" he asked. He was more subdued than usual, less jaunty and self-assured.

"I'd like to have another look at your field," Rudd told him.

"Help yourself," Spurgeon replied, shrugging.

"It shouldn't take long," Rudd said and then added casually, "I noticed you at the inquest this morning."

Spurgeon's eyes met his.

"Yes, I was there," was all he said in reply.

"The coroner wasn't expecting you to give evidence," Rudd said. It was phrased as a statement but the Inspector's voice had a questioning note in it. A small humorous quirk appeared at the corner of Spurgeon's mouth.

"No," he replied laconically.

It seemed to amuse him to fence with the Inspector in this way. But Rudd was too old a hand at dealing with people to be put off by this approach.

"Just curiosity, then?" he suggested.

It caught Spurgeon on the raw as he had intended it to. The blue eyes blazed.

"No, it bloody wasn't! I went because I wanted to know what they'd say."

"About you?"

Spurgeon backed down. This was too direct a line of questioning and it touched him too closely.

"I don't know," he mumbled. "I just wanted to hear what they said for myself."

"Of course," said Rudd mildly. "I can understand that."

He did, too. The man must have been desperately anxious to know how much would be made public of his own possible part in Mrs. King's death.

"It's still wide open," Rudd added. He said it as a kind of appeasement. "Anything may still turn up."

"Like him?" Spurgeon replied, pointing at Old Bill who was standing a little apart from them with Boyce, massive and disapproving, beside him.

"What have you brought him here for? Joined the police, has he?"

There was something of his old derisive, jeering manner in the question.

Rudd said, "He's helping us with our inquiries."

"And a fat lot of good he'll do you," commented Spurgeon. There was no malice in the remark and Rudd noticed Old Bill gave the farmer a shy, almost sheepish look. "You'll be lucky if he knows the time of day. You must be scraping the bottom of the barrel if you've got him in to help. Still, that's your business, not mine."

As he walked away, Old Bill said to Rudd, "He's a good lad, really."

There was no point in the remark except it was offered as an apology and explanation of what Spurgeon had said of him. His watery eyes blinked and then he added abruptly, " 'Ere, ain't you going to make a start? I ain't 'anging around 'ere all day. I've got things to do."

Rudd was wondering what possible things the tramp had in mind when, glancing round, he saw that old Mrs. Spurgeon had emereged from the house and was standing watching them from the back doorstep. The tramp's impatience seemed in some way to be connected with her presence.

Rudd could not resist saying, "There's Mrs. Spurgeon. You know her, I believe."

"I know 'er," replied Old Bill sullenly.

"Don't you want to go over and say hello to her?" asked Rudd.

"No. I don't," replied Old Bill. "And if you're going to 'ang around 'ere asking bloody fool questions, then I'm off."

"All right," said Rudd. "Come on. We'll take a look at where you had your fire."

They moved off towards the gate at the far end of the farmyard. But before they went through it into the field, Rudd looked back. Old Mrs. Spurgeon had followed them and was now standing, arms akimbo, watching them from the middle of the yard.

9

They moved slowly up the field, Rudd and Old Bill in front, Boyce a little way behind, dissociating himself from the others. The police driver, left behind in the farm gateway, had wound down all the car windows and stood leaning against the bonnet smoking a cigarette which he kept hidden, between puffs, in the palm of his hand in case Rudd should return unexpectedly.

Mrs. Spurgeon had gone back inside the house and Spurgeon was tinkering with the engine of the tractor.

Rudd and Old Bill came to the gate that led into the adjoining meadow and then walked back the little way on the far side of the hedge to the site of the camp fire.

The ash had been further scattered by the wind and what remained of it had solidified with the damp into a thick grey mass across which were printed the delicate footmarks of birds and small animals. The circle of half-burnt sticks, however, remained undisturbed.

The party halted.

"Now," said Rudd to Old Bill, "am I right in thinking that this was your fire?"

Old Bill studied it for a few moments and then said, " 'Appen it was."

"Come round to this side," Rudd went on and led the old man to the far side of the circle where he squatted down. Old Bill stood over him, his beard and hair blowing in the wind. He seemed amused at the sight of an Inspector of police sitting on his heels in a field. Boyce remained at a distance, keeping massively aloof from these proceedings.

Rudd patted the grass beside him invitingly and Old Bill lowered himself, with much puffing and grunting, into a squatting position beside the Inspector. The natural window in the hedge, with its view of the mushroom field and the

wood, was directly in line of vision of both men but Old
Bill did not glance at it. He picked up one of the charred
sticks and stirred the congealed ashes with the end of it.

"I reckon you sat just about here," said Rudd, "on the day
you lit this fire."

"Maybe," said the old man.

"There's no maybe about it," Rudd said sharply. "I
know."

The tramp gave him a quick, disbelieving look from under
his eyebrows and Rudd nearly laughed. He was thoroughly
enjoying the situation now, sitting under the hedgerow
with the old tramp, with Boyce looking on disapprovingly,
and perhaps Stan Spurgeon and his mother, concealed somewhere behind the farmbuildings, watching as well. Even the
white horse was there to complete the group and its long
mournful face was poking over the hedge looking down at
them. From time to time it blew whinnying breaths down
its nose.

Rudd felt like a conjuror about to produce a rabbit out of a
hat with a flourish and a roll of drums.

"Evidence," Rudd said. "That's what I base my knowledge
on. And the evidence tells me that you sat here. Right here,
I mean, on this very spot."

He cocked an eyebrow at Old Bill who said nothing, but
the faint grin had gone from his face and he looked
puzzled and a little uncomfortable. Rudd took his time,
drawing out the situation and making the most of it.

"See that bit of string?" he asked with an inconsequential
air, pointing to where he had tied it to the twig on the hedge
facing them as a marker on the day he found the camp.

Old Bill screwed up his eyes and followed the direction
of Rudd's pointing finger.

"Yes," he said.

"I found a bit of paper speared on that twig," Rudd
went on. "It was charred round the edges and, according
to my way of thinking, you'd used it to light this fire. I've
got it here, by the way," he added, getting out his wallet and,
opening it up with slow deliberation, he produced the scrap
of newspaper and unfolded it.

Old Bill watched him with an air of growing uneasiness.
His tongue flickered for a second across his lower lip.

"Evidence," said Rudd, putting the piece of paper and the
wallet carefully away again.

It was all a trick, a piece of psychological legerdemain which Rudd was performing deliberately. He wanted to get the old tramp into a state of such uncertainty that his derisive attitude would be broken down.

"Just a little bit of paper caught on a twig," Rudd went on, "but it tells me something important. It tells me which way the wind was blowing, for one thing; and as anyone sitting by this fire would want to sit with his back to the wind so as not to get smoke from the fire in his face, I reckon he'd be sitting right here, where we're sitting now."

Old Bill was watching the Inspector's face closely, taking in every word that he was saying and Rudd was pleased to see that even Boyce had lost his air of studied indifference and was listening, too, with every sign of absorbed attention.

Then the spell was broken. Old Bill laughed, showing his blackened stumps.

"Get away!" he said derisively. "That ain't much to go on!"

"Perhaps not," replied Rudd, "if it was all the evidence I had. But there's more. Take a look at the fire."

The old man stopped laughing, gave Rudd a hard stare and looked down suspiciously at the circle of charred sticks.

"Notice how the sticks are arranged," Rudd went on, with the tone of a lecturer expounding a scientific truth to a group of students. Boyce wandered nearer and stood at the far side of the circle, looking down too.

"On the far side of the fire, they're arranged singly. But," Rudd added on a rising note, "on this side, where we're sitting, they're grouped together; eight sticks, plus the one you picked up making nine, lying so close together that they're on top of each other in places; which also leads me to the conclusion that this is where you sat, feeding more sticks into the fire from this side."

Boyce looked at the Inspector and they exchanged a quick amused glance over the old man's head. They both knew that Rudd was making the best dramatic use of the situation.

Old Bill looked up at Rudd. The tramp was clearly uneasy again and baffled by the logic of the Inspector's argument. There seemed no way out of it.

"Well, maybe I did sit 'ere," he said unwillingly.

"There's no doubt about it," replied Rudd promptly, "and any court of law would accept the evidence as proof that you did."

Old Bill blinked his watery blue eyes.

"Who says anything about a court of law?" he asked with something of his old belligerency. But the spirit had gone out of him. He spoke with no real conviction and Rudd knew the first stage of the battle was over. Old Bill would come to heel from now on, like an obedient dog. But the Inspector did not want him so cowed that he would admit to anything. He needed a reliable and truthful witness.

"Let's hope it doesn't get as far as a court," Rudd said blandly. "And now that you've agreed you were sitting here, I want you to help me further by looking through that opening there in the hedge and telling me exactly what you saw when you were sitting here by the fire."

The old man glanced across at the opening as if it were a familiar movement. He was silent for so long that Rudd was prompted to speak.

"You saw someone?" he asked.

It was a shot in the dark and yet Rudd was convinced he had seen something. Otherwise everything, the field, themselves, even the horse, became meaningless.

"Where was this person?" Rudd asked. "In the field? In the wood?"

"On the edge of the wood," the old man replied, pointing a finger. "Just about there, by that oak tree."

Boyce's boots, on a level with Rudd's line of vision, moved excitedly and the Inspector looked up warningly. He tried to keep his own voice casual as he asked, "Who was it, a man or a woman?"

The old tramp turned troubled eyes in Rudd's direction.

"I dunno. I couldn't make them out proper. But whoever it was, they was just standing there, not doing nothing. Then they sort of waved and went back in the wood and I didn't see them no more."

"Waved?"

"Sort of," said Old Bill. "Sort of raised their arm."

"At you?" asked Rudd.

The tramp made a doubtful pout with his lips.

"Shouldn't think so. They couldn't see me, not where I was sat behind the 'edge, although they might 'a seen the smoke from me fire."

"Just a minute," said Rudd and, getting to his feet, he moved off a short distance with Boyce with whom he had whispered consultation. The old tramp watched them warily.

Boyce walked away at Rudd's instructions and Rudd returned to the fire.

"Tell me more about this person you saw," he said, rejoining the old man.

"Can't tell you much," Bill replied. "It was someone dressed in dark clothes and that's about all I can tell you."

"Did you get the impression it was a man or a woman?" Rudd persisted.

The old man sat deep in thought, his face puckered up with concentration. It was clear that he was doing his best to remember and Rudd waited patiently for him to speak.

"It could've been a man," he said finally. " 'E'ad a 'at on, a dark 'at, like a trilby."

Boyce had walked, as instructed, towards the wood and was now standing near the oak tree. Rudd directed the tramp's attention to him.

"Was the person, let's call him a man for the moment, standing where my Sergeant's standing now?" he asked.

Old Bill screwed up his eyes again and peered through the hedge opening.

"A bit more to this side," he said, raising his right arm.

Rudd stood up and, making a megaphone with his hands, bawled directions across the field to Boyce, who moved nearer to the tree.

"All right now?" he asked Old Bill, and the tramp nodded.

Rudd was amused to see that he was watching with intense concentration what was happening within the roughly circular hole in the twigs, like a child watching a television screen.

"Now," Rudd went on, "my Sergeant is going to make several movements with his arm. I want you to tell me when he makes a movement most like the one that person made. Do you understand?"

The old man had transferred his gaze from the hole to Rudd's face and was watching the Inspector's lips closely. As he seemed to follow the instructions, Rudd stood up and shouted to Boyce to begin. Then he squatted down again beside the tramp and the two of them watched the distant figure of Boyce standing under the tree and making painfully deliberate gestures with his arm like a man doing semaphore in slow motion.

"That's it! That's it!" Old Bill was saying excitedly.

Boyce was in the act of holding up his arm, bent at the

elbow and with the palm facing them, in the position of a policeman holding up the traffic.

Rudd jumped to his feet and signalled to Boyce to hold that position.

"Except the person I saw was moving 'is arm," said Old Bill, reaching up to grab at Rudd's jacket in his excitement.

Rudd cupped his hands again and shouted instructions at Boyce who, with an air of obedient passivity, jerked his arm about in puppet-like movements.

Old Bill watched him doubtfully.

"Well, it was summat like that," he said.

They had several more attempts but it was obvious that Boyce would never exactly repeat the spontaneous movement that Old Bill had witnessed.

It was pointless going on. In any case, the movement might mean nothing at all, although Rudd was convinced it had some significance. Someone had come to the edge of the wood, presumably through the wood itself, although this was not certain, and had stood near the tree and made a gesture with the arm not unlike a wave. Why? It was a question that intrigued Rudd.

The old tramp was out of sight behind the hedge. The person was not waving to him. To someone at the farm, then? To Stan Spurgeon or Mrs. Spurgeon? Unless, of course, the person at the edge of the wood had been one of them.

Rudd twitched his shoulders irritably and signalled to Boyce to come back. The Sergeant climbed awkwardly over the low tangle of bushes and brambles that skirted the wood and came towards them across the field registering, with every line of his body and every heavy deliberate step that he took, that he thought it was about time, too.

Rudd walked part of the way to meet him.

"Well?" asked Boyce sarcastically.

"A very creditable performance," Rudd replied. "I'm sure you could work it up into something really dramatic."

"Go on!" jeered Boyce. "If you ask me, this case has all the makings of a roaring farce. If it's not hunting for mushrooms or tramps stinking the place out, it's me standing up to my knees in nettles, waving my arms about. It only wants old Ma Spurgeon to lose her drawers and we'd have a West End hit on our hands."

Rudd laughed so much that Boyce forgot his ill-temper

and laughed too and the two men walked back companionably together.

Old Bill watched their approach uneasily.

"I don't know if I've been any 'elp," he began.

Rudd felt a twinge of pity for the tramp. The childlike absorption and excitement had gone. So, too, had the old derisive and disrespectful independence. He was reduced in stature to an old, broken-down man, nervous and unsure, asking in a quavering voice for their praise and approbation.

"You've been a great help," Rudd replied in a kindly voice.

"Can I go then?" Old Bill asked. "I'd like to be pushing off, if it's all the same to you."

"We won't keep you much longer," Rudd assured him. "But there's one or two details I must sort out first. Now, can you tell me which day it was you saw this person standing at the edge of the wood?"

Old Bill thought for a long moment and then shook his head.

"It was one day the week afore last," he said, "that's all I can tell you. I know that 'cos I moved on come the Sunday of last week."

"Do you know what day it is today?" Boyce asked.

"Tuesday?" the old man ventured. The Inspector and Sergeant exchanged glances. It was evidently going to be hopeless trying to establish a date for the incident.

"And what time during the day?" Rudd asked.

The tramp brightened.

"I can tell you that," he said. "It was the afternoon, round about four o'clock, or maybe a bit earlier. I'd had me bit of dinner and I lit the fire midway in the afternoon to brew up a cup of tea and finish off a mite of bread I had left over."

"That's fine," said Rudd encouragingly. "We'll take you back to headquarters and get you to sign a statement about what you saw."

"I can't read nor write," Old Bill said humbly.

"That won't matter," Rudd replied. "We'll write your statement out for you, read it over to you and if you agree with what's in it, you can sign with a cross if you like, provided it's witnessed. Then we'll treat you to high tea in the canteen. Will that suit you?"

Old Bill nodded and Rudd continued, "Right now, I want to have a word with Mrs. Spurgeon and her son. After that I'm going to take you into the village and buy you a new billy-can."

"Why?" asked Old Bill with a flash of his old spirit.

"Why not?" asked Rudd cheerfully and shepherded the old man back to the farm.

While Boyce waited at the car with Old Bill, Rudd briefly interviewed the Spurgeons. Neither of them had stood at the edge of the wood and waved or moved their arms about during the week in question and neither of them had seen anybody standing there, either.

Old Mrs. Spurgeon answered Rudd's questions abruptly. She was feeding the chickens when Rudd spoke to her, standing in the wired-in run, scattering grain in broad arcs while the hens scratched and pecked about her feet. Rudd, outside the run looking in, again got the impression of an almost archetypal figure despite her dirty macintosh and wellington boots.

Spurgeon answered the questions with the mock seriousness, keeping the Inspector waiting while he pretended to think deeply. Rudd had to keep his hands tightly clenched and rammed deep in his pockets to control his irritation. But, finally, the answer to both questions was "no."

Rudd also asked both of them if they belonged to the public library at Market Stratton and had borrowed a book from it recently.

"I don't get no time for books," old Mrs. Spurgeon replied emphatically and Spurgeon, after another pause for deep thought, said, "Is that the red-brick building in the High Street?"

"It is," Rudd replied impatiently.

"Then I ain't never been inside it," Spurgeon said with a slow grin.

Rudd turned and started to walk away when Spurgeon called after him.

"If that person comes back and waves again, Inspector, I'll get in touch with you straight off."

Rudd ignored him. Before he walked away, though, he had established one fact. At no point was the wood visible from the farmyard. In order to see it, one would have to walk beyond the buildings into the field.

Once more Old Bill was helped into the back of the car with Boyce, and Rudd got into the front seat beside the driver, giving him instructions to drive to the village.

The Inspector's decision to buy the tramp a new billy-can had a sound reason behind it. He ordered the driver to make for the Leacocks' hardware store. He wanted the Leacocks, as well as the Spurgeons, to be aware that he had contacted the tramp.

Gilbert Leacock was standing behind the counter in the same waiting attitude when Rudd ushered in Old Bill. Rudd watched his face closely but could see no expression on it other than distaste at the sight of the old tramp.

Rudd said, "We'd like to look at some billy-cans, if we may."

"I don't stock billy-cans," Leacock replied. He seemed torn between the desire to be polite to Rudd, to make a sale and to be rid of the pair of them before another cutomer came into the shop.

"Then a saucepan will do," Rudd replied cheerfully.

Gilbert Leacock emerged reluctantly from behind the counter and, giving Old Bill a wide berth, fetched a stack of saucepans from one of the shelves.

"There you are." Rudd said to the old man. "Choose yourself one."

Old Bill darted a glance at him full of quick apprehension but Rudd gave him a reassuring nod and the tramp turned to eagerly examining the pans, even testing the thickness of their bottoms by rapping on them with his knuckle, like any careful housewife.

While he was busy, Rudd drew Leacock to one side.

"I'd like a word with you and your sister," he said.

Gilbert Leacock looked at the door leading into the back room and then at Old Bill. He was clearly reluctant to leave the tramp alone in the shop.

"We can talk in here," Rudd said. "It's nothing secret."

Leacock went off to fetch his sister. Rudd could hear him talking to her and then her voice asking sharply, "What does he want now?"

When she came into the shop from the back room her little fat face was creased up with displeasure, which deepened when she saw Old Bill. She seemed about to say something when her brother nudged her warningly and she closed her mouth up tight.

"I shan't keep you long," Rudd said. "There's one or two questions I want to ask both of you. Firstly, do either of you belong to the public library at Market Stratton?"

He had produced a notebook deliberately in order to make the questions seem more important and official. Both the Leacocks said "No," and Rudd solemnly wrote it down.

"And did either of you borrow a book recently from the library?"

Amy Leacock shook her head and her brother said with a slightly superior smile, "That's hardly likely, Inspector, considering that we're not members."

Rudd ignored this and went on to the next question.

"Lastly, did either of you walk to the edge of the wood at the back of Spurgeon's farm any day of the week before last?"

Gilbert Leacock answered first.

"I certainly didn't. I've got the shop to run."

"But you do have a halfday on Wednesday?" Rudd pointed out.

Amy Leacock spoke up.

"We went to Market Stratton on the bus," she said, "the same as we do every halfday. We caught the 1:45 from the bus stop across the road, went to the pictures and had tea afterwards in the Blue Boy café. You can ask anyone. Our Wednesday afternoon outings are the one little bit of pleasure we get."

From the vehemence in her voice, Rudd guessed this was an old quarrel between them and that Gilbert Leacock only reluctantly escorted his sister on these outings.

"And were you at the wood any day during the week before last?" Rudd persisted, realising she had not answered his question.

"I've got better things to do," she snapped.

Rudd made another note and returned the book to his pocket. He noticed the Leacocks followed every movement.

"Is that all?" Amy Leacock asked. "Because if it is, I'll get back to my work."

As she turned away, she gave a quick, almost furtive glance at her wristwatch. It might have passed unnoticed, or as a gesture of little significance, except that Rudd remembered that when her brother had called her into the shop, she had again glanced at the time and on several occasions during the interview, she had turned her head in the direction of the shop door as if watching for something.

Old Bill had chosen a saucepan, a splendid white enamel one with a blue handle and a blue rim. He was clearly delighted with it but would commit himself to no more than a gruff "This'll do me, I reckon."

All the same, he watched closely as Gilbert Leacock warpped it up in brown paper and as soon as it was handed to him he stowed it away eagerly in his haversack.

Rudd wondered how long it would keep its pristine blue and white newness over a wood fire.

Outside the shop, Rudd consulted briefly with Boyce and stood on the pavement watching as the car drove away, with Old Bill installed in the back seat and the Sergeant, with obvious relief, seated this time next to the driver. It turned left, as Rudd had instructed, out of sight into Rectory Close.

There was a bus stop on the other side of the road, opposite Rene King's shop. Rudd bought himself a paper at the news-agent's and established himself at the bus stop, his back to the Leacocks' premises.

He did not have long to wait. The mystery of Amy Leacock's interest in the time was soon solved. About ten minutes later, a removal van turned the corner and pulled up outside the Bandbox. It was accompanied by a light blue Cortina with Roland King at the wheel. King got out of the car, unlocked the shop door and was followed inside by the men who had come with the van.

It had not taken the nephew long, Rudd reflected to arrange the disposal of his aunt's home. Nor did it take long for a small crowd to collect. Women with prams, women singly and in pairs, a few children and the old men, gathered on the pavement. People from the row of cottages opposite and the other shopkeepers came to their doors. Rudd tucked the newspaper under his arm and watched too. Almost at once, Amy Leacock's face appeared at the glass panel in the door of the hardware shop. A moment afterwards she emerged. She did not notice Rudd standing anonymously at the bus stop. Her interest was centered elsewhere and she joined the group of people clustered round the door of the Bandbox.

The men had already begun to carry out the furniture from the upstairs rooms. Rudd watched as the quilted bedhead was brought out; then the green velvet chairs and sofa; the pink-shaded lamps; the pretty gilt-framed mirror that had hung over the sitting-room fireplace; rolled-up carpets and crates of books and china.

The women jostled to look. Amy Leacock had somehow managed to work herself to the front of the crowd. Rudd could just see the top of her black felt hat.

Meanwhile Roland King was carrying out boxes of stock from the shop which he stowed in the boot of the car and on the back seat.

It was soon finished. The van left. The nephew locked up the shop and drove away. The small crowd began to disperse. Amy Leacock walked back to the hardware shop. At that distance, and with the brim of her hat shading her face, it was impossible to see her expression but there was an air of satisfaction in the way she walked. It was probably no more than curiosity that had drawn her to witness the removal; for King, it was a matter simply of business expediency.

Rudd folded up the newspaper and placed it in the refuse bin that was fixed to the bus stop. As he did so, he glanced at his watch. It had taken exactly thirty-five minutes to dispose of Rene King's home.

Thoughtfully, Rudd walked back to Rectory Close where the police car was parked, waiting for him. Boyce raised his eyebrows interrogatively but Rudd shook his head and remained silent on the drive back to headquarters.

There, Boyce was sent off to accompany Old Bill to the canteen for a meal. Alone in the office, Rudd pondered on the problem of how to keep in touch with the tramp. He hesitated to ask him to call in at police-stations to report his whereabouts. It would undermine his independence and Rudd already felt slightly guilty over the way he had dealt with him that afternoon. Old Bill had been humbled and Rudd disliked being the cause of any man's humility.

On the other hand, he would have to keep in contact with him somehow. If murder were ever to be proved and a case brought to court, the tramp's evidence might be vital.

In the end Rudd sent out for a dozen postcards which he stamped and addressed to himself at headquarters and when Old Bill was brought back to the office, Rudd explained that he wanted him to post one of the cards every week.

"You see," he said, "I may need to get in touch with you again and the postmarks on the cards will give me a rough idea where you're to be found. Otherwise," he added, as Old Bill was eyeing the pile of cards suspiciously, "you'll have to report in at the police-stations."

"What day d'you want them posted?" Old Bill asked. "I'll tell you, when I'm on the road I don't always know what day of the week it is."

"Sunday?" suggested Rudd. "You'll know it's Sunday because the shops will be closed and you'll hear the church bells."

"All right," said the tramp reluctantly and stowed the cards away in some inner recess among his layers of clothing.

"And if you don't post them," warned Rudd, "I'll have every copper in the county out looking for you."

The warning was meant to be taken seriously but Rudd softened it with a grin. The old tramp's reply was of so lewd a nature that even Boyce looked shocked and Rudd felt forced to say, "Now, now! Watch it."

A statement was drawn up, read over to Old Bill, typed out and then he made his mark at the bottom of each page, which was witnessed by two policemen. Rudd then asked him formally if he had recognised the person but Old Bill shook his head. It was as Rudd had suspected for he had seen no sign of recognition on Old Bill's part when he had been brought face to face with the Leacocks whom he had not previously known. As for the Spurgeons, whom he knew well, he would have mentioned it quite naturally. There would be nothing suspicious about seeing either of them at the edge of the wood so near to their own farm.

Rudd had arranged for a police car to take the tramp back to Stavely where he had been picked up, but he refused the offer.

"I'll get where I want to on my own feet," he said proudly. "I don't want no bloody police taxiing me around."

He left and Rudd immediately walked across the office and threw open the window.

"Do you know who he reminds me of?" Boyce asked.

"No. Who?" asked Rudd.

"Stan Spurgeon," replied Boyce.

"My God!" said Rudd. He could think of nothing else to say at the thought of that unholy alliance. But he could see the likeness now that Boyce had pointed it out to him. They had the same blue eyes, the same independent spirit and ironic humour.

"Makes you think, doesn't it?" said Boyce. "Imagine, him and her!"

"My God," said Rudd again.

But once more he felt that sense of the past come over him; of old loves and old alliances and possibly of old hates. And he made a mental note to talk to Holbrook about it the next day.

10

Rudd saw Holbrook the next day but the Sergeant was not any great help.

"Something that might have happened in the past?" he said when Rudd had explained what he wanted. "Well, that's a bit of a tall order. Like I said, I've only been here myself for five years. How far back in the past were you thinking of?"

"I don't know," Rudd said. "What about when Stan Spurgeon was young?"

Holbrook looked doubtful.

"I don't know much about events as old as that," he said. "Gossip dies down, given time, and certainly I've heard nothing. Leastways, I've told you all I do know."

"What about your wife?" Rudd asked, feeling slightly irritated by the Sergeant's impassivity.

"Betty? She's not one for gossiping usually. Keeps herself to herself, I'm glad to say. I don't like a long-tongued woman myself. But I'll call her though and ask her if you like."

Mrs. Holbrook was doing some washing and she came reluctantly into the little office, bringing with her the smell of soap and an air of domestic preoccupation.

"Detective Inspector Rudd wants to know if you'd heard anything in the village," Holbrook explained to her, "about the Leacocks or Stan Spurgeon; anything to do with their pasts."

She gave her husband an anxious look and he nodded at her reassuringly.

"What exactly do you want to know?" she asked.

Rudd shrugged his shoulders in a helpless and resigned gesture. The interview was doomed from the start. Instead of the three of them settling down to a comfortable, gossipy chat, Holbrook, with his heavyhanded approach, had made his wife thoroughly uneasy. There was an atmosphere of official procedure about it now and Mrs. Holbrook had been given the impression that she was on the mat in front of her husband's superior officer.

"Oh, anything," Rudd said casually, hoping to retrieve the situation. "Just any scraps of information you might have picked up. About Stan Spurgeon, for instance."

"I've seen him," she replied, "but not to speak to."

"A bit of a rogue, isn't he?" Rudd asked with a deliberate twinkle. But she did not respond.

"Not that I've heard," she replied and gave that anxious, sideways look at her husband.

"What about old Mrs. Spurgeon?" Rudd asked.

"What did you want to know about her?"

Rudd almost sighed out loud.

"Anything you might have heard. How does she get on with young Kenny, for instance?" Rudd suggested, thinking that the introduction of Spurgeon's son into the conversation might produce more positive results.

"I think they get on all right," she said, with a little more interest in her voice. "She doesn't keep him very clean, mind you, and I think he gets a walloping off her sometimes, but then it can't be easy bringing up a child that's not all there mentally."

"Oh, I agree," said Rudd warmly, glad to have got her started. "After all, she's not a young woman and it must be hard bringing up a grandchild without its mother."

"I can't think how she brought herself to leave him!" Mrs. Holbrook cried. "He couldn't have been more than two when she left. Fancy running off and leaving a poor little mite like that."

"Who did she run off with?" asked Rudd, not that the information was important to the case but now that she was speaking freely he was anxious to keep the conversation going.

"I don't know personally, it was years before we came here, but I've heard it was one of the men that was working on the school buildings. They were laying new drains and resurfacing the playground. An Irishman he was; he drove one of the dumper trucks."

"So Stan Spurgeon's mother had to look after the child after she'd gone?" said Rudd.

"Yes, and plenty she had to say about it too, by all

accounts. She'd been turned out of the farmhouse when Stan
married. His wife and mother never did get on and evidently
the wife said she wouldn't have the old lady living with them
any longer. Anyway, she left and went to live in a caravan
down in Nott's field. But he was glad enough to have her
back after his wife left him."

"Go on," said Rudd. This was an interesting piece of
information. If old Mrs. Spurgeon had been turned out of
the house by one wife, might she not dread the possibility
of it happening again if Spurgeon remarried?

"Has anything been said about Stan Spurgeon marrying
again at any time?" he asked, sounding as offhand as he
could.

"He's not divorced from his first wife, as I understand
it," Mrs. Holbrook replied.

"But suppose he was?" Rudd persisted. "What about Mrs.
King? Mighn't he have thought of marrying her?"

But Mrs. Holbrook looked doubtful.

"I shouldn't think so," she said. "After all, she was well
off enough as she was."

It was the same point of view that Mrs. Youngman had
put forward. Evidently the consensus of opinion in the
village was that Mrs. King would be foolish to marry Stan
Spurgeon even if he were divorced. Rudd wondered, all the
same, if old Mrs. Spurgeon had seen the relationship in
the same light. She might have considered Mrs. King as a
serious rival. It could certainly be a motive for murder.

He went on to ask Mrs. Holbrook about the Leacocks
but he could get nothing much from her except they were
quiet, respectable people. She seemed slightly in awe of the
fact that they were an old, established family, owned a
business and were older than she was, anyway, and she did
not seem prepared to talk about them as freely as she had
the more disreputable Mrs. Spurgeon whose good name in
the village did not stand so high.

After asking several questions which only elicited cautious
replies, Rudd gave up, thanked her for being so patient and
sparing the time and she returned, with obvious relief, to her
household chores.

Holbrook was looking a little worried. He knew the
Inspector was disappointed over the interview and he felt
his wife, and he himself too in some obscure way, had let
Rudd down.

"I'm afraid you didn't find out much," he admitted with

such a disarming air that Rudd could no longer feel annoyed with him.

"It couldn't be helped," said Rudd. "Obviously your wife doesn't know the kind of information I'm looking for. Look here, Holbrook, surely there must be someone in the village I can talk to; someone who knew Stan Spurgeon and the Leacocks when they were young; someone of old Mrs. Spurgeon's generation who wouldn't mind talking freely?"

Holbrook pulled thoughtfully at his lower lip. He was on his mettle, keen to re-establish himself in the Inspector's good books.

"There is one old lady," he said. "She's well over eighty and bedridden, but she's still lively enough. I drop in to see her from time to time for a chat."

"Bedridden?" said Rudd suspiciously.

"Only for the last few years," Holbrook hastened to explain. "She was up and about until her early eighties and, like I said, there's plenty of life in the old girl. She knows everybody in the village and she still takes a keen interest in everything that's going on."

"All right," said Rudd, "if you think she's the right person for me to talk to. I'd like to have a chat with her as soon as possible. Do you think you could fix it up for me to see her the day after tomorrow?"

"I'll certainly try," Holbrook replied.

"And look here," Rudd added, choosing his words carefully, "don't put her off by making it sound an official interview. I want a chat with her, not a question and answer session. But I'm sure I can rely on you not to put your foot in it."

The Sergeant's face coloured up. He was sensitive enough to perceive the point behind the remark.

"I'll be more careful about it next time," he said acknowledging his blunder and Rudd smiled, partly in recognition of the acknowledgement, partly to show the Sergeant he bore him no illfeeling.

"Then I'll look forward to seeing her the day after tomorrow," Rudd said. "Ring me at the office just to confirm it, will you?"

He rose to go and Holbrook accompanied him to the back door.

"The old lady'll enjoy it too," he assured the Inspector. "She likes a chat, does old Mrs. Turnbull."

"Turnbull?" asked Rudd.

He remembered seeing the name on several gravestones in the churchyard and he thought this augured well for the meeting.

Holbrook voiced his unspoken thought.

"There's been Turnbulls living in the village for generations, so I've been told," he said.

"Good," replied Rudd. "That's exactly the sort of person I'm looking for."

"By the way," Holbrook said inconsequentially, "did you know the auction's on today?"

"What auction?" asked Rudd.

"Of Mrs. King's furniture. It seems the nephew wants to get the stuff sold up and the shop put up for sale as soon as he can."

"He didn't waste much time," commented Rudd.

"Well, that's Londoners for you." Holbrook said with a countryman's contempt. "All bustle and drive and wanting to get things done. There's several people from the village gone; to the auction, I mean. I saw them waiting for the ten-past-nine bus this morning."

"Oh?" said Rudd, showing interest. "Who for instance?"

"Mrs. Youngman, for one. I think she wanted to buy something small to remind her of Mrs. King, sort of memento, like. I saw her at the bus stop. Then there was Mrs. Abstey and Mrs. Blaine; she'd not miss the chance of a bargain. Miss Leacock was there, too, surprisingly enough."

"Why surprising?" asked Rudd.

Holbrook laughed.

"Because she runs that house like clockwork. It's one morning for the washing, one morning for ironing, one morning for doing out the bedrooms. You don't usually find her out-of-doors before midday. 'If you only knew the amount of work there is in a place like mine!'" Holbrook added, giving a fair imitation of Miss Leacock's snappy voice. "'No modern conveniences, and the dust!'"

"Her brother must be thankful to see the back of her sometimes," Rudd remarked.

"He must that. Not that anyone's likely to marry her and take her off his hands, poor devil. Still, it can't be an easy life for her either."

"I might call in at the auction," Rudd said thoughtfully. "Any idea of the time and place?"

"It's being held in the Assembly Rooms in Market

Stratton, that's the white building just down the road from
the bus station, and I think it started at ten. I should imagine
it'll go on until all the stuff's cleared. It's not just Mrs. King's
bits and pieces. The auctioneers wait until there's a good
amount of stuff, so it'll take several hours."

Rudd glanced at his watch. It was just after ten-thirty and
he said good-bye to Holbrook and hurried to his car.

The auction had already begun when Rudd arrived and
the hall was so packed with people that he had difficulty in
squeezing himself in at the back of the crowd. The auctioneer,
a large, florid man in tweeds and a check waistcoat, a
carnation in his buttonhole, was seated at a small table
placed on top of a larger table, from which elevated position
he had a good view of the crowd and the crowd had a good
view of his handlebar moustache and huge thighs which
bulged over the sides of the rather small chair on which he
was sitting. Rudd suspected that the moustache, carnation
and bright waistcoat were all part of the act, for the
auction was being conducted in a rumbustious and highly
theatrical manner.

Rudd listened and looked about him, craning his neck. It
was almost impossible to distinguish any individual among
the crowd of people, most of whom had their backs to
him and were sitting, crushed together, on a motley col-
lection of chairs, sofas and settees that filled the main body
of the hall and that were, from the numbered stickers on
their backs, due to be put up for sale. More people leaned or
perched against bookcases, chests-of-drawers and sideboards
that lined the walls. He thought he caught a glimpse of Miss
Leacock's black hat over the back of a sofa towards the
front of the hall.

As for Mrs. King's possessions they were as impossible
to distinguish as the people. A pink-shaded lamp on top of a
sideboard might have been hers and Rudd was sure he
recognised the gilt-framed mirror that was propped up against
the auctioneer's table, where the more fragile and valuable
articles were placed.

Rudd stayed for two hours and then his conscience began
to trouble him. After all, fascinating as the auction was, it
was hardly relevant to the investigation and at a quarter-to-
one, he edged his way out of the door. Other people were
also leaving. It was lunchtime and Rudd made his way across
the road to a restaurant opposite where he got a table in
the window.

He was starting his pudding and was glancing in a casual way out of the window, when he saw Miss Leacock and another woman emerge from the door of the Assembly Rooms opposite. They hesitated on the steps, glanced across at the restaurant and then had a hasty consultation with each other. Miss Leacock indicated, with a gesture of her head, the bulky articles she was carrying: a rose-coloured eiderdown, inadequately wrapped up in brown paper, and a bed-side lamp, the one that Rudd had seen standing on the side-board at the auction and which he thought had belonged to Mrs. King. She seemed to be telling the other woman, who was less encumbered by parcels, that it would be inconvenient for her to have lunch in the restaurant. The other woman nodded her head in agreement and they walked up the road towards the bus station.

Rudd chewed and watched them go. He had recognised the lamp but he still could not place the eiderdown, although it seemed familiar.

As he was paying the bill, he suddenly remembered where he had seen it. It had been on the chair in Mrs. King's bed-room. It was a small point and yet it made him thoughtful. Miss Leacock, who normally did not leave the house in the mornings, had made a special trip into Market Stratton to the auction and had moreover bought two of Mrs. King's possessions, her lamp and her eiderdown. He doubted whether, like Mrs. Youngman, she had bought them as a memento of her friend. Perhaps it was nothing more than a desire for a bargain. He shrugged and left the restaurant.

At the office he found a list had been forwarded from the library of all the members with Abbots Stacey addresses. There were about fifteen people on the list but the names did not include the Leacocks, the Spurgeons or Mrs. Young-man. It merely confirmed what he already knew, but he filed the report away. The information might be useful should the circle of suspects widen to include others in the village even though, at the moment, there was no scrap of evidence to connect anybody else with the case.

His mail also included a report from the mycologist, Professor Harvey, in London on the specimens found in Spurgeon's field and the wood, which stated what Rudd had already suspected: the specimen from the field was an edible mushroom; those from the little glade in the wood were the fungus Amanita Phalloides.

Rudd was sitting looking thoughtfully at the report when Boyce entered.

"Penny for them?" suggested the Sergeant.

Rudd looked up.

"Tuppence, at least," he replied. "They're pretty dark."

He handed the report over to Boyce who read it through.

"Well," he remarked, handing it back, "it's what you expected, isn't it?"

"Except now it's in black and white," said Rudd, "and not merely a suspicion. You realise what this means, don't you, Tom? That fungus wasn't picked accidentally. Somebody went into that wood and looked for it."

"A kid could have done it, not knowing any better," said Boyce.

"Kenny Spurgeon, you mean?" said Rudd. "Yes, I suppose he could, although backward as he is, I still think he knows enough about country ways to know mushrooms don't grow in woods. Look, Tom, let's run over this together. It'll help to clear my mind. If Mrs. King was murdered, who could have done it? Means, first. Almost anybody from the village had access to the fungus growing in the wild. There's a footpath from the village that skirts the wood on the far side. Secondly, opportunity. Any of the Spurgeon family or the Leacocks could have put the fungus into the basket of mushrooms that Stan took to Mrs. King, either at the farm or later at her flat."

"So could Mrs. Youngman," Boyce pointed out.

"Yes, all right," Rudd agreed. "Personally, I can't see her a killer but we'll include her. Now, motive. And as far as I can see, there's not a damned motive among them, except for old Mrs. Spurgeon who may have thought her son might marry Mrs. King and she'd get chucked out of the house. Kenny may have feared having a step-mother but that seems a flimsy reason. None of the others seem to have any cause to wish her dead. Now, what have we got that's anything like evidence? An anonymous letter, the library book on fungus that someone borrowed shortly before Mrs. King's death and Old Bill's statement about seeing someone standing on the edge of the wood; all of which is inconclusive and as far as real evidence goes, doesn't add up to a row of beans."

Boyce scratched his head.

"There isn't much to go on," he admitted.

"There's damned all to go on," Rudd replied.

"Something'll turn up," Boyce assured him cheerfully. After all, he wasn't in charge of the investigation. It wasn't his responsibility.

"I hate a case that's not concluded properly." Rudd said. "I like all the ends tied off and *Finis* written on the file."

"You want a victim," Boyce replied.

"I've already got a victim." Rudd snapped back. "Mrs. King who died in her own vomit. I want to nail the person who caused her death."

"You're sure it was murder, then?" Boyce asked. "I know it looks like it but can we be one hundred per cent certain?"

"I'm ninety-nine per cent certain," Rudd replied, "and that's good enough for me."

"Come on," urged Boyce. "Cheer up. It's not the end of the world."

But Rudd refused to be comforted and sat scowling down at the mycologist's report on his desk.

"A cup of tea?" suggested Boyce. "Would you like me to nip down to the canteen for one?"

"In a minute," replied Rudd. An idea was beginning to form. The mention of the tramp had reminded him of the arm movement the old man had seen the unknown person making and Rudd remembered it had not yet been satisfactorily cleared up.

"Would you mind making that waving movement again, the one the old tramp told us about?" he asked Boyce.

"Oh, God, not again," Boyce groaned.

"All right. I'll do it." said Rudd, getting up and walking to the far end of the office. "Now, it was a bit like this, wasn't it?"

He tried repeating the gesture that Boyce had made and the tramp had said was most like the original.

Boyce frowned.

"It doesn't look much like anything," he said critically.

"What about this?" Rudd suggested, improvising on the movement.

"Like a kid doing underarm bowling?" suggested Boyce.

"Bowling?" said Rudd. "Throwing a ball awkwardly? Throwing something?"

Boyce caught his excitement.

"Yes, it could be!" he cried. "Do it again!"

Rudd repeated the gesture.

"Yes, definitely throwing," Boyce said. "But what?"

"Fungus?" suggested Rudd and was prevented from en-larging on this by the ringing of the telephone.

It was the desk sergeant who said that a Mr. Roland King would like to see the Inspector on official business.

"Send him up," said Rudd and rang off.

"Throwing fungus?" Boyce asked. He had followed the Inspector over to the desk in his anxiety to get the point cleared up.

"Or perhaps throwing away fungus," Rudd explained.

But Boyce remained baffled.

"I don't get it," he admitted. "We're looking for someone who picked fungus, not someone who threw it away."

"Perhaps the person was one and the same," Rudd replied enigmatically and could not explain any further as there was a knock on the door and Roland King was shown into the office.

"I won't waste words, Inspector," he said after he had sat down. "My late aunt's affairs have taken up a great deal of time, so I'll come straight to the point. I've brought the books, as you requested. You'll find them all in order. My accountant has gone over them very carefully and so have I. I don't understand why you need to inspect them but I suppose that's your business."

He gave Rudd a hard, questioning look but the Inspector merely replied, "Just a matter of routine, Mr. King."

There was an air of veiled hostility about the man and Boyce, sensing it, had gone to sit quietly at the far side of the office, keeping out of the way.

"The books are here," King went on and, opening his expensive leather brief-case, produced a small pile of account books, tied together with tape, which he placed on the desk. One small black-bound ledger remained loose on the top and King kept his hand on it as if to signify its importance. Rudd noticed this and waited.

"Yesterday I was making a final check on my aunt's personal expenses," King continued, "and I happened to flick over the pages of her household ledger. It was then I noticed the last two pages were written on. I might add that they had escaped my accountant's notice."

The last remark was said with a certain smugness and self-satisfaction. Rudd shifted in his chair but still said nothing.

"It appears," King said and one well-manicured fingernail

tapped on the small black book, "that my aunt had been lending sums of money to a certain Mr. Spurgeon; quite large sums in fact, amounting to £250, of which only twenty pounds has been repaid."

Rudd sat silent for a moment.

"Mr. Stan Spurgeon?'" he asked at last.

"That's right," King replied. There was an odd smile on his face, as if in some subtle way he had got the better of the Inspector.

"May I see the account?" Rudd asked.

King picked up the book and, turning to the last two pages, handed it open to Rudd.

"My aunt was a careful bookkeeper. I'm sure you'll find the figures are correct," King was saying with deliberate politeness.

"I've no doubt," Rudd murmured, his attention on the book. Boyce, aware of an implied sarcasm in King's voice, cleared his throat in an embarrassed way.

Rudd ran his eye quickly over the account. It was clearly headed "Personal Loans to Stan Spurgeon," and the figures showed that the farmer had been borrowing money from Mrs. King over a period of sixteen months, usually in amounts of ten or twelve pounds. The largest loan was of twenty-five pounds. He had repaid, as Roland King had said, a total of twenty pounds in small sums of not more than two or three pounds at a time.

The accounts were written in a firm, clear handwriting. No interest appeared to have been charged on the money. Mrs. King had lent it freely but, good business woman as she was, she had kept a detailed record of each transaction.

"I assume you'll want to keep the books for the time being?" King was saying. He seemed put out by Rudd's silence and the Inspector roused himself to reply.

"I'll see they're returned to you as soon as possible," he said. "You'll receive an official receipt for them, of course."

"I'd be grateful if you didn't keep them too long," King said stiffly. "I haven't yet wound up my aunt's affairs. I still have the income tax people to see and they'll no doubt want to go over the figures for themselves." He hesitated and then added, "This Mr. Spurgeon . . .?"

"A local farmer," Rudd explained. "I'd rather you didn't approach him about the debt until I've had a chance to speak to him first."

"All right," King replied. "I'll leave it for a few days, but this money will have to be returned and I can't hang about indefinitely. I want my aunt's estate settled up as soon as possible."

He snapped shut his brief-case and pulled on a pair of pigskin driving-gloves, revealing as he did so initialled gold cuff-links. All the man's possessions, his fashionable suit and shirt, his watch with its heavy gold bracelet, his hand-made shoes, spoke of material success and yet Rudd did not envy him for it. Although still young, there was already a grey and careworn air about King, a used-up quality.

"About my aunt's death," he began. But Rudd was not going to be drawn.

"Certain lines of inquiry are being investigated," he said, assuming his official and non-committal voice. "You'll be informed of any important developments."

For a moment King looked as if he might argue the point, then he picked up his brief-case and stood up. But he was not prepared to leave without a parting shot. At the door he turned.

"I understand from my wife that a police sergeant called at my flat, making inquiries about a street accident."

"Really?" murmured Rudd. "When was that?"

"A few days ago," King replied. His eyes flickered across to Boyce who had got to his feet for King's departure. "A big, broad-shouldered man, my wife said. He seemed interested in the whereabouts of my car on a certain evening."

Rudd raised his eyebrows in polite inquiry.

"It crossed my mind," King went on, in a louder voice, tightening his grip on the handle of his brief-case, "that you might have been checking up on my movements."

Rudd's expression remained bland.

"A local accident was it, Mr. King? Something that happened in this district?"

"No, it wasn't," King replied impatiently. "My wife couldn't remember the details, but the man mentioned the Tottenham Court Road."

"Oh, I see," said Rudd, smiling and lying cheerfully. "Then it wouldn't be one of our men. It'd be outside our area. You'd best get in touch with the Metropolitan police."

"I may do that," King replied, turning away. Behind his back, Rudd dropped an eyelid at Boyce, half-humorous, half-serious.

"My Sergeant'll accompany you downstairs," Rudd continued. To Boyce he added, "See that Mr. King gets a receipt for the account books."

Boyce, stiff-faced, walked heavily forward.

"I'll see they're returned to you as soon as possible," Rudd said to King. He held out his hand. "Thank you for your co-operation."

Baffled, King offered a reluctant gloved hand for the Inspector to shake. "If you need to get in touch with me over the next couple of days, I'm staying at the George in Market Stratton," he said. "My aunt's funeral is tomorrow and I have several other matters of business to see to as well."

He left, accompanied by Boyce, and Rudd returned to his desk, thinking that it was a strange mind that could consider a funeral as a "matter of business."

He was re-examining the accounts in the small ledger when Boyce returned.

"Do you think he suspected something?" the Sergeant asked.

"Who?" asked Rudd, his mind on the figures.

"King. About me checking up on his movements."

"Oh, that," said Rudd. He had dismissed it from his mind. "He may do but I doubt if he'll do anything about it. I'm more interested in this."

He tapped his finger on the ledger.

"It's certainly a turn up," Boyce commented. "Two hundred and fifty quid's a lot of money."

"Enough to give Spurgeon a motive for murder," Rudd replied. He remembered the final demand bills tucked in behind the clock in Spurgeon's living-room and the other indications about the house and the farm of a hand-to-mouth existence.

"Where does the other person fit in, then?" asked Boyce. "The one who was supposed to be chucking fungus about?"

"I don't know," said Rudd. A feeling of weariness came over him. "Perhaps nowhere. It may mean nothing at all. All I can go on is the facts, and the facts are that Spurgeon owed Mrs. King over £200, which he's never uttered a word about and which, if I've read the signs right, he'd've been hard put to it to repay. I shall have to go and see him."

He glanced at his watch. It was still quite early, only a little past three o'clock. He could easily drive to Abbots Stacey there and then and interview Spurgeon.

Rudd began to heave himself out of his chair. He was reluctant to go. He rationalised his indecision by telling himself it would be better to postpone the interview until the morning, when Kenny would be at school and Mrs. Spurgeon busy in the house. But he realised there was another motive that he was only half-aware of himself and which he did not care to examine too closely; and that was a wish to give Spurgeon a few more hours of grace before he confronted him with the truth.

"Are you going to see Spurgeon now?" Boyce was asking.

"Yes," said Rudd, making up his mind. There was, after all, no room for sentiment. "Get the pages in that ledger photocopied, will you, Tom? I'll have the other accounts looked over tomorrow but with King out of the case, I don't think they're going to be relevant. It's Spurgeon that interests me now."

There was no sign of Spurgeon's battered van as Rudd drove into the farmyard. But old Mrs. Spurgeon was there, splitting logs into kindling sticks on a chopping-block outside the barn. She stopped briefly in her work as the car drew up and then, as Rudd got out and walked towards her, she began again as if the Inspector's presence was of no consequence to her at all.

Rudd strolled over and stood watching. Her gnarled and very dirty hands were surprisingly deft in their movements. The chopper blade bit neatly into the log, splitting it down the middle, and then each half log was split and split again and the sticks were swept off the block with a sideways swipe of the blade to fall into the apple box that stood ready at the side to receive them.

"Stan's out," she said after a long silence.

"Never mind," Rudd replied equably, showing no reaction. "I'll wait if it's all the same to you."

She gave him a look and then returned to her task.

"Please yourself," she replied ungraciously. "He'll be gone some time, though."

Rudd, not at all put out by her unwelcoming attitude, looked about for somewhere to sit down. There was a sawing horse a little distance away, against the barn wall and he perched himself on it and, leaning back against the warm brick, half-closed his eyes.

The farm cat walked round the corner of the barn and came up to Rudd, rubbing its body inquisitively against

his trouser legs. He put a hand down to stroke it and felt
it arch its back to press into the palm of his hand, the
spine hard and flexed under the soft covering of sun-
warmed fur. Its tail lifted and quivered with pleasure at the
contact.

"Did you know Mrs. King?" Rudd asked casually, still
stroking the cat's back.

Old Mrs. Spurgeon paused and then laid the chopper
down on the block. There was a look of unwilling resignation
on her face, as much as to say, if you're going to talk, I
suppose I'll have to stop and listen to you.

"I'd seen her about the village," she replied grudgingly.

"To talk to?" Rudd asked.

"No," she said, and made as if to pick up the chopper
again, indicating that as far as she was concerned the
conversation was at an end.

"What did you think of her?" he asked.

"I didn't," she replied shortly.

"Not even as a friend of your son's?" Rudd asked.

Still stooping, she glanced at him over her shoulder, her
face closed, almost grim, giving nothing away.

"It was his business, not mine," she said after a moment.

"They say she was a bit more than a friend," Rudd said
boldly, wanting to test out her reaction. He wondered how
much she knew about Stan's relationship with Mrs. King; if
she knew that he had borrowed money from her.

Old Mrs. Spurgeon gave him a strange, lop-sided, bitter
smile.

"They say a great many things," she replied. "They've had
plenty to say about me, too, in their time. I know. I've
heard them. I've learned to turn my back on them. They're
muck, that's what they are. Dirt. And I wouldn't so much
as pass the time of day with them."

Rudd was taken aback by the fierceness of this speech
although he tried not to show it.

"There's always gossip," he remarked defensively.

She stopped and turned towards him. For a ridiculous
moment he was aware of the full strength of her formidable
personality and felt a little in awe of her.

"I know what else they're saying," she said angrily,
standing over him, "that it was Stan's fault she died. You ask
your questions, mister. You dig about in the dirt as much
as you like. But you won't find a thing against my boy, no
matter what they tell you. And as for them so-called

Christians, mealy-mouthed as they may be, the devil'll claim his own in the end."

In spite of the enigmatic quality of this remark, Rudd had the feeling that she was referring to someone in particular. Miss Leacock crossed his mind and he was about to lead the conversation round to her, when old Mrs. Spurgeon turned away, adding abruptly, "I've said my say," and began chopping into a log with such ferocity that Rudd was afraid to speak to her in case he should distract her and cause the flashing blade to slip.

He leaned back, hoping that if he waited quietly for a time, her anger might subside and he could persuade her to talk again. He was curious, for one thing, about her relationship with the Leacocks which he had never before considered, and he wondered if the old woman had some grudge against them.

They remained in silence for several minutes, Mrs. Spurgeon ignoring him completely and Rudd seemingly absorbed in drawing patterns with the toe of his shoe in the dust. "I don't think I'll wait any longer, Mrs. Spurgeon. Perhaps you'll tell your son that I'll call to see him tomorrow," he said, at last.

She did not reply but Rudd was pleased to see a look of uneasiness come into her face and it was with the jaunty mood of having scored the final point that he went across the yard to his car and drove away.

11

Rudd returned to the farm the following morning. This time Spurgeon was there, forking fresh straw into the heifers' pen. The sweet clean smell of it filled the air as the animals trod it underfoot.

"Oh, so it's you again," the farmer said in greeting.

"I called yesterday, but you were out," Rudd replied.

The farmer did not answer and Rudd guessed that old Mrs. Spurgeon had told him of his previous visit.

"Well," Spurgeon said after a pause, "what do you want this time?"

"Another chat with you," Rudd replied.

There appeared no change of expression on the farmer's face. He merely shrugged, stuck the fork into the straw-pile and, wiping his hands on the backside of his trousers, replied, "You'd best come into the house then."

Rudd followed him into the kitchen where old Mrs. Spurgeon was scraping carrots at the sink. Rudd said "good morning" but the old woman ignored him and the two men went into the livingroom where Rudd took the precaution of closing the intervening door quietly behind him. As he did so, he noticed that Spurgeon's best suit, the one he had worn at the inquest, was hanging on the hook behind the door. A bunch of late asters and chrysanthemums, picked from Spurgeon's garden, Rudd guessed, but carefully arranged and tied together, was standing in an enamel pail in the empty hearth. It seemed that Spurgeon had made his preparations for attending Mrs. King's funeral that afternoon.

Spurgeon indicated chairs and the two men sat down at the big oval table.

Rudd turned over some pages of his notebook slowly, as if looking for the right place. As Rudd had intended,

Spurgeon was made uneasy by this sign of officialdom. Neither man spoke and the only sounds were the slow scrape of the pages being turned and the subdued clatterings made by Mrs. Spurgeon in the kitchen. Then Spurgeon swallowed and, as if this had been a signal, Rudd began.

"I was approached yesterday by Mr. Roland King, Mrs. King's nephew, with some important new information," Rudd said. He looked up at Spurgeon. The farmer's eyes met his but the opaque look had come over them as it had at the first interview, giving them a dazed, blank expression.

"Yes?" said Spurgeon.

"Mr. King had been going through his aunt's accounts and he found that since May of last year you have been borrowing money from Mrs. King."

There was a long silence and then Spurgeon said with a sulky, defiant air, like a schoolboy confronted by a headmaster with irrefutable evidence of misbehavior, "I paid some of it back."

"I've taken that into account," Rudd replied sharply. "You borrowed a total of £250 and paid back £20."

Spurgeon said nothing and Rudd was forced at last to speak.

"Why did you say nothing about this to me?"

"It wasn't none of your business," Spurgeon replied. "It was between me and her."

"Good God, man!" Rudd cried. "Don't you realise what this could mean? I've been investigating the possibility of murder. You must have known that. And yet you kept silent about the money you owed her. What am I supposed to make of that?"

"You can make what you bloody well like out of it," Spurgeon replied. The opaque look had gone and there was a hard blue glare in his eyes. "All I know is I didn't kill her. I wouldn't've touched a hair of her head."

Rudd lowered his voice. He had no intention of turning the interview into a shouting match.

"You must try to see my point of view," he said, with an air of reasonableness. "If you were innocent, why didn't you admit to borrowing the money off her?"

"Because I didn't think it'd be found out," Spurgeon replied.

"You thought you'd get away with it?" Rudd asked.

"If you like," the farmer said defiantly.

"Like the seed potatoes?" Rudd suggested.

Spurgeon gave him an odd look, half-angry, half-amused.

"Been gossiping with Sergeant Holbrook?" he asked, jeering.

"I have my sources of information," Rudd replied primly. "Why did you borrow the money?"

"Because I needed it," Spurgeon said, implying in his voice that he considered the Inspector a fool to ask such an obvious question.

"What for specifically?" Rudd persisted.

"I don't see that it's got anything to do with you," the farmer replied.

"Hasn't it? Mrs. King is dead and that's something to do with me."

"All right then," said Spurgeon. "If you must know, it was to pay off a repayment on a bank loan. I'd got behind once before and they'd threatened to foreclose. And some of it was to settle up some bills I owed for feedstuff. The supplier said he wouldn't serve me any more if I didn't pay his account. I couldn't see my animals starve, could I?"

"So you asked Mrs. King to lend you money?"

"Yes," he said sulkily.

"Did she object?" Rudd asked.

"No. She said she'd lend it and not charge me interest. I said I'd pay her back when I could."

"And you had paid her back only twenty pounds when she died?"

"Her death's got nothing to do with it!" Spurgeon shouted. "I'd've paid it all back if I could. I just couldn't manage any more at the time."

"But you hoped you wouldn't have to pay the rest back after she died," Rudd pointed out. "As you said yourself, you hoped you'd get away with it."

"I didn't mean it that way," Spurgeon protested. There was an air of desperation about him now.

"Then how did you mean it?" asked Rudd.

"I don't know. I just hoped when I heard she'd died that nobody'd find out about the money. If I kept quiet, I wouldn't be asked to pay it back. After all, her nephew's well off. What's a couple of hundred quid to him? He'll get enough out of selling her business to more than cover what I owed. I was short of cash and he wasn't. There didn't seem anything wrong about it."

"I see," said Rudd non-committally. He closed his note-book, put it away and rose to his feet.

"Will he ask for the money to be paid back?" Spurgeon asked anxiously. Rudd looked down at him. The man would have to know the truth.

"I think he will," he replied.

Spurgeon put his elbows on the table and propped his head in his hands. He was silent and Rudd, after looking at his bent head for a moment, asked, "How will you manage?"

"God knows," said Spurgeon.

He lifted his head to look at the Inspector. His face was quite bleak.

"But I'll have to manage it somehow, I suppose. I'll have to find a job. Fred Bailey might take me on as a cow-man and I'll just have to fit the work in here as best I can."

"You can't run this place and work on another farm as well," Rudd protested.

"I'll have to, won't I?" Spurgeon replied. "One thing's certain, I won't sell up this place."

Rudd started to say something but the farmer broke in.

"I'll not sell up, I tell you! This is my land, my fields, my farm! And I'd go through hell first afore I'd part with them."

The emotion was genuine enough. The man's eyes were glaring fiercely at Rudd and the Inspector wondered how a rundown smallholding, a few scrubby acres and a decrepit old house could have such a hold over a person's heart. It strengthened too, Rudd realised, the motive Spurgeon might have had for killing Mrs. King. He might easily have con-templated murder in order to save his farm for which he obviously cared so passionately.

Rudd turned away but not before Spurgeon had caught something of the Inspector's expression. He stood up and confronted Rudd.

"You think I killed her," he said, "so as not to have to pay back the money. But you're wrong. She was a friend. She understood about the farm. She said, 'Anytime you're in a corner, come and see me. But don't sell up.' "

He paused and then added, "I was going to her funeral this afternoon, to pay my last respects. I can't go now. Somehow, you've spoiled it." He swallowed with a convulsive movement of the throat muscles and blinked his eyes rapidly.

"I'll see myself out," said Rudd and walked to the door.

Old Mrs. Spurgeon began busily to scrape carrots again as Rudd went through the kitchen. He wondered how much she had heard. He wondered, too, how much she had known about the money owing to Mrs. King. Perhaps Stan Spurgeon had confided in her? If he had, and if she realised how desperate the. situation was, she might have had a stronger motive for killing Rene King than her fear of Stan remarrying.

Rudd turned the car in the yard and drove down the short lane to the road. The table was set out beside the gate; on it, a few flowers, a basket of windfall apples, some onions tied in a bunch. It was a pathetic display.

Had Spurgeon been genuine when he had spoken so feelingly of Rene King's funeral? Rudd was not sure. The farmer was a more subtle man than he might at first appear. He had covered up successfully the fact that he owed Mrs. King money, hoping to get away with it. Had he hoped to get away with murder as well? Certainly the farmer's moral sense did not seem all that fine or well-developed, but whether it would bend far enough to accommodate murder Rudd was not so sure.

He was certain of one thing, however: as the case stood at the moment, he had not enough evidence to charge Spurgeon, although he would have him in to make a statement. He doubted, too, if the man would make a confession even if he were guilty. There was a strong instinct for self-preservation about him that would not be easily broken. All that Rudd could do was to plod on, hoping to scrape together evidence that might be used.

The church was packed with people for Rene King's funeral that afternoon at half-past two. Rudd deliberately waited until the last.

When the service ended, the vicar spoke a few words about the dead woman. He said her death had been a tragic loss to their little community. Although Mrs. King had not lived in the village for very long, she had made many friends and had contributed generously to many local activities and charities and had been a regular worshipper at the church in which her body would now find its last resting-place.

Mrs. Youngman's quiet sobbing could be heard above his words and her husband put an arm round her shoulders and drew her to him.

The hymn "Abide with Me," was sung and the coffin was then carried out to the churchyard, followed by Roland King, the rest of the congregation filing quietly out of the pews behind him.

Rudd remained in his place, scanning the faces as they went past. Stan Spurgeon was definitely not among them.

When the last person had gone, Rudd walked out into the churchyard towards the gate. He did not wish to see Rene King placed in her grave. His concern was with those living who might have brought about her death.

As he drew near to the gate, he noticed a man standing under the yew trees that lined the walls. The Inspector could not make out who it was; he had drawn back behind the protection of the low branches but Rudd got the impression that he was watching him closely. He caught a flash of colour, yellow and red and purple, and then the man walked rapidly away from him down Rectory Close. It was Stan Spurgeon in his best suit, clutching a bunch of flowers.

Rudd began to hurry after him and then changed his mind. After all, he had no reason to pursue him. Spurgeon had every right to be there, whatever suspicions might be hanging over him.

Seconds later, Rudd heard the spluttering cough of an engine as the farmer started up his old battered van and drove away.

Rudd walked on. He was too preoccupied with his own thoughts to notice if the face was again at the cottage window and he did not remember it until he reached the end of the lane and it was too late to look. Motive. That's what it came down to in the end. Out of all the suspects, Spurgeon was the only one who appeared to have any reason for killing Mrs. King.

An hour or so later the hearse and the other cars had gone. The churchyard was empty of people. All that remained was the long hump of earth, covered with flowers. Rudd bent down to examine some of the cards. On Roland King's wreath of white carnations a black-bordered card read: "To darling Auntie Rene from her ever-loving nephew." As he read it, Rudd gave a small grim smile. The Leacocks had sent yellow chrysanthemums inscribed "With our deepest sympathy." Other cards carried messages from local people. "From Mr. and Mrs. Abstey with our fondest love." "From Jack and Norah, always remembered." And from Mr. and Mrs. Youngman a bunch of dahlias, Mr. Youngman's prize blooms, and the words, "To a dear friend who is sadly missed."

Rudd almost overlooked Stan Spurgeon's flowers. They lay, as if humbly, at the foot of the grave, overshadowed by the larger wreaths, but Rudd recognised them as soon as he saw them. Their stems were tied together with string and a little white tag of paper showed where the farmer had torn off the accompanying card. Rudd wondered what had been written on it but he thought he understood why it had been removed.

It was all he wanted to know and he turned and walked back to the car.

Sergeant Holbrook was at home and had changed back into his uniform. Mrs. Holbrook made tea and they sat together in the living-room, drinking and talking about the funeral. Holbrook took it as a matter of personal pride that so many people had been present.

"I'm glad she had a good send-off," he said. "There's nothing worse than a half-empty church at a funeral."

"Stan Spurgeon wasn't there," his wife commented. "I'd've thought he'd've come. After all, he knew her and it shows respect."

"He waited at the gate," Rudd said. He felt he ought to say something to excuse the man. "And he left flowers on the grave."

He decided not to tell Holbrook anything about the money that Spurgeon owed Mrs. King. Holbrook would be unlikely to add anything of value and besides, Spurgeon had admitted it and Rudd had seen enough evidence to show that the man was short of money.

They finished their tea and Rudd rose to go. At the door, he mentioned the real purpose of his visit.

"Have you fixed up a meeting yet with Mrs. Turnbull?" he aked the Sergeant.

"Yes, I dropped in to see her this afternoon, after the funeral. I was going to phone you. It'll be all right for tomorrow afternoon. Like you told me, I didn't say much; just mentioned you wanted to have a chat with her. She seemed quite keen on the idea; but, then, she doesn't get a lot of company."

With that back-handed compliment the two men parted, Rudd smiling to himself.

At the office, he wrote up his report on the interview

with Stan Spurgeon. Sometime, in the near future, he would have to have Spurgeon in to make an official statement, but Rudd hesitated to make the move quite yet. As a police-man, he persuaded himself that this would be an astute decision. It was better to let the man stew over it for a few days and then have him in for further questioning. It might break him. It had been known to work before.

As a man, though, Rudd knew he was moved by other motives. Spurgeon had enough on his plate with his debts, his run-down farm, his retarded son. Rudd was letting him have a breathing space in which, the Inspector hoped, God knows what might turn up and force his hand.

Rudd moved restlessly about the office. The case became more and more unsatisfactory every day. The only evidence he had was an anonymous letter and some fingerprints and even those might be valueless. It certainly did not add up to enough evidence to bring a charge.

Boyce came into the office at that moment.

"Seen Spurgeon?" he asked Rudd cheerfully.

"I did," Rudd replied.

"And did he admit it?" Boyce went on.

"He could hardly deny it," Rudd said sourly.

"It's a motive," Boyce pointed out. "And one of the strongest: greed."

"Not greed," said Rudd. "A kind of love."

"Love?" asked Boyce, not understanding.

"One of the oldest forms of love there is," Rudd ex-plained. "The love of the land. I don't mean the pride of ownership, of the landed gentleman. It's something more primitive and fundamental than that. It's loving the actual soil, the earth itself. It's what makes an exile kneel down and kiss the ground when he returns."

Boyce shrugged.

"It's still a motive," Boyce pointed out.

"It is indeed," Rudd agreed.

"Well, then," said Boyce, not sure what he was expected to say.

"I don't know," Rudd admitted.

He went to stand at the window, his back to the room, looking out at the sooty tree in the yard.

"Spurgeon had means, opportunity and motive," he said. "He's our strongest suspect so far. And yet I'm not sure. Poison's a mean crime, Tom, and I don't think he's a mean person. He's passionate; he's quick-tempered; he has his own standards of honesty which aren't all that straight-forward. I can see him cheating someone better off than himself and thinking he's doing something clever. I can see him losing his temper and clobbering somebody with the first thing he can lay his hands on. But I can't see him going into that wood and deliberately picking that fungus and carrying it off to Rene King as a present. It just doesn't fit in with what I know of the man."

"That's not evidence," Boyce pointed out.

"I know," said Rudd, "and Rene King's accounts are. But it's people that count, Tom, not figures."

A complex look passed over Boyce's face. It contained a kind of puzzled pity and Rudd realised that, in Boyce's opinion, he was losing his grip.

"It'll work out," he promised Boyce, but it was poor compensation. The Sergeant looked at his feet and asked, in a restrained way, if the Inspector needed him for anything else.

"No," said Rudd. "You can cut off home."

He left, too, shortly afterwards and took his sister to the cinema that evening. It was a good film but he could not keep his mind on it.

When they came out, it had begun to rain, that fine melancholy drizzle of early autumn and the streets were sad and smeared with damp.

As they walked to the carpark, Dorothy touched him gently on the arm.

"Is anything the matter?" she asked.

Her face, ghastly in the glare of the sodium lights, looked anxiously up into his. Rudd thought of Boyce's face, pitying him; of Spurgeon's expression when he said, "somehow, you've spoiled it."

"It's nothing," he replied. "I'm just tired, that's all."

"Mrs. King was buried today, wasn't she?" his sister asked.

"Yes," replied Rudd.

"I'm sorry," she said simply. "It can't be easy for you."

12

The second anonymous letter was delivered the following morning. Rudd recognised it as soon as he saw it. It was the same cheap quality envelope and was printed in the same crude capital letters, only this time it was addressed to him by name.

"Our chum's at it again!" he announced triumphantly and Boyce came over to watch as Rudd slit the envelope and shook it over his blotter. A small beige-coloured cardboard oblong fell out. Rudd turned it over with the tip of a pencil. It was a membership ticket for Market Stratton public library and the name on it was Mrs. R. King.

Boyce looked puzzled but Rudd realised its significance at once.

"That's cleared up one mystery," he said. "How our unknown person managed to borrow *British Mushrooms and Toadstools*."

"I don't quite——" Boyce began.

"Whoever it was used Mrs. King's ticket; probably saw it lying about her flat and took it. So we're back again with our old list of suspects, Stan Spurgeon, the Leacocks, or Mrs. Youngman." He added her name reluctantly. "It must have been one of them. Nobody else had access to her flat, as far as we know."

"Someone might have asked to borrow it," Boyce pointed out.

"That's true," Rudd agreed. "Although it'd have to be someone with the devil of a nerve. Anyway it's a possibility we can't afford to ignore. But we know one thing, we needn't bother any more about that list of library members. Whoever borrowed that book certainly wasn't a member or they'd've used their own ticket. And it tells us something more. Our

149

anonymous friend feels we need a little more information. We've certainly stirred up interest there."

"I wonder how the letter writer got hold of the ticket to send it to us?" Boyce said.

Rudd looked at him with sudden interest and excitement.

"That's bright of you, Tom!" he said. "I hadn't thought of that. But you're right. It must have been someone fairly close to the person who took it in the first place, or had access to their home. Mrs. Spurgeon would fit that bill. So, too, would either of the Leacocks."

Rudd picked up the ticket and the envelope with tweezers and dropped them into plastic bags.

"Get those sent up to forensic straightaway, will you, and tell them I want a rushed job on them, especially on the ticket. I doubt if they'll find much on the envelope that's useful, but if we can find prints on the ticket then we're practically home and dry. We'd have to back it up, of course, with other evidence; it'll mean digging around for more proof, but at least we'll know the identity of the person we're looking for and that's more than half the battle."

"Right," said Boyce. "I'll get these sent off."

When Boyce had left the office with the plastic bags, Rudd sat at his desk thinking over the case. He had a feeling that, at last, it was beginning to go his way and he reckoned it was about time it did too. All the luck so far had been on the other side.

He was opening the other letters when Boyce returned.

"I've sent Pierce with them," he said.

"Fine," said Rudd vaguely, tearing open the envelope he had in his hand and taking out the sheet of paper it contained.

"Oh, bloody hell and damnation!" the Inspector said violently and Boyce almost ran across the office.

Rudd silently showed it to him. Unlike the first anonymous letter, this one was typewritten. It read: "Did you know that Mrs. Youngman had been stealing money from the shop till for several weeks and Mrs. King was going to sack her and tell the police just before she died?"

"Is this true?" Boyce asked.

"How the hell should I know?" Rudd snapped. "But I'll have to find out."

He thought of Mrs. Youngman's cardigan, mended at the elbows, the shabby furniture, the cage of Angora rabbits kept to help out the family income. He thought, too, of her plain, round, anxious face and her eyes brimming up with tears.

"But she found the body," Boyce pointed out. "She'd've hardly murdered Mrs. King and then found the body the next day, unless she's as hard as nails."

He was trying to raise objections to soften the impact of the letter without knowing why he felt he must do so.

"She could hardly have done otherwise," Rudd replied. "She'd naturally be the first person to find her. After all, she worked there."

All the same, Boyce had a point. It would have been more in character if Mrs. Youngman had made some excuse for not going to work that day or had got someone else to go into the shop first on the pretext that she did not have a key. Or would she? A woman with five children faced with possible arrest might be desperate enough to see it through to the end and to find the body, even if it was merely to satisfy herself that Mrs. King was dead. On the other hand, from the normal long-drawn-out symptoms of Death Cap poisoning she might not have expected to find Mrs. King dead. The poisoner could not have known beforehand that Mrs. King would die of asphyxiation. It would be more in the murderer's interest to make sure that medical attention was delayed for as long as possible so that the effects of the poison would have greater time to take effect.

Rudd knew that Amanita Phalloides poisoning took several days. Dr. Foreman had told him. But it suddenly occurred to him that the book *British Mushrooms and Toadstools* had not given a lot of medical facts. He could not remember if that information was in it or not. He turned quickly to Boyce.

"Get hold of that library book, Tom," he said. "I think it's back from having the photocopies made of the illustration. And you'd better get these sent off to forensic as well."

He slipped the letter and its envelope into bags.

"I want them fingerprinted, saliva tests made and a report on the typewriter that was used. We may be able to trace it."

Boyce once more left the office and Rudd got up from his desk and went to stand at the window, thinking about the implications of the letter.

Mrs. Youngman's state of shock had seemed genuine

enough. Dr. Foreman, that shrewd and experienced medical man, had certainly been taken in by it. It could though, Rudd supposed, have been a nervous crisis brought on by guilty conscience or hysterical relief that Mrs. King was no longer alive to accuse her of theft.

Boyce, returning with the book, found Rudd standing with his hands in his pockets, looking out of the window with an air of abstraction. He handed the Inspector the book and then withdrew. He knew better than to try engaging him in conversation when he was in one of those moods.

The book fell open as it had done before on the page featuring Amanita Phalloides with its now familiar illustrations. Rudd ran his eye over the text. The medical information was scanty. "This fungus," it stated, "is one of the deadliest. The symptoms include vomiting, diarrhoea and acute stomach pains and, unless prompt medical attention is given, the patient invariably dies."

That was all. There was nothing about the symptoms appearing to subside or death following after a protracted illness of three to ten days. Mrs. Youngman, therefore, with that inadequate knowledge might very well have expected Mrs. King to be dead the following morning.

Rudd bit his thumbnail savagely. There was no way out. She could as easily have taken the library ticket as any of the others under suspicion, and put the fungus into the basket of mushrooms. The identity of the person who had forwarded the library ticket to him was less obvious. He did not think that Youngman himself had done so. His affection for his wife was too genuine. And it was unlikely to have been either of the Spurgeons or the Leacocks. None of them seemed to have any connection with Mrs. Youngman or to be on friendly visiting terms at her house where one of them could have picked up the ticket. But it might be a friend or neighbour who, already suspecting Mrs. Youngman, had written the first letter, suggesting Mrs. King's death was not accidental, and had, afterwards, come across the ticket and sent it to Rudd.

Boyce came in with a cup of tea which he placed apologetically on the Inspector's desk.

"I thought you needed it," he said.

"Thanks," said Rudd, touched by his sign of concern. "I'll have to go up to London and see Mrs. King's nephew. He's been through the books to do with her business and he may be able to trace if any money's missing."

He suddenly remembered his appointment that afternoon with Mrs. Turnbull and, as he drank his tea, he telephoned Sergeant Holbrook to cancel it.

"Something's turned up here," he said, "and I may not be back in time."

"The old lady'll be disappointed," Holbrook replied with a note of regret. "She's been looking forward to having a chat with you. Shall I fix it up for another day?"

Rudd nearly told him to cancel it altogether and then hesitated. Because a new line of inquiry had come up, that did not mean that he had to abandon all the others. On the other hand, he was not sure how long the inquiries into the allegation against Mrs. Youngman might take and he did not want to make fresh arrangements, only to cancel them again.

"I'm not sure when I'll be free," he said.

"Well, it can't be helped," replied Holbrook with that disarming air of his. "I'm off duty tomorrow afternoon, so I'll probably drop in on the old girl anyway. She enjoys a bit of company."

"Look," said Rudd. "Give me her address and I'll do my best to meet you there. Say around half-past two. But if I don't turn up, make my apologies."

"All right," Holbrook said. "You won't have any trouble finding it. She lives in the cottage next door to the Youngmans, the second along the row."

"I know it," said Rudd and rang off.

So the face at the window was not a child's as Rudd had supposed but old Mrs. Turnbull looking out at the world from her bedroom. She might be well worth talking to anyway. As next-door neighbour of Mrs. Youngman's, she might have some useful information.

But the first person to interview was Roland King and Rudd telephoned him to ask for an appointment. King agreed to see him that morning and, without going into any details, Rudd rang off.

He caught the next train to London, leaving Boyce in charge of the office to deal with reports from forensic as they came in.

Roland King's business was in a street of clothing wholesalers in Whitechapel. From the outside it was unimpressive. Behind a dirty plate-glass window a few coats and dresses were on display. An alley at the side led presumably to the warehouse at the back. A van with the firm's name on it was parked at the entrance, its rear doors open and Rudd, glancing inside, saw tightly-packed rails of clothes, covered with plastic sheeting.

Roland King's office showed more signs of affluence. Although it received no sunlight and the barred windows overlooked a yard, the floor was covered with expensive carpeting and the desk was large and well polished. But it was a place of work as well. The room was lit with daylight fluorescent lighting and swatches of material lay on the desk and a long workbench.

Roland King, smartly dressed as usual, came forward to meet the Inspector at the door and showed him to a chair.

Rudd got straight down to business.

"I've called this morning, Mr. King, because I'd like to check over with you one or two points concerning your aunt's business accounts."

"Is it something to do with the money Spurgeon owed my aunt?" King asked.

"No, it's another matter entirely. I understand you went carefully over Mrs. King's books?"

"I did. Very carefully."

"Would you know from the figures if any small sums of money had been missing from the till over a period of several weeks?"

Roland King gave the Inspector a very sharp, surprised look which turned to sudden understanding.

"Are you suggesting the woman who did the cleaning had been pinching money?" he asked.

"I'm afraid I can't give you any details," Rudd replied.

"Well, it can hardly be anyone else," King replied peevishly, as if he thought the Inspector was taking him for a fool. "Apart from my aunt, she was the only person who was ever in the shop regularly."

Rudd kept his expression perfectly pleasant but he did not reply and, after a few moments, King's face hardened. The man seemed more aggressive on his home ground, more sure of himself and it was clear he resented Rudd's assumption of authority.

"Have you brought the books with you?" he asked abruptly.

"I have," Rudd replied.

He produced them from his brief-case, a scarred and battered object, very different from the elegant pigskin one that King possessed. He placed them on the desk and King sorted them through rapidly, chose one and opened it.

"As I've already pointed out," he said, "I went over the accounts very carefully and as far as I could see there was no record of any money missing."

"As far as you could see?" Rudd persisted. "Can you be more definite than that?"

"Of course I can," King replied shortly. "I don't know how much you know about bookkeeping but I'll try to explain how my aunt kept her daybook."

"Thank you," said Rudd gravely. It did not matter to him that King wanted to put him in his place. In fact, the Inspector was amused by King's assumption of the role of shrewd man of affairs. He even drew his chair nearer to the desk and adjusted his shirt cuffs, before running his finger down a column of figures. Rudd sat patiently and waited.

"Here we are," said King and half-turned the book so that Rudd could see the relevant pages.

"These are the accounts for the last three weeks. I don't know if you're familiar with the type of till my aunt used in the shop? Well, it was a good quality one that I got cheap for her. Everytime she rang up a sale, the amount was recorded on a paper roll, so that at the end of the day, she only had to add up the figures to know exactly what amount she'd taken. She started every morning with a £5 float, mostly in small change. Otherwise the till was empty of money. The amount of the float was deducted from the total when she closed the shop, the till was cleared of money and was placed in the small safe she had in the office. She banked once a week. So if any money was missing, even a few coppers, she'd know about it."

"I see," said Rudd thoughtfully.

"So if it's been suggested the cleaning woman was stealing from her, then someone's having you on," said King with an air of satisfaction. "My aunt was no fool where the shop was concerned."

"But suppose somebody had?" Rudd asked. "What would have been her reaction?"

"She wouldn't have let it go on for several weeks, I can tell you that," King replied promptly. "If it was the char, she'd've confronted her with it the next day."

"And dismissed her?" Rudd asked.

"Probably. My aunt didn't like dealing with people she couldn't trust."

"Would she have gone to the police about it?"

King looked doubtful.

"I don't think so. It wasn't her way of treating people. She preferred facing them herself. And as far as the char's concerned, you can knock her off your list. I know for a fact my aunt trusted her. I saw her myself about ten days before she died. There'd been a bit of bother over an order, some second standard nylon stuff that had been invoiced as best, and she rang me up and I said I'd come down myself and sort it out. The char, Mrs. What's-her-name, made coffee for us and my aunt happened to remark how lucky she was to have her. So up until then, she hadn't any reason for giving her the sack."

"Thank you, Mr. King," Rudd said. "You've given me some very useful information. By the way," he added, as King began to push the ledgers towards him across the desk, "I'll leave the account books with you."

"You've finished with them already?" King asked. There was a small, tight, sarcastic smile on his face that suggested he considered a great deal too much fuss had been made over them in the first place.

Rudd pretended not to notice it.

"For the time being," he replied equably. "If we need them again, I'll get in touch with you. I haven't returned the household ledger yet but we should be finished with that in a day or two."

"The one containing Spurgeon's account?" King asked. "Have you been to see him about it?"

"I have spoken to him," Rudd replied cautiously.

"Well, I wrote to him," King went on, "and I got this reply. You might care to read it."

He went to the filing cabinet, opened a drawer and took a letter from a grey folder and handed it to Rudd.

It was written on cheap, lined paper, in a sprawling handwriting and said:

"Dear Mr. King,

I got your letter and I'm sending you £2 towards paying back the money your auntie lent me. I can't pay it all back at once but I'll do my best to send you a couple of pounds every week. I'd like to say how sorry I am about her death. She was a good friend to me and I miss her very much."

It was signed S. Spurgeon.

"Touching, isn't it?" said King.

Rudd looked at him sharply, wondering if he was still being sarcastic but he saw the man really meant it. So even King had an element of sentiment in his character.

"He seemed to like her," Rudd replied in a non-committal voice.

"I'm glad she had a few friends," King continued. For once he sounded almost friendly. "I didn't get the time to visit her all that often. As a matter of fact, I was very pleased to see so many people at her funeral."

Passing the can, was Rudd's silent comment. It eased King's conscience to think his aunt had not been lonely.

"At least Mr. Spurgeon's making an effort to repay the money," Rudd said, hoping for some comeback. But it was too much to expect that King's sentimentality extended to business matters.

"As long as he makes small regular payments, I shan't press him," he replied.

So much for that, Rudd thought. Spurgeon was going to be made to repay the loan and Rudd could not really blame King.

He rose to go.

"I suppose it's no good asking you again why the police should be so interested in my aunt's death?" King asked.

"At this stage, I'm afraid I can't give you any information," Rudd replied.

King lost the brief friendliness that he had shown during their talk about Spurgeon. The hard look returned.

"I wasn't born yesterday, you know," he said angrily. "There must be something fishy about it or the inquest wouldn't have been adjourned."

"I'm sorry," replied Rudd. "I can tell you nothing."

"I've got a good mind to write to your superintendent," King said. He was working himself up into a state of angry indignation. "As a taxpayer and her next-of-kin, I'd be within my rights."

"You must do as you think best," Rudd said. He was displeased that the interview was ending on this note. "All I can say is that, like you, I have a job to do."

Roland King made no reply to this but turned to his desk and Rudd saw himself out.

There were no taxis and he walked back to Liverpool

Street station through the dingy streets. The next train for
Chelmsford left in twenty minutes and he whiled away the
time drinking a cup of coffee in the station buffet among
the clatter of china and the refined voice of the station
announcer booming out the times of train arrivals and
departures.

The urns hissed. People came and went. A coloured woman pushed a trolley between the tables and gathered up the
dirty cups in a bored, languid way.

Rudd drank his coffee and thought over what he had
learned from the interview. It seemed certain from what
Roland King had told him that Mrs. Youngman could not
have stolen money from the shop without Mrs. King being
aware of it. The letter writer, then, had not known that
this could be proved. It was merely dirt-slinging of the most
malicious type. But someone had made the allegation hoping
that it would stick.

"Someone's been having you on," had been King's comment and it was true. There was an air of hysteria about the
accusation, a desperate clutching at straws.

It was time for him to get his train and Rudd walked
across the station, under the huge, dirty, echoing arch of the
roof, showed his ticket and got into a compartment, still
deep in thought. The train pulled out and slid slowly between
high brick embankments. Rudd summed up his thoughts.
Firstly, the writer of the original anonymous letter, which
had been printed in capital letters, had given him useful
information. The accusation of murder appeared to be ac-
curate. The library ticket had added important new evidence.
But although the writer of the other anonymous letter, the
typewritten one, had made a definite accusation, naming
Mrs. Youngman, the information in it was incorrect.

This would suggest that there were two separate writers,
one attempting to help the police, by however a devious
and underhand method; the other trying to throw the police
off the scent by making false accusations.

It also occurred to Rudd that the second anonymous
letter writer was not as shrewd as the first. Handwriting, if it
is cleverly disguised, is not easy to trace, although it can be
done. But a typewritten letter is another matter. Providing
the typewriter can be found, a specimen typed out on it can
easily be checked against the original and certain irrefutable
comparisons made.

It might also be possible that the second writer had made an even more serious blunder and had left fingerprints on the paper.

But here Rudd was disappointed. On returning to the office, he found Boyce had taken notes on the reports telephoned through from the forensic department, a written copy of which would be forwarded later. The typewritten letter, like the others, was clean of anything except smudges.

"And the saliva test didn't tell us much either," said Boyce. "The writer of the typed letter was a non-secreter and the nicotine tests were negative, so that means a nonsmoker as well."

"What about the library ticket?" asked Rudd.

"No prints there, either," Boyce replied. "Wiped as clean as a whistle."

"Oh, blast!" said Rudd moodily. "That's another hopeful lead down the pan. What about the typewriter? They've surely found something positive to say about that?"

Boyce consulted a sheet of paper.

"Elliot type. Well-used ribbon," he read from his notes. "Several letters blocked with ink and damaged in some instances, so probably an old model. Letter 'e' very worn and so bunged up with ink it's almost indistinguishable from an 'o'. Probably a portable as some of the upper case letters aren't properly aligned. Person who typed it not an expert. Uneven pressure and several typing errors are overprinted."

"Well, that's something to go on at least," said Rudd. "If we can only find the tpyewriter, we still might be home and dry."

"How did you get on about Mrs. Youngman?" asked Boyce.

"Nothing there," said Rudd. "She can't possibly have been pinching money. And I must say I'm glad. She's the last person I'd want to arrest on a murder charge."

"So what do we do now?" asked Boyce.

"We go back to the old lines of inquiry," Rudd replied. "We'll follow up the prints on the library book, although I don't hold out much hope there. You can make a start there, Tom, tomorrow. Get the prints of all the library staff. And we'll have the wood behind Spurgeon's farm and the footpath thoroughly searched. We'll make door-to-door inquiries in the village about the typewriter and we'll put the frighteners on a few people by having them in to have their prints taken and samples of their handwriting, starting with the Spurgeons and the Leacocks."

"Do you want me to do all the fingerprinting?" asked Boyce, looking depressed at the thought.

"Yes, take a constable with you. I'll get Holbrook and a couple of other men to start the door-to-door inquiries in the village about the typewriter. I'll interview the Spurgeons and the Leacocks myself. And we'll get the search organised for tomorrow afternoon. You should be finished at the library by then. You can be in charge of that. I'll see that you've got enough men to help you. The footpath starts just behind the church, so you can begin there and work your way along to the wood."

"We've already searched the wood once," Boyce pointed out.

"Well, I want it searched again," snapped Rudd. "I want every dead leaf turned over and every twig inspected and I don't care how much rubbish you bring in as long as there's something among it we can use for a positive identification."

"You've got a hope," said Boyce. "And where will you be, sir, if I need you?"

Rudd noticed the Sergeant's use of the word "sir" and grinned to himself. It was one of Boyce's ways of showing disapproval.

"I'll be interviewing a lady," said Rudd. "The second cottage along the row in Rectory Close. If you need me, come upstairs. I'll be in the bedroom."

"Very good, sir," said Boyce, without a flicker of expression.

"She's bedridden and over eighty," said Rudd, laughing, "and she probably won't be able to tell me a damned thing that's any use, but it's worth a try."

Rudd spent the rest of the afternoon making preparations for the following day's investigations. He telephoned the library and arranged for Boyce and a constable to call the next morning to fingerprint the staff. He then arranged for the search party to comb the path and the wood under Boyce's direction. Last of all, he rang Holbrook about the inquiries in the village.

"About a typewriter?" asked Holbrook.

"I'll send a couple of men over to help you," Rudd said. "Leave the Spurgeons and the Leacocks to me; there's a few other questions I want to ask them. But I want you to go to every other house in the village. If the occupier has a typewriter, get a specimen typed out on it. Also ask if any member of the family belongs to the library at Market Stratton, has ever been inside Mrs. King's flat and keeps paraffin on the premises. I'll get a questionnaire made out and sent over to you first thing tomorrow. And get a full list of every adult. We may need to take fingerprints later."

"Of everybody?" asked Holbrook.

"If necessary," said Rudd.

"I see," said Holbrook. He seemed stunned by the news. "I'll get that organised then, sir."

"And I shall want you to meet me at Mrs. Turnbull's cottage in the afternoon," said Rudd. "I shall be free at two-thirty. You can leave the other men to carry on with the door-to-door inquiries for the time being, but I think you'd better be with me to make the introductions."

"Very good, sir," said Holbrook. He sounded subdued.

Rudd rang off and, taking a piece of paper, began to write out the questionnaire. Boyce had gone off to arrange about a constable to accompany him to the library. Turner, another sergeant, had been detailed to draw up the list of men for the search party. Things were moving. All Rudd could do was hope that out of all the activity something useful would emerge at last.

13

The following afternoon Rudd drove over to Abbots Stacey and turned into Rectory Close. Holbrook had evidently just arrived as he was still locking up the car door as Rudd drew up. Ahead of them a police van and two cars were already parked but there was no sign of Boyce or any of the constables. The search of the path must have begun.

"How are the door-to-door inquiries going?" asked Rudd as Holbrook approached.

"Not too bad, sir," Holbrook replied. "We've been to over twenty houses so far and found three typewriters; one at the doctor's house, one at the rectory and one at the school. I've had specimens typed out on all of them and lists of people who were likely to use them. The school's typewriter is in the most general use, but I think I've got all the names."

"Good man," said Rudd.

"Well," said Holbrook modestly, "the questionnaire you sent has been more than useful. I thought I'd finish the inquiries and then make up separate lists from it; all the people who keep paraffin and so on."

"That's what I call using your head," said Rudd. "And it'll save me a devil of a lot of work."

Holbrook looked down at his feet.

"I don't know if I ought to ask you this, sir," he went on. "But it is my village, so to speak, and I feel I must ask even if you tell me to mind my own business."

"Well?" said Rudd, although he had a good idea what the question was going to be.

"It's all these inquiries. I see there's a group of men out now, searching the footpath. Are you likely to be making an arrest soon?"

"I can't tell you," said Rudd, "not because I don't want

to but because I haven't got enough facts. You won't need telling who's on our list of suspects. I've got scraps of evidence against all of them but nothing I can base a charge on yet."

"I've been thinking again about putting in for a transfer," Holbrook said. He glanced at Rudd, hoping for some reassurance. But Rudd had no comfort for him.

"You must do as you think best," he replied shortly. "But while you're on these inquiries, you're to keep your ears and eyes skinned for anything that might be useful."

"Of course, sir," Holbrook replied, sounding low-spirited.

"Now shall we go in and see that old lady of yours?" Rudd said.

They walked up the long garden together. Rudd had not noticed before how neatly tended the garden was and he commented on it.

"A few of us younger chaps in the village put in an hour or two on it every so often," Holbrook replied. "Old Mr. Turnbull can't do much gardening now."

Rudd said nothing but he wished now that he could have satisfied the Sergeant over the question of his transfer. Holbrook obviously was at home in the village and a good local policeman meant a lot to a small community.

Old Mr. Turnbull must have heard them coming for he was at the door to greet them. He was a tiny, fragile man, whose small skull and thin bones put Rudd in mind of a bird.

"How's things, Dad?" Holbrook asked with easy familiarity, after he had introduced Rudd.

"Not too bad. Mustn't grumble," the old man quavered in reply.

"And how's Ma?"

"She's well. She's upstairs waiting for you coming. She's been on about it all day. I've been up and down them stairs more times than I care to count, tidying this and straightening that."

Holbrook laughed. "She keeps you at it."

"She does that," Mr. Turnbull replied, with affection. "You'd best go up to her. I'll make you a cup of tea later."

"Now see here," said Holbrook firmly. "You're not carrying a tray of tea up them steep stairs. You give us a shout when it's ready."

"All right then, lad," Mr. Turnbull replied. "I'll holler you to come down."

Rudd thought, as the two of them mounted the precipitous stairs to the upper floor, that the old man seemed incapable of uttering any sound louder than a chirrup. At the head of the stairs, they turned right on a tiny landing into the front bedroom.

As soon as he entered it, Rudd was reminded of his grandmother's bedroom. She had been dead for years but in his teens he had visited her every day after school during her last illness. There had been the same kind of rag rug on the floor, the same marble-topped wash-hand stand with its bowl and jug and soap-dish of flowered china, the enamel slop-pail with a lid standing discreetly underneath it. The pictures on the walls were of the same period, too; pre-Raphaelite prints in Oxford frames of cherubs' heads and impossibly beautiful women in Greek draperies standing by marble pools.

The room was dominated by the bed; a high Victorian bedstead with an iron frame and brass knobs, and the bed was dominated by old Mrs. Turnbull, sitting propped up among a great many plump pillows, with her fine white hair pinned up in a little circular plait on the top of her head, a handknitted bed-jacket round her shoulders and a very bright and inquisitive look on her face.

"So you've come," she said.

Holbrook introduced Rudd and she held out a thin knotted hand for him to shake. He was surprised by the vigour in her grip.

"I'm sorry we couldn't make it yesterday," Holbrook said.

"So am I," she retorted. "I'd done my hair up specially, but you'll have to put up with it as it is. I can't go combing and coiling it every day for policemen who don't come when they're supposed to."

"It was my fault," said Rudd with a twinkle. He was already hugely enjoying the interview and he gave Holbrook top marks for finding such a delightfully sharp and acid old lady.

"I've no doubt it was," she replied, giving him a look. "I've seen you before in the lane. You waved at me. Well, sit down, sit down. I can't crane my neck all afternoon looking up at you two great gawks."

Rudd drew a rush-bottomed chair up to the side of the bed and Holbrook perched himself at the bottom of the bed. Old Mrs. Turnbull looked at them both with an air of satisfaction.

"It's a good few years since I've had two men in my bedroom," she remarked. "Now, I suppose it's you," she added, turning to Rudd, "who wants to ask me some questions."

"I'd prefer a gossip," said Rudd disarmingly and she laughed.

"And who do you want to gossip about?"

"What about Old Bill, the tramp?" Rudd suggested, choosing a non-controversial person as a beginning.

"Is he still about?" Mrs. Turnbull said. "I remember seeing him around the village when I was a young married woman and that's more years ago than I care to remember. I can't tell you much about him, except he's supposed to have taken to the roads, during the depression when he was quite a young man, looking for work, and he got a taste for the life and never settled down again. He used to do casual farmwork but he must be past that now."

"What about old Mrs. Spurgeon?" Rudd asked, working his way up the list. Mrs. Turnbull gave him a quick look, full of laughter.

"If you meant a connection between those two names," she said, "You won't be the first to make it."

"Go on?" said Rudd encouragingly.

"Now that's really raking up the past," she replied. "And if she did, who's to blame her? Old Mr. Spurgeon was a proper old devil, more often drunk than sober and Stan's been a good son to her, whoever his father was."

"Let's talk about Stan, then," said Rudd. "I know a bit about him already; the fact that his wife left him and the child, and there was some trouble when old Mrs. Spurgeon got turned out of the house."

"Well, if you know that, there's not much more I can tell you. She, his wife that is, was a girl from Copse End; used to do the milk-round with Fred Bailey's father. Stan met his match there, right enough. He's always been a bit of a lad where women were concerned, but he couldn't wriggle his way out of that one, not with her in the family way."

"Had he wriggled out of many situations?" Rudd asked innocently.

"He's upped and offed more than once," the old lady replied with something like admiration in her voice. "And he's got away with it. But he's always been like it. Up to all kinds of mischief as a lad, he was; scrumping apples, breaking windows with his catapult, teasing the girls, the backside hanging out of his trousers more often than not. But you couldn't help liking him. I've clipped his ear for him more than once and all he did was look at me with those blue eyes and grin."

"What about Mr. Leacock and his sister?" Rudd asked. "You must have known them, too, as children?"

She sniffed. "I did and I didn't take much to either of them. Gilbert was one of those quiet boys although there was a lot more to him than he let on. I remember the rector we had then, Mr. Babberton, he's been dead and gone these past twenty years, and a nicer gentleman you couldn't wish to meet, but he gave Gilbert a good hiding once. I don't know what about, something to do with some baby birds, but old Mrs. Leacock, she was alive then, went round there and threatened the police and I don't know what else. Anyway, Mr. Babberton must have told her straight because no more was heard about it. She was a proper old harridan was Mrs. Leacock. She was bedridden like me for the last five years of her life and I've been in their shop many a time and heard her banging on the floor upstairs with her stick so hard that big flakes of whitewash fell off the ceiling. So their life hasn't been easy. Amy was run off her feet, fetching and carrying and running up and down stairs to her every five minutes. It was old Mrs. Leacock who put a stop to her marrying Stan Spurgeon."

"Amy Leacock was engaged to Stan Spurgeon?" Rudd asked. It was the kind of information he was hoping to find, although he could see now that he might have guessed it for himself. They were both of the same age. It wouldn't have been all that unusual in a small village for them, as young people to form some relationship.

"Well, not exactly engaged," Mrs. Turnbull was saying. "They were more what we used to call 'walking out together.' No ring, mind, and nothing formal, but a kind of understanding. Mind you, I don't think Stan ever took it very seriously. But his father had just died and he'd been left the farm and a whole pile of debts, so he was looking around for someone with money who might make him a wife. The Leacocks were comfortably off at the time, so he started calling on Amy. Old Mrs. Leacock was never that keen on the match. Stan was as poor as a church mouse and he'd got this reputation with women; there'd been others before Amy and she didn't think he was very steady. Anyway, Stan cleared off after a time and, if you ask me, I think he'd had enough of her. She wasn't a bad-looking girl, then, although you'd never think it to look at her now; a bit on the plump side but pretty hair and quite good features. But right stuck-up and fancied herself a cut above everybody else because her father had a shop and she'd had piano lessons. Poor old Stan used to turn up at their place in his best suit with his boots polished and his hair combed flat and they'd go out walking together, all prim and proper. They'd never have suited. Anyway, I reckon it was him who'd had enough and the next thing we know he's calling on a young widow out at Latching with two children and a bit of money her husband had left her. That came to nothing either, but Amy was furious, the silly little cat. And to make matters worse, old Mrs. Spurgeon had been going round the village saying she was glad she wasn't going to have Amy as a daughter-in-law. That put the tin lid on it and Amy was all for suing the pair of them, Stan for breach of promise and his mother for slander."

"And did she?" Rudd asked, fascinated.

"Not her," said old Mrs. Turnbull contemptuously. "When it came to it, she lost her nerve, although she did go as far as seeing a solicitor in Market Stratton. It all died down in the end, but it spoilt any chances Amy had of marrying someone else. None of the other young men would risk asking her out in case she had him up in court, so you might say she cut off her nose to spite her face."

"And Gilbert never married either?" Rudd asked.

"I've never got to the bottom of him," Mrs. Turnbull admitted. "Although I had an uncle like him who stayed single. There's some men born to be bachelors. Maybe they're afraid of women or don't like them, I wouldn't know. But Gilbert's always been a bit of a loner. I remember going past the school many a time and seeing him standing in the playground all by himself. Not that he seemed to mind. He's one of those people who don't seem to need company, they're happiest on their own. Mind you, he's had his bellyful of women over the years, what with his mother and then his sister. His father, poor man, was nagged into his grave. He was the quiet type, like Gilbert, and Mrs. Leacock treated him like a servant. It was 'do this, do that' from morning to night."

A faint cry from downstairs interrupted the conversation.

"That'll be my Wally with the tea," said Mrs. Turnbull and Holbrook, who had been sitting quietly at the foot of the bed listening, got up and went downstairs.

Rudd glanced casually out of the window.

"You've got a fine view of the lane," he remarked.

"That's one reason why I like being up here," Mrs. Turnbull replied. "I can see a bit of life, not that they'd be able to get me down the stairs now. I saw your lot arriving this afternoon; a van load of bobbies. They've parked out in the lane now."

"You must be able to see everybody who goes past," said Rudd, thinking of the footpath that led from behind the church. "Can you remember seeing anybody going past fairly recently, somebody who doesn't live in the cottages?"

"How recently?" she asked. "I see them all but I can't be expected to remember every one of them."

"In the last fortnight?" suggested Rudd.

"That's a tall order," she said. "It may be a quiet little lane with not much going on, but there's a good few pass by, especially on a Sunday, going to church."

"What about a weekday?" Rudd asked. "Can you remember any person you saw in the past two weeks?"

She leaned back against the pillows and closed her eyes for a few seconds. The eyelids, thin-skinned and delicately creased, had a bluish tinge to them.

"There was Mrs. Tingley and Mrs. Martin," she said, opening her eyes again. "That'd be on the Fridays. They do the brasses and the flowers in the church. And old Charlie who helps tidy up the churchyard, but he might go by any day. He pleases himself. Someone called at the rectory in a car; insurance, I'd say; he had a brief-case. The doctor's been a couple of times to the end cottage; there's a child there with measles. And Miss Leacock went past to do the family grave."

"Oh yes," said Rudd. "I saw her myself. That'd be last Wednesday."

"And the week before that," said Mrs. Turnbull. "I said to Wally, she'll scrub the lettering off that stone one of these days."

Holbrook came up with the tea-tray at that moment and Rudd gave him a quick glance, full of warning. The Sergeant took the hint and, placing the tray on the wash-stand, quietly poured out the tea without speaking.

"Which day was that?" asked Rudd.

"I can't say for sure. It was early on in the week, maybe the Tuesday, but it could have been another day. You should have asked me sooner. I might have remembered better, but it's more than a fortnight ago now."

Rudd silently wished he had asked her earlier.

"But you definitely saw her twice recently?" Rudd asked. "Once last week and once the week before?"

"That's right," Mrs. Turnbull said. She fixed the Inspector with a bright knowing look. "You seem very interested in what Amy Leacock gets up to."

"I'm only checking a few dates," he replied. "And both times you got the impression she was going to tidy up the grave?"

"She was carrying a bucket and that little rubber mat of hers rolled up under her arm, so she'd likely be."

"Of course," said Rudd. "Can you remember how long she was gone both times?"

"It was about an hour but I couldn't say for sure. I didn't look at the time."

"Well, what about a cup of tea?" said Rudd, dropping the subject.

Holbrook, on cue, passed the cups and they talked for a little longer. From time to time, Mrs. Turnbull turned an inquiring look at Rudd but he smiled and chatted and pretended not to notice. Eventually she seemed to forget about his questions and shortly after Rudd took his leave.

But if he thought she had forgotten, he was soon corrected. As he was leaving and was bending down to take her hand, she said, "You'd be wrong to set much store on her doing the grave twice. She'd not been by for several weeks before that and there'd be a lot of tidying up to do."

"I expect there would be," Rudd replied, smiling down at her, "and it looked very nice when she'd finished."

Outside, Holbrook and Rudd parted in the lane, Holbrook to continue his house-to-house inquiries. The Sergeant was clearly longing to discuss with Rudd what he had learned from the interview but the Inspector was not going to be drawn. Rudd watched him walk back to his car, a little heavy-footed and round-shouldered, as if dispirited.

As soon as he had gone, Rudd walked briskly down the path to the Youngmans' cottage. There was one question that he wanted to ask of Mrs. Youngman and he had given it some considerable thought.

She showed him into the little parlour. Rudd noticed that she looked better, more relaxed and less anxious. She even managed a tentative smile.

"There's only one small point I'd like to clear up," he said, refusing a chair. "And it's this: did Mrs. King ever say recently that she'd manage to run the flat without your help?"

Mrs. Youngman's reply was immediate.

"Oh, no," she said. "Whatever gave you that idea? She'd've liked me to do a bit extra some days but I couldn't oblige, not with my own family to see to."

"I see," said Rudd cheerfully. "Well, that's all, Mrs. Youngman. I don't think I shall need to trouble you again."

He walked away, leaving her at the door with a puzzled expression on her face. But Rudd had seen and heard enough to convince him finally of her innocence, even if Roland King's evidence had not already done so. Nobody, certainly not Mrs. Youngman, could have produced that look of genuine surprise when asked that question. Mrs. Youngman clearly had no fear of dismissal. It ruled her out of the case entirely.

From her cottage, Rudd drove straight to Spurgeon's farm. The yard gate was open and Spurgeon, helped by Kenny, was driving half-a-dozen rather poor-looking cows in from the adjoining pasture for evening milking. Rudd went straight up to him.

"I want a word with you," he said firmly.

"I've got cows to milk," said Spurgeon. He seemed in a sulky mood.

"They'll have to wait," said Rudd. "If you're sensible, this won't take long."

"It hadn't better," grumbled Spurgeon. "I'm working mornings for Fred Bailey and I can't see to my own work and spare much time to talk to you. Do you want to go into the house?"

Rudd looked at Kenny, who was regarding them both with a flicker of apprehension in his eyes.

"I think that's best," he replied.

Rudd came straight to the point.

"I want the truth, Mr. Spurgeon," he said.

"What about?" the farmer replied belligerently. "I ain't told you no lies, except about the money and you didn't ask about that anyway."

"It's not about the money," said Rudd. "It's about the mushrooms you took to Mrs. King."

"I told you the truth," Spurgeon said slowly.

"No, you didn't," retorted Rudd. "You told me part of the truth. And now I want it all. I noticed the first time I was here and asked you about it, you hesitated. I want to know why. Or we can do it the hard way and go over what you said step by step until we come to the real facts. What's it to be?"

Spurgeon looked at him and wiped his hand across his mouth.

"It wasn't far off the truth," he said sulkily.

"Oh, for God's sake, man, come out with it!" cried Rudd.

Spurgeon sat himself down in the worn armchair by the fire. He avoided Rudd's eyes and gazed into the hearth.

"All right then, I'll tell you. But I can't see how it makes a happorth of difference. Like I said, I picked the mushrooms in the morning and put the basket out on the table by the roadside, but I went back later that evening and picked a few more."

"You're still not telling me the whole truth," said Rudd. "Why did you trouble to cover up something as unimportant as that? Or shall I tell you?"

He waited but Spurgeon refused to speak or raise his head. Rudd continued, "You lied because you didn't want to seem mean, because some of those last mushrooms you picked weren't in fact growing, were they? You found them lying on the ground and you didn't like to admit you'd picked them up as they might not have been as fresh as the others?"

"So what if I did?" Spurgeon asked, looking up at last. Now the truth was spoken he seemed ready to brazen it out. "There wasn't no real harm. The old horse kicks them up sometimes and providing they ain't been squashed, I put them in with the others."

"No harm," said Rudd, "except what you picked up loose from the ground that evening weren't mushrooms."

The farmer stared at him and then said "Oh, my God!" and put a hand to his face.

"You'd better show me where you found them," said Rudd.

Spurgeon got up silently and preceded the Inspector out of the house, through the yard and up the slope of the meadow. He paused at the top of the field, about ten feet in from the boundary of the wood, near to the oak tree where Boyce had stood.

"It was about here," said Spurgeon. "I'd picked most of the good 'uns from the lower part of the field that morning and come the evening, after we'd had our tea from them, there weren't enough left for Mrs. King. There was only half a basket, so I went back up the field and picked a few more. The loose 'uns were lying about here."

"How many?" asked Rudd.

"Only a couple," Spurgeon said. His tone was eager and apologising as if the small number of them was an excuse.

"Were they small ones?" Finch asked.

"Yes, they were just like button mushrooms. I saw them lying in the grass and I didn't give them a second thought."

"Thank you," said Rudd wearily. "That's all I want to know. I may have to ask you to come into headquarters sometime to make a statement."

He started to walk off down the field. Spurgeon hurried after him.

"But who put them there?" he asked. "Was it Kenny? If it was him, he'd not have done it deliberate. He'd've just picked them and thrown them down, not thinking, like."

"No," said Rudd. "It wasn't Kenny. You can set your mind at rest there."

They came to the gate that led into the yard. Spurgeon suddenly stopped and leaned against it, his hand over his face.

"I'll never forgive myself," he said. There was a rough catch in his voice as if he was choking. Rudd put his hand out as if to touch him on the shoulder and then withdrew it.

"You weren't to blame," he said.

"It was my fault," Spurgeon repeated. "I should have left them bloody things lying there. I knew they weren't fresh and I had to bloody pick them up all the same and because of that she died."

Rudd humped his shoulders. He could think of nothing to say to the man.

A mournful lowing sound came from the shed.

"You'd better see to your cows," said Rudd.

Spurgeon straightened up and followed Rudd into the yard.

"You're keeping on with the farm, then?" Rudd asked, for the sake of something to say.

"I told you I would," Spurgeon replied. "I'm not selling up."

"Well, good luck with it," said Rudd.

There was a fleeting return of Spurgeon's old ironic expression.

"You must be bloody joking," he replied and turned and walked away.

14

Rudd drove a little way up the road and then, parking his car in a gateway, got out and leaned over the gate. From where he was standing, he had a view across the fields to the distant tower of Abbots Stacey church, just visible among the elm trees that surrounded it, and a few slanting angles that he knew to be the roofs of houses.

The wind had dropped and a great calm lay over the countryside, the peace of an autumn evening, with a chill to the air and a faint smoky quality about the atmosphere that rose from the damp fields. The summer was definitely over. The far clumps of trees no longer had the rounded shapes of the high season, quilted with leaves. Now their intricate structures of branches and twigs were visible and the grass in the fields had a shabby look, as the lush growth died down.

Rudd lit a cigarette and folded both arms along the top bar of the gate. His immobility was part of the landscape, of the still hedges and patient trees. But his mind was busy. In his imagination he was following someone, across the fields, to the wood, through the wood to the little clearing where the Death Cap fungus pushed its rounded head through the dead leaves of last summer.

It all fitted. Means, Motive. Opportunity. All he lacked was proof. Without bothering to unfold his arms, Rudd dropped the smouldering butt of his cigarette between his feet and trod on it. Then he got back into the car and drove through the grey-blue smoky light of the gathering dusk towards the village.

The police van had gone from the lane. Boyce was just leaving, too. Rudd flashed his headlights at him as a signal to stop and then beckoned the Sergeant over to the car. Boyce got in beside him.

"Any luck?" asked Rudd, although he knew already from Boyce's face that there hadn't been.

"We found about half a hundredweight of waste paper," Boyce replied, "an assortment of old metal, including several beer cans and a bicycle chain. Two old shoes. One French letter, used. And a very dead rabbit."

"No evidence," said Rudd. He pinched his eyelids wearily between his finger and thumb.

"I suppose you'll want me out fingerprinting again tomorrow," Boyce said gloomily.

"No," said Rudd. "It's all over. I know who did it but I don't think I'll ever make it stick."

"Who?" asked Boyce, half-turning in his eagerness.

Rudd told him.

"And there's not one single scrap of evidence," he concluded.

Boyce said, "But there's still the library book. There might be prints on that."

"Maybe," replied Rudd. "But even if there are, borrowing a library book, even on someone else's ticket, isn't a crime. And I can't use Old Bill's evidence. It's too vague. I've got a beautiful theory, Tom, that I'm damned sure is the right one and I can't prove it."

"Something may turn up later," Boyce said optimistically.

"You must be joking," Rudd replied and then remembered they were the same words that Spurgeon had used.

"You get home, Tom," Rudd continued. "You've had a hard day. I'll see this through to the end."

There was one long shot that he had left. It might pay off. It had been known to happen before.

Boyce got out of the car and Rudd turned in the narrow lane, his headlamps glittering briefly on the windows of the Youngmans' and the Turnbulls' cottages. There was a bitter scent in the air of burning leaves.

The Leacocks' shop was closed, the blind drawn down over the glass panel in the door. Rudd rapped loudly on it several times and, at last, a light sprang up in the shop and someone fumbled at the bolts.

Gilbert Leacock's head appeared cautiously round the doorframe.

"We're closed," he said.

"I want to speak to you and your sister," Rudd replied.

"Oh, it's you," said Leacock, recognising the Inspector. "I suppose you'd better come in. We're just finishing supper."

He had taken off his overall and appeared unfamiliar in a brown woollen cardigan that had dropped in an irregular line round the hem.

Rudd followed him through the shop, dimly lit by the one bulb that had been switched on over the counter. The smell of the shop was stronger in the semi-darkness, the musky odour of old wood and plaster mixed with the sharper, newer smell of paraffin and paint.

In contrast, the room beyond was brightly lit and smelt of warm gas and food. The table had been cleared of plates but the white table-cloth was still in place, harshly bright under the ceiling light.

Amy Leacock was sitting at the table, her head turned to see who it was that had been knocking on the shop door so late, her expression ready to be suspicious of such an unexpected caller.

"It's the Inspector, Amy," said Leacock. "He wants to speak to both of us."

"You'd better sit down then," she said.

Leacock made as if he was about to pull the table away from the wall as he had done at the first interview but Rudd had no intention of saying what had to be said sitting squashed up behind it. He drew out one of the upright chairs so that it was back to the sideboard and sat down firmly on it, facing the pair of them. Gilbert Leacock, after a moment's hesitation, sat down at the table and placed his fingertips on the cloth. He seemed about to say something but Rudd crossed his legs sharply and the sudden movement silenced him.

"I'm making inquiries into the ownership of a typewriter," Rudd began. "Do either of you possess one?"

"No," said Amy Leacock. "We don't."

"We used to, though," said Gilbert Leacock, with an air of being helpful. "An old portable one that belonged to my father. It's upstairs in the attic."

"That? I threw it out," snapped Amy.

"When?" asked Rudd.

"I don't remember," she replied. "Quite a time ago."

"A year? Two years?" persisted Rudd.

"Is it important?" asked Gilbert Leacock. One hand had come up to hold his chin and the listening air that Rudd had noticed before was quite pronounced.

Rudd said nothing but tilted his head towards Miss Leacock.

"It was some time last spring," she replied.

"And what did you do with it?" Rudd asked.

"I put it in the dustbin," she said.

"Oh, Amy," said Leacock reproachfully. "You shouldn't have done that. We could've sent it to the church jumble sale."

"It was broken," she said. "It wasn't working properly."

Rudd felt like a spectator watching a game, the rules of which he was not yet sure of, although he now understood the point of it.

"The dustmen might remember seeing it, then?" he asked.

"I doubt it," she replied. "It was in a box along with a lot of other stuff I cleared out at the same time. Including your old stamp catalogues," she added, looking at her brother.

"I might have needed those sometime," he said mournfully.

"Well, they've gone now," she said.

One point to her. Leacock ducked his head sideways.

Rudd settled back in his chair. He was more sure of himself now. A kind of relaxed awareness came over him, like a tennis player who, after a few shots, has got his eye in and can judge the pace and flight of the ball.

"And I suppose you threw out at the same time any papers that had been typed on?" he asked.

"I expect so," she replied. "I gave the attic a good turn out."

"No samples left at all?" asked Rudd. "Nobody in the village likely to have a letter, say, or a bill that was typed out on it?

Her eyes met his.

"I wouldn't know," she said.

"Then I'll have to ask, won't I?" said Rudd pleasantly.

"What's all this leading up to?" asked Leacock. The tips of his fingers were pressed down on the cloth, splaying out the pads so that they were white round the nails.

"Just routine inquiries," said Rudd. "And while I'm here, I'd just like to check again on the question of library membership. I am right in thinking, aren't I, that neither of you belong to the library at Market Stratton, or had occasion to borrow a book from it recently?"

"You asked us that before," said Leacock.

"I'm asking you again," said Rudd.

"The answer's no," said Leacock.

Rudd looked at Miss Leacock, who merely shook her head. Her face had a puckered-up, closed tightness about it that reminded Rudd of a clenched hand. Leacock was leaning forward with that listening, deaf person's intentness. Rudd saw him give his sister a quick sideways glance but she showed no sign of having seen it.

"Is that all?" asked Leacock.

"Oh, no," said Rudd. "It's by no means all. There's the question of the footpath, the one that runs behind the church to Copse End. You know the one I mean?"

"Yes," said Leacock.

"And you?" Rudd asked of his sister.

"You've already asked me that once," she said.

"So I did," said Rudd. "It skirts the little wood behind Stan Spurgeon's farm. I don't suppose either of you have used it recently?"

"Not for years," said Leacock. He was more relaxed now. He even permitted himself one of his little tucked-in, superior smiles.

"Of course not," said Rudd. "You haven't the time. But I expect you used it as children? Blackberrying? Or blue-belling?"

"Nutting," said Leacock promptly. "There's a lot of hazel trees in the wood. We used to pick them. Do you remember, Amy?"

"That was years ago," she said.

"Do you remember seeing anyone going along that foot-path recently when you were in the churchyard tending your parents' grave?"

"I can't say I do," she replied. "Only you, that afternoon."

"I was thinking about the other occasion," said Rudd. "About eight days before that."

"What occasion?" she snapped.

"Didn't I make it clear?" asked Rudd. "I'm sorry. I'll start again. I'm talking about the week beginning September 7th, the week that Mrs. King died."

"I don't remember," she replied.

"You don't remember the occasion or you don't remember seeing anyone going along the footpath?" Rudd asked.

"I don't remember the occasion," she said.

"Oh, I see," said Rudd on a note of faint surprise.

"I can't be expected to remember everything I did all those days ago," she said.

"Quite," said Rudd reasonably. "But if someone said they

saw you going to the churchyard one day that week with your cleaning things, then you'd accept that you must have done so?"

"Which day?" she snapped.

"Any day," said Rudd.

"And who said so?"

"Someone who saw you."

"Well, I can't recall it."

"But you remember seeing me on the second occasion when I spoke to you in the churchyard?" Rudd asked.

"Yes, I remember that."

"You'd been scrubbing the headstone," said Rudd, "and pulling up grass from the grave."

"I like to keep it tidy," she replied.

"Quite long grass," said Rudd. "I saw it in a little pile beside the path."

She did not reply and Rudd, after waiting for her to speak, went on, "Did you pull up the grass the time before when you tidied up the grave?"

"I've already told you, I don't remember," she replied.

"And scrub the headstone?" Rudd persisted.

She kept her lips tight shut.

"I don't see what you're driving at," said Leacock in a soft voice.

"Don't you?" said Rudd. "I think your sister understands the implications only too well."

He looked across at her and she returned his gaze defiantly. For several seconds their eyes held. She would never give in, Rudd realised. Any hope he might have had of breaking her down was gone. She would brazen it out to the end. Perhaps she knew, or guessed, that he had no proof. He could have left it here, got up and gone away, but a perverse sense of honour, of seeing it through to the end, even though there would be no victory, made him go on.

"Do you want me to explain?" he asked. "Mrs. King died as the indirect result of fungus poisoning. There is no disputing that fact. The only facts that were in question were whether she had died accidentally or, if not, who had killed her. I have the answer to both of those questions now."

He saw them exchange glances, Amy first with a hard, disbelieving look, answered by her brother with a little pursed-up smile.

"It's a story with its roots in the past," Rudd continued. "It doesn't make sense otherwise. It began about twenty years ago when Stan Spurgeon came courting you, Miss Leacock."

He saw her open her mouth to speak.

"If you're not prepared to listen to me," warned Rudd, "I can make this interview official. I can send for a squad car and have you taken in to headquarters. I don't think you'd like that very much. May I go on? Well, as I was saying, Mr. Spurgeon came here courting you and you began walking out together, as the saying is. Then Stan Spurgeon's attentions ceased. We needn't go into the reasons. I expect, as happens in such cases, there was more than one. Your mother objected, I believe, and perhaps he was afraid of committing himself too far. Anyway, people talked about it as they were bound to do in a small place like this. Your pride was hurt, wasn't it, Miss Leacock? You, the daughter of a local tradesman being let down by a good-for-nothing, penniless farmer. You made up your mind to get your own back. You even went as far as to threaten him with a breach of promise case and then you withdrew. So far but no farther. It was a revenge that didn't quite make the grade. And then Stan Spurgeon married and that was that.

"Now we come to more recent times. About three years ago, Mrs. King moved into the village; a widow, comfortably off, with her own little business and modern flat, and Mrs. Youngman coming in every day to do the housework. I wonder what you really thought when you went round to her flat to play cards? I think I know. She had so much, didn't she? Fitted carpets and a fridge, a new bathroom suite and nice furniture. As soon as she died, you made it your business to acquire some of those things for yourself, her bedside lamp and pink eiderdown. I saw you carrying them out of the auction rooms.

"But Mrs. King had something more besides: Stan Spurgeon's attention. He was always taking her little presents; half a dozen eggs, a basket of soft fruit or mushrooms. There was talk. There's always talk. People thought she'd be a fool to marry him. Oh, I know he's not divorced. And I don't think he wants a divorce. He's quite happy as he is, just as Mrs. King was quite happy as she was. But that didn't stop the gossip, linking their names. And it didn't stop you from seeing them laughing and joking together. He'd once walked out with you and yet there he was, all friendly with Mrs. King who had so much anyway, and people wondering whether they might get married one day. It brought it all back, didn't it, the pain and the hurt pride of the other time, twenty years before, when he'd turned you down?"

Her mouth opened very slightly but she made no reply. Her eyes were fixed on Rudd's face with a kind of mesmerised fascination. Leacock's face could not be seen. He had cupped one hand round his chin and his fingers were spread out to cover the side of his face.

"At one of the Wednesday evening card parties you overheard Stan Spurgeon promise Mrs. King some mushrooms the next time he saw her. He wasn't very honest about them. He told me first of all that he'd picked them that morning. That was rather confusing. But today he came out with the truth. He'd gone back that evening to pick some more to fill up the basket and he found one or two lying on the ground. Naturally, he didn't want to be thought mean so he didn't let on about it. After all, nobody likes to admit taking mushrooms to a friend that might not be quite fresh, ones that a horse had kicked up, or so Stan thought. So he picked them up and said nothing. That was on the Wednesday before Rene King died.

"But let's go back to the day before, to the Tuesday. I think it must be the Tuesday. I'm right, about that, I'm sure. You set off with your cleaning things to tidy up the grave. So far so good. Some time that same afternoon, as I believe, Old Bill, the tramp, who was sitting behind the hedge at the back of Stan Spurgeon's farm, glanced up and saw someone in a dark hat come to the edge of the wood and make a gesture with an arm, like this."

Rudd repeated the throwing movement.

"It was my Sergeant who suggested a child bowling underarm. Now children aren't the only ones who throw a ball that way. Ever noticed a woman bowling to a kid in cricket? No? Well, take my word for it, they invariably bowl underarm. I've watched them on the beach. A man usually throws overarm. So, I think to myself, it's probably a woman. But what was the woman throwing? Certainly not a ball. Fungus, then? I think that's what it was. In fact, I'm certain that's what it was because Stan Spurgeon found the loose mushrooms, as he thought, lying in the field a few yards from the place where Old Bill had seen this mysterious person standing.

"So, it was a woman, I tell myself. A woman in a dark hat, a bit like a trilby, as Old Bill described it. Who could it possibly be? And then I came up with the answer. It was you, Miss Leacock.

"I got some more useful information this afternoon, about your visit that week to the churchyard and I also happened to remember that I'd seen you myself, only just over a week later, tidying up the grave. Twice, I thought? But the grass you'd pulled up was quite long and there was lichen on the headstone. Grass doesn't grow that quickly at this time of the year, and lichen certainly doesn't. Which led me to the conclusion that your previous visit to the grave hadn't been very productive, not if it wanted weeding and the stone wanted scrubbing only ten days or so later. So I asked myself, if Miss Leacock hadn't been tidying up the grave that afternoon, what had she been doing? And I think I know the answer. You had been walking across the fields by the footpath, entering the wood, picking the fungus and then throwing it away again. Well, I thought, that's not criminal. There's no case to answer. There's no law to stop people from picking things in woods, even if they are poisonous, and then chucking them away. It was the revenge fantasy again, wasn't it? Like you did with the breach of promise case, going so far and yet not all the way? You'd thought up a nice scheme to punish Mrs. King and then you changed your mind at the last moment. Am I right?"

"It's all a pack of lies," she said.

Rudd ignored her.

"But then I got to thinking about it a bit more carefully. I stood leaning over a gate this evening and I imagined you in that wood, in your black hat and your dark tweed coat, bending down, picking some of the fungus that looked so much like button mushrooms that anyone would be fooled into eating them. I saw you with them in your hand and I imagined you changing your mind and throwing them away. But, you see, Miss Leacock, I have to go on facts and the facts tell me that you walked, with the fungus in your hand, to the edge of the wood twenty feet away, through low-growing scrub and brambles and then you threw them away into the field. I pictured the scene. I imagined the smoke from Old Bill's fire behind the hedge, and the horse, and you in your black hat throwing the fungus as far as you could. And I asked myself, why? Why, if you'd changed your mind, didn't you just throw them down where you'd picked them, or chuck them under the nearest bush? Why go to the trouble of making your way twenty feet to the edge of the wood to throw them away in the field where the mushrooms were growing? It didn't make sense. If you wanted to revenge yourself on Mrs. King, it was a clumsy way of going about it. You couldn't be certain she'd get those particular fungus. You couldn't be certain that Stan Spurgeon would pick them up, or, even if he did, whether they'd be eaten by him or his mother or his child. And then it dawned on me that it didn't matter."

All the time that he had been speaking, she had been looking at him, her expression closed and sullen, as if she was listening unwillingly to something that did not concern her. Now, as he said those last words, Rudd saw a tremor pass over her face and a gleam of recognition come into her eyes and he knew that she had, in that moment, learned the truth about herself and come to a sudden and terrible understanding of her own hidden motives. The black-columned clock on the mantelpiece ticked slowly and Rudd felt the atmosphere in the room thicken until it had an almost tangible quality that enclosed the pair of them. Gilbert Leacock, forgotten, remained outside the circle of their silent and intense concentration.

There was still a chance, Rudd told himself with a quickening sense of power and triumph, that he could break her. In her new awareness of herself she might give in and admit the truth. He felt his own willpower, like a steel point, bore into hers.

He said softly, "You persuaded yourself, didn't you, that you were doing nothing wrong? You were simply throwing the fungus away. But you realise now, don't you, that deep down you hoped someone would suffer? There was more than one old grudge to pay off: Stan Spurgeon for turning you down; Mrs. Spurgeon who had gone round the village saying she was glad her son wasn't going to marry you; Mrs. King who had so much when it seemed you had so little. Even the child, Kenny Spurgeon, didn't matter in your reckoning, or did you see him as the means by which Stan Spurgeon's wife had trapped him into marriage when you had failed. Eeny, meeny, miny, mo, and if someone got counted out, then you told yourself you weren't to blame. All you had done was to throw the fungus away in the field and if it got picked up, it wasn't your fault. But as bad luck would have it, it did get picked up and was put in with the mushrooms that Stan Spurgeon took to Mrs. King. Can you now go on telling yourself that you're not guilty of her death?"

He stopped and looked hard at her. The tremor which had passed over her face and made her fat cheeks tremble had gone. The closed, tight expression had returned and although she could no longer meet his eyes, Rudd realised he had lost the last chance of forcing a confession out of her. Her pride was stronger than her sense of guilt. He could see it in her rigid mouth and the inflexible angle of her head even as she turned away.

"Not guilty, Miss Leacock?" Rudd repeated.

It was Gilbert Leacock who spoke.

"I suppose you realise these are very serious accusations?" he said.

"Oh, yes," said Rudd. "They are. Very serious indeed."

Amy said, "Say nothing. He can't prove anything."

"There's the tramp," said Rudd.

"He couldn't . . ." she began, and then shut her mouth like a trap.

"See you?" suggested Rudd. "Because he was behind the hedge? But he certainly saw somebody. Then there's the little matter of the library book, *British Mushrooms and Toadstools*, which was borrowed from the Market Stratton public library shortly before Mrs. King died and which fell open on the page about the Death Cap fungus. And then there's Mrs. King's library ticket that someone so kindly sent to me, and two anonymous letters, one handwritten and one typed. It was the handwritten one that first suggested Mrs. King had been murdered. Then there's fingerprints and saliva tests and handwriting experts."

"Fingerprints?" said Leacock. His tongue glistened along his lower lip.

"Not on the letter you sent me," said Rudd. "You were careful to wipe the paper clean."

The remark, spoken so casually, fell into a great silence in the room.

Leacock half-rose from his chair but Rudd waved him to sit down.

"Don't bother to deny it," Rudd said. "I know it must be true. It's the only answer that fits. You were playing your own revenge game, Leacock, and, as the winner, you had the chance of quite a good prize. Peace. You wanted to see the back of your sister, didn't you? Or you hoped you might.

So you dropped little hints and took little steps and wondered how far you'd have to go, like in that kid's game, before the big, bad wolf of an Inspector shouted 'Dinnertime' and turned round and made a grab at her. It was you who sent that first letter, of that I'm certain, and the library ticket that Miss Leacock had seen lying around Mrs. King's flat and had helped herself to in order to borrow a book about fungus from the library. What first put you on to her? Did you find the book in the house? Did you then hunt about and find the ticket later? You see, it was you who remembered that your sister had left the room to fill up the milk-jug. Perhaps, like me, you were convinced that the fungus had been put in with the mushrooms some time that evening. And you couldn't resist the hint. And it was you who remembered the old typewriter up in the attic, which your sister so conveniently got rid of last spring. What did you do with it, Miss Leacock, after you'd typed out the letter accusing Mrs. Youngman of stealing from the shop? Dump it somewhere?"

Amy had turned to look at her brother. Her face was expressive of so much hatred that Rudd averted his eyes.

Leacock was spluttering, "That's a monstrous suggestion! I didn't write any letters! I shall ask for legal advice."

"Do that," said Rudd. He had had enough of both of them. "But I don't think any solicitor would advise you to take legal action. You see, you don't know what cards I still hold in my hand. And you might find the publicity unpleasant. But if, like your sister, you want to play the revenge game further, then go ahead. I'm willing to bet, though, that you won't take the final step."

The Inspector stood up and pulled down his jacket sleeves.

"You see, the game may not yet be over," he said. "There's still a few more moves I could make. I've had the wood searched today and the footpath leading to it. I could get a warrant to have this place searched for the typewriter. Or the whole damned village if need be. I could have every pond dragged and every rubbish tip dug over. I could have the pair of you put up for identification, by the tramp or the library staff. I could have your fingerprints taken and handwriting tests made. I shall certainly have you both in to make a statement. The file on Mrs. King isn't closed and it never will be. And while it's still open, there's always the chance someone may come forward with fresh evidence. Or there's always yourselves."

Rudd cocked his head at Leacock.

"How much do you really know or were you only guessing? I can tell you one thing for certain, you won't get much peace now, will you?"

He walked to the door.

"I shall be sending a squad car over tomorrow morning to bring you both in to make statements. I advise you to think very carefully about what you will say, I'll see myself out."

Their faces were turned towards him, Amy Leacock's tightly shut, her mouth nothing more than a thin line; Gilbert Leacock's ducked down, looking at him with that nervous, fluttering spasm of his eyelashes. Then they turned to look at each other and it was in that exchange of glances, so briefly glimpsed by Rudd before he left the room, that his satisfaction rested.

He had no proof and there was small chance that a charge could ever be brought. But there was a justice, after all, beyond the law, beyond judges and lawyers, beyond the sentencing of the courts; a justice that the village would mete out when the police car was seen the next day outside their door; and a justice that Rudd recognised in the faces of the brother and sister as they looked at each other.

ABOUT THE AUTHOR

JUNE THOMSON's other Detective Rudd novels include *A Question of Identity*, *The Habit of Loving*, *Case Closed* and *The Long Revenge*. She lives in the beautiful Essex countryside outside of London.

INSPECTOR RUDD
Books by June Thomson

June Thomson is a highly praised British mystery writer whose series of books features Inspector Rudd, a likeable policeman who cleverly but without a great deal of flash, investigates and solves unusual murders in English towns. The following are the first American paperback appearances of Ms Thomson's books.

DEATH CAP

In the quiet Essex village of Abbots Stacy, Detective Inspector Rudd of the local CID becomes involved with murder—someone has slipped a poisonous mushroom in Rene King's food. Rudd is at his wits end until he discovers a piece of village gossip that had long ago been swept under the carpet.

THE HABIT OF LOVING

This time Inspector Rudd's case involves a bizarre triangle —Maggie Hearn, a middle-aged spinster who has befriended handsome young Chris Lambert and Jess Lambert, a beautiful young girl who has a date with death.

A QUESTION OF IDENTITY

When the local archaeological society asks permission to excavate a meadow they hope to find bones. They do. However they are the badly decomposed remains of more recent vintage. The only clue is a corroded cross on a chain. Rudd's investigation leads to a man who had disappeared several years before.

Read these Bantam Books by June Thomson, available wherever paperbacks are sold.

A Special Preview of
the pulse-pounding opening pages of

THE
ROSARY MURDERS

By WILLIAM KIENZLE

"I do believe the Rabbi will have to move over—and make way for Father Koesler. The book is well-paced, tightly written, exciting as hell . . . the best mystery I've read in years."

—*Dallas Times Herald*

Monday, February 28

"Was it an interesting funeral?"

Father Bob Koesler stubbed out his third afterdinner cigarette. Dinners at old St. Ursula's rectory were painfully elongated experiences for Koesler for the simple reason that he tore through his food like a starving European child, while Father Paul Pompilio, pastor at St. Ursula's, toyed with his.

Father Pompilio carefully cut a sliver of meat from his porterhouse, placed the knife beside his plate, transferred the fork from his left hand to his right, and began to swirl the meat in its juice. "Not particularly. You've seen one priest's funeral, you've seen 'em all."

Koesler lit another cigarette. There were a million places he'd rather be, but, for politeness' sake, he always waited until Pompilio finished eating. Which was always a good forty-five minutes after Koesler finished. Which was not helping Koesler's effort to cut down on cigarettes.

"Was Monsignor O'Brien there?"

Pompilio's fork and knife were resting on his plate as he thoughtfully chewed a morsel of steak. "Old O'Brien? It wouldn't have been a valid priest's funeral without O'Brien. He was there, all right, from the first psalm of the Office for the Dead until they wheeled the body out the door. They were great buddies, you know." Pompilio resumed knife and fork and began sawing away at another cut of meat. "Old Father Larry Lord and O'Brien. Funny thing. Before they closed the lid on the casket, O'Brien tried on Lord's glasses—took them right off the old man's face and tried 'em on. Looked around the church, decided his own were better, put the glasses back on Lord, and went back to his pew like nothing happened. It's a good thing O'Brien didn't need teeth."

Koesler's stomach turned. He was glad he'd finished eating. Pompilio built a forkful of mashed potatoes.

"How was the sermon?" Koesler asked, crushing out his fourth afterdinner cigarette. He had tried early on to monopolize dinner conversations on the chance that, with nothing to do but eat, Pompilio would finish sooner. But by actual measured time, Koesler had discovered that it didn't make any difference.

"The arch is out of town, as you know . . ." Pompilio speared his last sliver of meat. ". . . so Bishop Donnelly gave the sermon. Same old Donnelly stuff, very spiritual. Told how Lord had died on Ash Wednesday. How significant that was. Can't see it myself. Good Friday, maybe. But Ash Wednesday just isn't a very significant day to die. By the way . . ." Pompilio shoved aside his well-scoured plate and tinkled the small bell that stood next to it. Sophie, five feet in every direction, entered the room, cleared the table, and served coffee. ". . . why weren't you at the funeral?"

Koesler lit another cigarette. "Couldn't. Had negotiations with the newspaper guild. Contract's up in another couple of months."

Koesler was priest-editor of the diocesan weekly paper. He wasn't exactly assigned to St. Ursula's. He was in residence there, said Mass daily and Sundays, heard confessions, helped out as much as he could. But his primary assignment was at the paper. He sipped his black coffee. "Did anyone say anything about the plug?"

"Plug? What plug?" Pompilio stirred the third spoonful of sugar into his coffee.

"Come on, Pomps," Koesler chuckled. "You know there's a rumor that somebody at St. Mary's Hospital pulled the plug on Lord. Not that anyone, including God, would mind. The poor old guy had no place to go but out."

"Now that you mention it, there was some talk about that rumor at the priests' brunch after the funeral. Say, Bob, if you print any of this," Pompilio was grinning from ear to ear, "you will protect your sources, won't you?"

Koesler grinned back. Of all people on earth, Pompilio would be among those who most wanted to see their names in print. The problem, as usual, was not protecting sources but keeping the whole damn story out of the paper. He remembered just a few weeks back. Tony Vespa, the newly appointed Archdiocesan Delegate for the Laity, had called and asked if the *Detroit Catholic* would consider running an "Action Line" similar to the column in the *Free Press* that solved everybody's problems. He had explained, "Look, Tony, besides the expense of hiring a staff to run a column like that, most of the problems Catholics have with the institution don't have solutions." Tony, after careful consideration, had withdrawn his suggestion.

"Don't worry, Pomps, you'll be well protected. But, go on, did the guys at the luncheon think it really happened?"

There wasn't any question of anything like that appearing in the diocesan paper. Koesler was simply a mystery buff. He read mystery novels like some priests read the Bible. He loved a mystery. And he felt this was as close to a real-life mystery as he was likely to get.

"Disputatur apud peritos." Pompilio didn't know much Latin, but when he tripped over an appropriate phrase like "The experts are in dispute," he liked to throw it in for everyone's amazement. "Some thought yes. Others, no. Jack Battersby made a great point that according to Church teaching, nobody is bound to use extraordinary means to support life, and all those tubes and plugs certainly could be described as extraordinary. Ed Carberry, who, as you know, is still in the thirteenth, the greatest of centuries, argued that God was surely reducing Father Lord's purgatory time with all that added suffering, and to shorten his time of expiration was thwarting God's plan and so, against the Natural Law—or some damn thing—and gravely sinful."

Koesler, now bored, was about to yield to a gigantic distraction.

"However," Pompilio droned on, "Pete Baldwin's sister is a nurse at St. Mary's. And she told Pete somebody at the hospital definitely detached Lord's respirator system. And that finally put the old man out of his misery."

Koesler, alert to the first bit of genuine news, fought off his distraction. "You mean they actually know the respirator was unplugged?"

"According to Pete's sister, yes."

"Is anybody at the hospital trying to find out who did it?"

"I dunno. I get the idea that if it actually happened—and remember, Father Editor, this is still rumor—nobody at the hospital wants to know."

"Did anyone call the police?"

"I don't think so. If anybody did, there'd have to be an investigation. Pete, who seems to know more about this than I would have given him credit for, says the police couldn't sweep something like this under the rug. If they knew about it, they'd have to investigate, and if they found who did it, there'd be a prosecution. I guess nobody at the hospital wants that. Especially a Catholic hospital with a dead Catholic priest whom nobody cared about anyway."

"I'll bet they don't." For the umpteenth time, Koesler found himself wishing he belonged to a somewhat more legitimate news medium instead of being boss of what was little more than a religious house organ. Nevertheless, he felt drawn to speculate about who might have done it. He pictured a holy nun—one still covered from head to toe with yards and yards of habit—stealthily entering Lord's quiet room, looking every which way to be sure no one was watching, then, with utmost compassion, jerking the plug out of the wall socket. Then, later, in great remorse, confessing her sin. Or maybe it was an agnostic doctor strolling into Lord's room. No one around. He casually lifts his foot and kicks the plug out. Leaves the room. Thinks nothing of it. Never will.

"So the consensus seems to be that Lord's unplugged respirator is gonna be swept under the institutional rug, eh?" Koesler asked, lighting yet another cigarette. He counted the butts in the ashtray. This was his sixth. He shook his head.

"Guess so." Pompilio had finished his coffee. There was the usual residue of undissolved sugar at the bottom of his cup. He gave a little shove to the table. Nothing moved. It was just a signal that the dinner ritual was concluded. "Funny thing, though, about the rosary Lord was holding when he died."

"What's that?"

"It wasn't his."

"Wasn't his?"

"Didn't belong to him. Lord's rosary was mother-of-pearl. It was in the drawer of the table near his bed. The rosary he was holding was an ordinary black one. But I guess a rosary is a rosary is a rosary."

Nelson Kane, city editor of the *Detroit Free Press*, stood looking around his large, rectangular, well-lit city room. As usual, at least whenever he was there, the dozens of reporters seemed to be developing Pulitzer Prize—winning stories. On those rare occasions when Kane wasn't there, feet were propped on desks and typewriters, mobs formed at the coffee machine, after-hours dates were made, and gossip passed. Fortunately for the paper's welfare, Kane was usually there, barking orders and being generally unsatisfied and demanding.

Kane was looking for Joe Cox. Cox had come to the *Free Press* only three months before with an award-winning book under his belt and excellent references. For years, the *Free Press* had had no religion writer as such. Kane learned quickly from experience, and he had experienced a memory full of inaccuracies from past religion specialists. Cox was a staff writer, and a good one, who, among other things was given most of the religious assignments. He handled them well.

Cox came in and had just reached his desk when Kane spotted him.

"Cox!" Kane's practiced tone rose well above the noise of typewriters and ringing phones.

Cox smiled at his master's voice and hurried over to Kane's centrally located desk.

"Did you check that hospital lead?" Kane talked around his never-removed cigar.

"Yup."

"And?"

"And nothing. I talked to just about everyone on the floor Father Lord was on. Nurses, nuns, orderlies, nurses' aides, doctors, interns, even the chaplain. Couldn't get anything from anybody. Not even for nonattribution."

"What did your gut tell you?"

"It happened."

"Goddammit, I know it happened! Are the cops in on this at all?"

"I don't think so. I made the tour of headquarters, real slow, and nobody's movin' on it."

"Whaddya think?"

"Catholic hospital, Catholic priest, they don't wanna admit they got a problem."

"Any more leads?"

"One. There's a nurse I talked to, a . . ." Cox flipped through his small notebook "a . . . Nancy Baldwin. She just didn't seem too sure of herself."

"How's that?"

"Nobody wanted to talk about no plug in no respirator. But she hesitated. Like she really did want to talk—or already had—to somebody. I thought I'd give her a day or so and get back to her. The story's still there. All locked up in the priests' pasture at Mt. Olivet Cemetery. It won't go away."

"And it won't get so old nobody cares. Not a Catholic priest getting knocked off in a Catholic hospital. That's the closest to an eternal story we got at this goddam paper."

"Right, Nellie."

"Stay on it and keep me informed."

"Right."

Joe Cox, Kane mused, was his kind of reporter. Just as interested in and dedicated to a breaking news story as Kane ever was. With the young legs Kane no longer had.

Wednesday, March 2

It was Wednesday, the day the *Detroit Catholic* weekly newspaper was put together and sent to Brown Printing for publication. It was also one week, to the day, since Father Lawrence Lord had died at St. Mary's Hospital.

Father Koesler pondered as he paced back and forth in his cluttered office at the paper on Forest Avenue close to downtown Detroit. There had been no mention of the unplugged respirator in any of the local media. There certainly would be no mention of it in the *Detroit Catholic*. It would be a straight priest's obit, on the bottom of page one: picture, brief biography, length of service, number of buildings built, survivors, interment. In Lord's case, there would be lots of buildings but no survivors. Few besides priests and other bachelors left no survivors, Koesler mused.

Maybe there was no unplugged plug. It was, after all, just a rumor. And the other media, particularly the two daily papers, had the means to dig out the story if it were really there. If they had, it would have been the *Detroit Catholic*'s lot to react and defend the hospital in every way possible. Koesler had learned long ago that the guys in the chancery, from the archbishop on down, didn't like waves. They could live with criticism being aimed at almost anybody or anything, as long as the target was not a member of the Catholic institution, especially another bishop. They were particularly happy when a controversial Catholic doctrine, such as abortion, divorce, or birth control, was being defended. On that score, they were often not happy with the *Detroit Catholic*. However, the archbishop had never suggested that Koesler be removed as editor. And that, in this day and age, Koesler reflected, was no small virtue.

The tall, thin, blond priest's pacing was interrupted

when Irene Casey appeared in the doorway. "The editorial page is done, Father; do you want to look it over before we pack it up? And do you want another cup of coffee? It's going fast."

Dear Irene. She'd been with the paper nearly fifteen years. It wasn't a great deal of money, but it did help get her five kids through an increasingly expensive parochial school system. Irene, technically, was women's editor. But on a publication with the *Catholic*'s small staff, everyone did a little bit of everything.

"No, thanks, Irene, I don't want any more coffee. And, yes, I'd like to see the editorial page. Did you change anything in my editorials?"

"Does the pope change anything in the Bible?"

"It probably hasn't occurred to him."

Koesler was on his way into the editorial office when his phone rang. He backtracked.

"Father Koesler," he said guardedly into the phone. As often as not, he was greeted on the office phone by a hostile voice. He figured he got more calls and letters from Catholic nuts than any other priest in the archdiocese.

"Father, you don't know me. I don't live in St. Ursula's parish, but I go there every Sunday for Mass. I've got a problem, and I wondered if I could talk to you about it?"

"Why me? Father Pompilio is home at the rectory today. Or there must be a priest in a parish near where you live . . ."

"This is a complicated problem, Father. And I . . . well, I like your sermons and the things you write in the paper and I just . . . I'd rather talk with you if you could give me just a few minutes." Her voice was strained and shaky with emotion.

"Well, O.K. then. What's it about?"

"I'd rather not say over the phone, Father. Could I come and see you? I know where your office is, and I drive."

"All right. When do you want to come?"

"Well, this is my day off. I could come this afternoon if that would be convenient with you."

"Two o'clock?"

"That would be fine."

"All right. There's a parking lot next to our building.

Use that . . . this is not your Grosse Pointe neighborhood. By the way, can you tell me your name?"

"Nancy Baldwin. I'll see you at two."

Nancy Baldwin. The name rang a bell. Could she be Father Pete Baldwin's sister, the nurse? And, if so, why wouldn't she see Pete instead of him? Koesler was still wondering about that as he entered the editorial office.

Sister Ann Vania, a tall, handsome woman in her middle thirties, was preparing the second graders of St. Alban's parish in Dearborn for their first communion. Sister Ann (she had been known as Sister Paschal before her order decided to return their real names to the sisters as part of post-Conciliar renewal) was religious coordinator at St. Alban's. As such, she was responsible for the religion program for the entire parish. As a professional administrator, she seldom got involved in actual teaching. But second graders and their first communion were a special delight to her, and she would delegate their training to no one.

"Michael, can you tell us the story of the Good Samaritan?"

"Yes, Sister. There was this guy who was goin' somewheres. And some bad guys jumped him and beat him and mugged him and cut him up and . . ."

"That'll be enough of the violence, Michael. Go on with the story."

". . . they wouldn't help him. And then this Summertan . . ."

"Samaritan."

"Yes, Sister . . . Samaritan came by. And the guy thought this Samaritan was his enemy. But the Samaritan helped him."

"Very good, Michael. And do you know what the moral of that story is?"

"No."

Sister Ann sighed and suppressed a giggle. "Does anyone? Andrea?"

"The moral is that everybody is our neighbor and that we should love everybody. Even people who want to hurt and kill us."

"Do you think you could love somebody who wanted to hurt and kill you, Andrea?"

"Yes, Sister."

Sister Ann didn't think she could go quite that far herself. Fortunately, she knew of no one who wanted to hurt or kill her.

It was two o'clock. Father Koesler had been helping proofread for the past four hours, with a break for a sandwich and coffee, and he'd forgotten his appointment. Judy Anderson, the receptionist, bobbed briefly into the editorial room. "Your appointment's here, Father."

Appointment . . . appointment . . . ah, yes, Nancy Baldwin. "O.K., thanks Judy."

As Koesler moved from the editorial room to his adjoining office, he pulled his black suit jacket from the coat rack and slipped it on. Since he was already wearing his clerical collar and vest, he was now in full uniform and ready to face whatever.

He opened the door leading from his office to the reception area, and there was Nancy Baldwin. He recognized her immediately, though he had not hitherto known her name. Ten o'clock Mass on Sundays, toward the middle of the church, left side. Somehow, most regular Massgoers formed the habit of occupying the same place at the same Mass every week.

She was shaking the late winter snow from her imitation fur coat. With her was a small, bundled boy, perhaps five years old.

"Nancy Baldwin, I presume."

"Hello, Father." She smiled.

"Hi, God," said the little boy.

In his twenty years as a priest, Koesler had been called many things. But not until now, "God." He stood staring at the boy, speechless, then glanced at Nancy. "Yours?" he asked.

"Oh no, Father. Billy's my nephew. I'm babysitting today. I'll explain the 'God' bit in a minute. I know this is an imposition, but is there someplace we can leave Billy while we talk?"

"I think I know just the place." He leaned into the editorial room. "Irene . . ." He turned back to Nancy. "Even after five of her own, Irene Casey is still a sucker for little kids."

"Irene, this is Nancy Baldwin and her nephew Billy. Would you please show Billy some of the fun we have putting together a weekly newspaper?"

"I recognize you from your picture in the paper. It's nice meeting you, Mrs. Casey." Nancy extended her hand.

"Please to meet you, too, Nancy. Come on, Billy. It's never too early to start a journalism career."

Some people just have a natural way with kids, Koesler thought as Billy trotted off after Irene. If I had invited the kid to come with me, he'd probably have hit the floor kicking and screaming.

"Won't you come into my parlor?" Koesler waved his guest into his office. "May I take your coat?"

Nice trim figure, he thought as he hung up her coat. Carefully pressed pleated skirt, white ruffled blouse under a blue cardigan, small metallic cross on a thin gold chain. Nice legs, nice bottom, small breasts, short wavy hair. He had the intuitive impression she was the proverbial "nice Catholic girl."

"Father, what we talk about, can it be a secret?" She removed a handkerchief from her purse and began winding it through her fingers.

"Sure. If you want to go to confession, that's a very special kind of secret. If you just want to talk to me, that's a professional secret. In either case, I won't tell anyone whatever it is we'll talk about."

"Oh, good." A brief, nervous smile crossed her lips.

"Are you a nurse at St. Mary's Hospital?"

"How did you know?"

"I won't tell anyone what you tell me. And I can't tell you what somebody else tells me."

"You're just full of secrets, aren't you, Father." There was a trace of bitterness in her voice.

Koesler was angry at himself. This, obviously, was what she had come to discuss, and he had led her into the matter prematurely. He'd been a priest long enough to know that people have their own time to talk about troubling things, and there was no hurrying that time.

"I'm sorry," he said. "Everything in life is not a secret. Your name came up in a conversation about Father Lord's funeral. You were supposed to have said that his death might not have been due to natural causes."

"It must have been my brother, Father Pete." She was slightly flustered. Koesler didn't know if he could recoup the moment and gain her trust. "But I didn't actually say that to Pete. I tried to tell him about Father Lord's death, but he got so excited he scared me and I couldn't. I just couldn't. Sometimes Pete hears what he wants to hear."

"I see. Would you like some coffee?"

"No, Father."

He let things be quiet for a while. She had to have a chance to think it out. She spent perhaps a couple of minutes—it seemed much longer—staring intently at the handkerchief she had tortured through her fingers. Finally, she raised her eyes to Koesler very calmly. Unsure if she were ready to tell her story, he said, "You were going to tell me about why your nephew called me 'God.'"

She laughed. "I never thought it would turn out that way. I live very near my sister and brother-in-law—Billy's their child—and sometimes I take him with me to church on Sunday. To keep him quiet, I tell him that's God up there at the altar and he shouldn't disturb God. Only it's usually you up at the altar. I didn't think he'd put the two thoughts together. But when he saw you here today . . ."

"Gotcha." Talk about Santa Claus and the Easter Bunny! This was wild. But it was all in the interest of peace and quiet in church and, he thought, he'd drink to that.

They seemed to be on friendly terms again. The time appeared to be right.

"Now, would you like to tell me about it?"

"Yes, Father, I would. I've got to tell someone. And I want to tell you. Are you sure this will be between just the two of us?"

"You have my word."

"Well, it really did happen. Someone disconnected Father Lord's respirator. And that's what killed him. It didn't kill him much before he would have died anyway. But it—the lack of a life support system—caused his death."

She paused. Koesler said nothing. Nor did he show any sign of emotion, though he was slightly shocked. He'd learned long ago that when people tell a priest—or, he supposed, a minister or a psychotherapist—something shocking, they knew damn well it was shocking and they needed no response, not even a raised eyebrow, to confirm their conviction.

Assured they both knew what she was saying, and encouraged by his silence, she continued. "I was the one who found him. Just the day before, he'd been moved to this private room from the intensive care unit. The head nurse on the floor—that's me—was supposed to check him regularly. There was no need for a private duty nurse. God, Father, he was practically dead. We all expected him to slip away at any moment. We just tried to make sure he was as comfortable as possible, that he wasn't in any pain. I'll never forget it. I had just come back from the chapel—it was Ash Wednesday and we'd just received the blessed ashes. I went right to Father Lord's room to check on him. Right away, I noticed there was no chest movement. And there was the smell of death in the room. Do you know what I mean, Father?"

Koesler nodded. He couldn't define or even describe it. But long ago he had discovered, for instance, on entering a home where someone had just died, that there was indeed a very special odor of death. Once you experience it, you never forget it.

"I checked for his pulse. There was none. And then I saw the plug hanging loose by his bed. My first impulse was to reconnect it. But that would've been futile. He was gone. If he had been a younger person, I'd have called for emergency equipment. But Father Lord had been hanging on by a very fragile thread. It was just too late for anything." She paused again, this pause clearly indicating she was finished with her story.

"And now, Nancy?"

"And now, Father, I don't know what to do. And I feel just all torn up."

"Does anyone else at the hospital know? I mean, for sure?"

"The only one I know knows for sure is Sister Mildred, the supervisor on my floor. I got her right after I discovered Father was dead, and showed her the disconnected respirator. She didn't know what to do, either. We sort of agreed that someone in the hospital tried to do Father a favor and didn't know he or she was committing a crime. Sister Mildred decided that, all things considered

—Father's condition and all—that it would be better to say nothing. She put the plug back in its socket. And that's where things stand right now."

"It's not possible that Father Lord might have made one of those 'living wills' or that some authorized person, like his doctor, might have done this?"

"Not to the best of my knowledge. And I really would have been informed of something like that."

"The police haven't been called, nor have they investigated Father's death, have they?"

"No. They don't ordinarily investigate hospital deaths unless they're called."

Koesler hesitated. He knew what had to be done. And he was pretty sure Nancy knew also. She only wanted, he surmised, to be encouraged. But cautiously.

"Nancy, in effect, you're living a rather crucial lie. The longer it continues, the worse it's going to get, and the worse you're going to feel." Her face brightened slightly and the furrows in her brow smoothed almost imperceptibly. Yes, this was right and she knew it. "Right now, you're aiding and abetting a crime. But I'm quite sure it's not too late. If I were you, I'd go to the police and tell them the whole story. Undoubtedly, it would be good to clear it first with Sister . . . what's her name?"

"Mildred."

". . . Mildred. But no matter how she reacts, I'd go to the police in any case. I'm sure they will not hold it against you. And I can't see them sending a sweet little old nun up the river. But this *is* a crime, and it has to be investigated. Whoever did it, probably, as you suggest, had noble motives. Whoever it is, all things considered, I wouldn't mind being the accused's attorney. It wouldn't take Perry Mason to get him or her off lightly."

It was evident nearly all the tension was gone. Nancy had relaxed the rigid position she'd held throughout the interview. She replaced the now refolded handkerchief in her pocketbook.

"I can't thank you enough, Father. I guess I knew all along what I had to do. I just needed someone to say it."

"You're welcome, Nancy. This is still going to be rough and I'll pray for you. It's going to be a can of worms. But, sometimes it's just necessary to open the can."

"Yes, Father. Oh . . ." She rummaged through her pocketbook. ". . . there's something I wanted to give you." She produced a small black rosary. "This is the rosary Father Lord was holding when he died. It wasn't his. His was a mother-of-pearl rosary. When we prepared his body for the mortician, we sent his rosary with him. He was such a holy man, I kept this—sort of like a relic. I'd like you to have it."

"Thank you, Nancy. I'll prize it." He slipped it into his pants pocket where it clinked against the rosary he always carried. You can never have too many rosaries, he thought, though he was coming close.

He helped Nancy on with her coat. As she buttoned it, she looked into the editorial room. "Come on, Billy, we're leaving." There followed the pitter-patter of little feet.

Koesler accompanied them to the door leading to Forest Avenue.

"Good-bye, Father. And thanks again, more than I can say."

"Good-bye, Nancy. And, good luck, God be with you."

"Goo'bye, God," said the almost forgotten Billy.

"So long, kid." After all, it was in the interest of quiet in church.

Everything was about to hit the fan. Only, Koesler had no notion that this was not the beginning of the end but the end of the beginning.

This death is just the first in a series of bizarre murders that shock the Detroit Catholic community. Father Koesler and his friends must use every trick in the book to trap the ingenious killer.

Read the complete Bantam Book, available March 1st wherever paperbacks are sold.